the
laws
of
return

the
laws
of
return

[Cameron Stracher]

William Morrow and Company, Inc. / New York

Library of Congress Cataloging-in-Publication Data

Stracher, Cameron.
    The laws of return / Cameron Stracher.—1st ed.
      p. cm.
    ISBN 0-688-14902-2
    1. Young men—United States—Religious life—Fiction. 2. Jewish men—United States—Fiction. 3. Spiritual life—Fiction.
    I. Title.
PS3569.T67578L39   1996
813'.54—dc20
                                        96–8053
                                          CIP

Printed in the United States of America

First Edition

1 2 3 4 5 6 7 8 9 10

BOOK DESIGN BY GRETCHEN ACHILLES

For Christine

And when Abram was ninety years old and nine, the Lord appeared to Abram, and said unto him, I am the Almighty God; walk before me, and be thou perfect.

And I will make my covenant between me and thee, and will multiply thee exceedingly.

And Abram fell on his face. . . .

—GENESIS 17:1–3 (*King James Version*)

the
laws
of
return

bondage

ontogeny
and
phylogeny

I am eight days old. The *mohel* hovers above me, a scalpel in his hand. I scream. He slices. I am shorn from my foreskin, that fatty overcoat, exposed and raw before the world. *Cha'yim ben Binyamin*, proclaims the rabbi. Colin, son of Benjamin. Grow in vigor to a love of *Torah*, to the marriage canopy, and to a life of good works.

Later I lie wrapped in bandages, while the guests drink sweet wine and vodka, and my parents sip Chablis. *Mazel tov! L'chayim!* They dance around me.

Who are these people? I wonder. Whose eyes, whose hair, whose teeth? Each Jew's life is a cold swim in a deep pool. We crawl to the surface, shake water from our backs, stand upright.

We begin.

Above my bassinet a Calder mobile swings a lazy arc. Beneath the bookshelves Mozart's *Jupiter* Symphony spins on my father's new hi-fi. My mother, who can't operate mechanical devices, has left one side playing all morning—an endless loop of violins and violas. I'm squirming against the soggy mass in my diapers, but my mother can't hear my cries over the music and her books.

Finally, she notices me. She lifts me out of the crib and places me on the kitchen table alongside her books. Freud's *Jokes and*

Their Relation to the Unconscious, Babel's *Collected Stories*, and some other titles that I don't recognize. She is writing her dissertation. She will change topics three or four times, her academic adviser will die, but eventually she'll graduate with a Ph.D. in comparative literature.

"Okay, okay," she says brusquely, a million things to do. "Mommy's here."

She plucks the diaper off my rear, snapping my feces into the trash. While she wipes me clean and squirts me with mineral oil, I read:

> If we did not already know it from research into the psychology of the neuroses, we should be led by jokes to a suspicion that the strange unconscious revision is nothing else than the infantile type of thought-activity. Thought is put back for a moment to the stage of childhood so as once more to gain possession of the childish source of pleasure.

Unity for our fractured selves, I speculate as her hands grease my bottom. A return to childish pleasures. If only humor were so simple! He has forgotten ironic distance, alienation, the twin plagues of a modern dialectic. Even the joker is a victim of society.

She flips me onto a swatch of clean cotton, pulling the ends up through my legs. She rolls me to one side, then the other, pinning the fabric at my hips. I gurgle and drool. She sighs heavily and lifts me to her breast for the morning's meal.

It's not easy being a woman in a generation torn between career and family, the only child of immigrants, a professor trapped in a housewife's body. And I, the first offspring in the third generation, in the Year of Their Lord 1961.

Her breast knocks against my cheek. I tighten my grip on her nipple, sucking as if I'm afraid the milk will run out.

The milk will run out.

My father, the scientist, asleep on the rigid sofa in our Scandinavian living room. A *Journal of Biological Chemistry* folded over his chest.

The quiet, busy lives of platelets and proteins his source of domestic excitement.

In the kitchen my mother poaches eggs for dinner. Her specialty. She eases them into the boiling water, careful not to break the yolks. Tonight she may even make some toast.

She calls to my father, wakes him from his reverie. He nearly squashes me as he stumbles off the couch. I'm two years old; shouldn't I be walking already? He swabs my saliva from his shoes with the sports section, untangles me from his legs, and carries me to my high chair.

My mother has an announcement. That explains the bottle of wine and the home-cooked meal. She waits until we're all seated.

In her womb floats my brother, David, a tiny fish with gill slits and flippers. Ontogeny recapitulates phylogeny. Each Jew's life narrates the biblical tale: bondage under a cruel master, a hasty freedom, worship of false idols, forty years of wandering, the Promised Land. He will lead our people from the desert while I build the golden calf.

Two boys! My father won't believe his good fortune when he finds out. If only his father were still alive to see the strength of his son's seed, the skill with which his sperm have succeeded in giving him not one, but two male heirs. He would be proud of his bookish son, who, though not exactly a doctor, at least wears a white lab coat.

They gaze moonishly at each other, their big eyes like the flying saucers landing in our backyard. Our president says we should mobilize; the Cubans can see in the dark. The neighbors have stored powdered milk in the basement, safe from fallout and Soviet missiles. They've offered to dig us a shelter.

The world is not safe for the young and democratic. Crackpot republicans lurk in the shadows of Camelot. But my parents aren't worried. They're pregnant, upwardly mobile, a generation on the edge of a New Frontier. They've vaulted the gender gap and bridged the racial divide. Religion is donned for special occasions. They love their neighbors, such interesting lights and plastic dioramas. It's too bad their house is for sale.

I toss a banana to snap them from their reveries. They exchange a knowing look. They have just read the "New Sibling" chapter in their baby book.

"He'll be fine," my father says. "They're always fine."

But his unswerving faith in the arcane powers of biology fail to placate me. I regurgitate my food, soil my diapers, and twist my head around in a complete circle.

From a grassy knoll, a hidden gunman puts an end to Camelot.

A photograph of my parents at Coney Island shortly after they met: He is tall, wavy black hair cut close to his head, impossibly thin wrists poke from his shirt cuffs; she is barely out of high school, Lolita's sister, blue eyes, black hair, painted lips. They lean into each other, elbows and knees, their faces lit like Ferris wheels.

I stare at the photo in the front hallway. My eyes barely reach to the table's edge. How could two such attractive people produce an ungainly, buck-toothed, slope-headed boy like me? I am pale, freckled, blue-eyed, blond. A mutant in our increasingly Semitic ghetto.

Jews don't have blond hair, my uncle tells me. I must be the postman's son.

My new brother is perfect. David, the beloved. Strangers stop us on the street, marvel at his olive skin, while I, with my Frankenstein haircut, am ignored. Pale, spindly, my head like a deflated football. I wear long shirts and trousers outdoors. My parents take me to a pediatric dermatologist, a neuroendocrinologist. Nothing to worry about, they say, perfectly normal development. But I know, I know, that's what happens when the People of the Word crossbreed with the Deliverers of the Letter.

My mother claims I inherited Grandma Miriam's Polish genes. But Grandma Miriam is fat and gray-haired. My father's mother, ageless, epochal, who mangles the language with a babel of tongues. She visits us once a year, the anniversary of her husband's death. The house is so quiet in spring.

"Such a *goyisheh boychik*," she says, touching my hair.

"He has beautiful hair," my mother says.

"Why shouldn't he?" asks Grandma Miriam.

At night she sits at the edge of my bed. *"Cha'yim,"* she cries.

My father listens from the hallway, worried that his mother's melancholia endangers his son's normal development. I will become listless and depressed, unable to play with other children. "Let him sleep," I hear him whisper as he creeps into the room. Then, in a quieter voice, as if he's embarrassed: *"Luz em alein."*

But Grandma Miriam resists. She wants one more look at the *shayner bubeleh*. Her husband's namesake. The dead grandfather I never knew.

How can my father deny her happiness? Her visits are so rare. If he had never left the frozen Niagara winters, she wouldn't be so alone.

Five more minutes, my father relents, then I really have to get to sleep.

My beautiful golden locks, my sweet blue eyes. She smothers me in her ample bosom.

I am the promise of immigration made manifest, the Lamarckian product of the drive to assimilate, as if the simple will to be American, to breathe American air and eat American food, could produce a blond-haired, blue-eyed child.

Like the ugly duckling, I discover there's virtue in not looking like a duck.

And then she is pregnant again. This time, it's a girl. Rebecca. Becca, my mother explains, not Becky. Another olive-skinned beauty. Our little baby, our little girl, they coo.

Grandma Miriam can't make this one, she's exhausted from all the travel; but my mother's parents arrive with enough food to stock our neighbors' abandoned fallout shelter. How proud they are! Their Brighton Beach walkup cluttered with pictures of their only daughter and grandchildren. My grandfather's bakery plastered with flour-covered photos; his boss prefers them to pamphlets. This one, the daughter they sent to Columbia. She refused to live at home; *no one lives at home anymore*, she told them. They paid her dormitory fees with my inheritance.

"Hold the head," Grandma Esther recommends. She's round as Grandma Miriam but dark and sharp-featured, her nose like a hawk's claw.

"I think I know what I'm doing, Mother, thank you," says my mother.

"What's a little suggestion?"

"Too many suggestions," says my grandfather, the anarcho-syndicalist.

"You know better?"

He knows enough not to argue with her. Her Hungarian temper like fiery paprika. If he didn't work all night and sleep all day, they might have a minute to kill each other.

My sister latches to my mother's breast like a bat. My grandparents think it's normal. She doesn't cry; she doesn't even breathe. They will thank me when I drive a stake through her heart.

My father closes the door. We've seen enough for the day.

"How lucky to have a brother *and* sister," Grandma Esther tells me while Grandpa Isaac bounces me on his lap.

"You want them?" I ask.

She laughs. I am such a joker. If only I could return to one.

Now we are three. A triumvirate of joy for any mother.

"Go play somewhere else, children," she says. "Mommy is trying to work."

We gallop back to the living room, where Dad is asleep on the couch. The poor man is tired. All day in front of a microscope, stirring beakers with foul-smelling solutions, test tubes and petri dishes scattered about his lab. When he comes home, he wants "a little peace, not a three-ring circus."

Into the first ring David and I toss Becca, hair glued to her head like papier-mâché. Upstairs, in the second ring, we arrange Matchbox cars into special configurations visible only by alien spacecraft. And, in the third ring, we perform daring experiments in the bathroom. Watch us mix baby powder, milk, shampoo, and dirt clods in the sink. We add a splash of Drano. We have replicated conditions on primordial earth, creating life from a hot thin soup! Stockholm is calling!

My mother re-emerges from the study, a pencil behind her ear, a paper clip between her teeth, reading glasses dangling from her neck.

"What's all the noise?"

My father lifts his head, rubs his hands across his eyes and mouth, focuses on his daughter crying at his feet.

"Where're your brothers?" my mother asks. "It's too quiet upstairs."

"Is something burning?"

My mother rushes to the kitchen to rescue the chicken that's been baking since noon. The recipe said six hours at two hundred degrees. But who moved the temperature dial on the oven?

One and a half pizzas later Mom retreats to her study while Dad does the dishes. Becca helps by breaking two plates. Dad is calm; he sings show tunes; he knows that in a mere two hours he'll be back on the couch and we'll be Mom's problem.

"I have often walked / Down the street you live."

I, unfortunately, have inherited my mother's voice, a tin screech like an extinct bird. Dad, you gave me those bony knees, that sparrow chest; why couldn't you have given me your larynx too?

He sings like a choirboy. Sunday morning, hair slicked back, his brown eyes in a sea of blue. The Lord's Prayer trips lovingly off his tongue. His parents thought it would bring them business, a connection to the American community. It was so hard to make people see past the accents, the ill-fitting clothes, the embarrassing idioms. And my father loved to sing. What did he care about whose god? Religion is a curiosity, to be examined under the microscope, dissected, analyzed, extrapolated. Soon the *Jew tailor* did a very good business.

My father scoops Becca off the linoleum and marches her up to bed. David and I follow, good little Crusaders battling the Infidels. He rearranges our Matchbox cars into perfect rows, accidentally signaling the orbiting aliens to perform medical experiments on our internal organs while we sleep. When we're clean, he tucks us into bed and sings us a lullaby. Then he slips downstairs and collapses on the couch.

Ten minutes later I'm at the study door.

"There's no sleep," I say.

She lays her book on the desk; there's no more working tonight. "That's one trait you didn't inherit from your father," she says. Then she shuts the light and carries me back to bed.

❉   ❉   ❉

The scrawny, tinselly, ersatz tree droops in our living room. While we wait upstairs, my mother arranges our presents around its base (one each night, trumping our Christian friends by seven), Dad thumps a "Ho, ho, ho, it's the *Hanukkah* man," and we come tumbling down the stairs.

The incredible visible woman! A chemistry kit! Binoculars!

"The kids need ceremony," my mother explains to Grandma Esther.

"There's not enough ceremony with *Hanukkah*, the Festival of Lights?"

"Esther, you make a nuisance," says my grandfather.

My grandmother raises her hands in exasperation. She has braved city buses and trains, the vagaries of the suburban public transportation system, to see her daughter put up a Christmas tree?

"It's a *Hanukkah* bush," my mother says.

"God help us."

Later, as I disassemble my binoculars, scratching the ocular lens with my fingernails, my grandmother tells me that *Hanukkah* commemorates the re-dedication of the Temple destroyed by the Romans.

"Caesar drove them from the city a second time," she explains. "Afterward, the *diaspora*."

I can't remember which way the lens fits into the eyepiece. And I seem to have lost all the screws.

"Your mother forgets."

Assimilation is a terrible thing, I agree, but we live in Rome.

"Leave the boy alone," my grandfather says. "This is America." He pats me on the head. "Colin," he says. "Such a good name."

My grandmother fixes him with an evil eye. "God watches," she says.

He laughs deeply from a belly rolling in pastries and fresh bread. I laugh with him though I have no idea what is funny. But *he* is funny with his shiny head and his hooded eyes, his clothing always too loose and his shoes curled up at the ends. A roly-poly, red-faced, sweat-stained baker.

"I spit at God," he says.

❀   ❀   ❀

GI Joes napalm innocent villagers, torture suspected informers, sabotage industrial facilities. When they're finished, they troop to their barracks in a shoebox beneath my bed.

"They're Israeli soldiers!" I scream when my mother discovers them during one of her erratic sorties through my room. Purchased with change slowly stolen from my father's bureau, they represent months of painstaking labor. My industry and patriotism are not rewarded, however, and the soldiers go in the trash.

Despite my heavy losses, I am undaunted in my plan to overrun the Sinai and the West Bank. I'll rout the combined armies of Jordan, Syria, and Egypt with military assistance from well-connected friends in the United States. Afterward I'll sweep low across the desert, dipping my wings in triumph, my sonic boom heralding a new age. No one messes with the Jews.

My mother tacks a purple poster to my bedroom wall: War Is Not Healthy for Children and Other Living Things. Her brown hair has grown long, her loopy reading glasses like basketball hoops.

But who's going to fight the Arabs, the heathen, and the Nazis? They'll never forget you're a Jew, that's what Grandma Esther says. You think you're safe, you think they've forgotten, you sing in a choir, buy a *Hanukkah* bush then POW!, your windows are blown in. Go home, Jews!

"There are no *pogroms* in the United States," my mother explains as she removes jet decals from my wall. "We don't need guns here."

My grandfather disagrees. "The coloreds have guns," he says. "You can't even walk the streets." The edge of my bed sags toward his thick frame.

"Crime is caused by socioeconomic inequalities," explains my mother. "No one ever made peace with a gun."

"Two coloreds robbed your uncle Asher's jewelry store," Grandma Esther says, "and he wasn't even a religious man."

Satisfied that she's made her point, Grandma returns to the kitchen to grind liver for chopped liver, my favorite dish until I discover what a liver is.

Grandpa thinks I should learn to use a gun. "I was ten years old when I left Romania," he says.

"My son will not have a gun. He will not have plastic soldiers. He will not pretend to kill human beings."

My mother's naïveté is charming. As a girl she lived in books while a world war raged and the uneasy peace that followed killed millions.

"I refuse to argue over ideology," she says. "He's my child."

"Ideology?" he says. "Who's arguing?"

But she knows him. Even the labor unions didn't like his politics. Soft-headed Leninists, he called them. Vanguards of the middle class. He crossed more picket lines than a blitzing army.

"You won't get your way," she says. "Not this time."

He lowers his heavy shoulders like a drowsy bull. She is my mother, after all, despite her convoluted sociological analysis. Beneath the covers I feel his raspy knuckles tap my knee. I reach out and clasp his hairy hand.

Into my greasy palm he slips a folded and well-creased ten-dollar bill.

A rare night off. My father packs us into his rambling Dodge. Through the cookie-cutter suburbs, into the dilapidated borough of Brooklyn. The little city that couldn't: squat buildings and shabby storefronts like a lack of nutrients. The aged and infirm shuffle down the sidewalks, stop and spit at the curb, comb their fingers through thinning hair. All roads lead to the end of the road.

My grandparents' apartment building smells like cooked onions. On every floor, the crackle of frying liver. Ancient tenants peek through the doors as we clomp up the stairs, their features elongated and fish-eyed in the peepholes.

Grandma clicks four locks before the door opens. Her face is flushed and damp with heat. She throws her fat arms around us. Welcome to her home, the dark apartment where my mother was born. The stained couch, the dusty figurines, the photographs curling on waterlogged walls. David rushes inside, spins the handles on the radiators, explores the network of pipes and wires poking from the cracking plaster. I follow reluctantly, Becca clamped to my leg.

When I turn to my father, he has vanished, leaving us stranded in Grandma's clutches.

She bustles about the kitchen, slicing, dicing, chopping, frying. Are we hungry? She has pickles and kohlrabi, pale green rinds that look as if they've failed to ripen. Becca chomps at their skins while I shovel the food behind the sofa for an imaginary dog. Later there'll be kasha and cashews, butterfly egg noodles and onions, orange soda, ice cream, and prunes.

Grandma calls us to the table to light the candles. Welcome, the Sabbath bride. She strikes a match and holds it aloft, muttering words in an ancient tongue. Becca laughs, her demon face shadowed by fire. Grandma holds Becca's hand and moves it over the candle. The wick smokes, then bursts into flame. Grandma bows her head and summons the light into her arms.

After dinner we play cards. Grandma teaches us pinochle and lets David win. Becca cries when she catches me looking at her hand. If she knew how to play, I protest, I wouldn't have to help. We drink warm strawberry Jell-O from glass teacups and suck on peppermint candies. When it's time for bed, I am woozy with sugar, practically diabetic, inches from a coma. I fall into a jittery sleep.

Grandpa returns when the last candle has melted. Long ago he gave up on her religious gibberish. Let the rabbis babble; what he won't hear can't hurt him. But the children are young, their minds soft and impressionable. Why does she fill their heads with bubbles?

I listen to their argument from my edge of the sofa bed. David's elbow juts into my ribs. Becca's hand splayed across David's back. It's the darkest part of dawn, the lightest slice of night. Somewhere in the intersection, I fall back asleep.

When I awake, the house is full of police officers. My mother sits on the arm of the sofa, mascara running down her cheeks like black scars.

"Grandpa, Grandpa," I cry out from bed.

He's had a heart attack, she explains. One half of his heart killed the other. They've put him in a box and taken him to heaven.

She holds my hand, the black tears dripping off the end of her long nose. Grandma Esther sits on a crate in the middle of the floor, mumbling a prayer.

"Are you speaking to him in Jewish?" I ask. I never had a chance to say good night.

She nods her head; her lips move rapidly.

"Will you thank him for the gun?"

"Cha'yim!" Grandma Miriam wails.

I hold the telephone from my ear. I wonder how such a large woman could fit into such a small receiver. I place the phone on a coffee table and run off to find my parents.

"Why does she call me that name?" I ask my mother.

"She's lonely," my mother explains.

"But it's not my name."

"It's my father's name," my father says.

"Does she think I'm your father?" I know that old people are often confused. The other day Grandma Esther called me David until David began to cry.

My mother tells me that Jews have two names—one English and one Hebrew. In Hebrew I am named for my grandfather.

"Who am I named for in English?"

"You're yourself," my mother says.

In Hebrew, I conclude, I must be someone else. I share a hidden identity in a secret language with my long-dead grandfather, a man I never met.

I examine my face from all angles in their bedroom mirror. Is there a puckered old man beneath that baby skin? A dead man clawing to get out? He wants to know why I've changed my name; what was wrong with his? *Cha'yim, Cha'yim,* I cough it up from the back of my throat.

"I wish she would stop," I tell my parents.

My mother looks at my father. His spectacles droop along the bridge of his nose. His eyes, behind them, are magnified beach glass, an ocean glimmering on their rounded and worn surface.

"I'll tell her," he says.

"Good," I say, turning back to the mirror. But I know I've done something horrible; the face that stares back at me is wretched and hollow.

An old man's face.

✿   ✿   ✿

My mother thinks I should spend more time alone with my father. "Wouldn't that be nice, Colin?" she says after an early dinner. "Just you and your father going for a swim?"

I hate swimming. The cold water; the naked, hairy backs of older men; the ease with which my father glides through the pool.

"Buoyancy is a function of lift," my father explains as he maneuvers the car into a parking space with one finger on the steering wheel.

I nod dutifully while he lies about my age to the attendant. I follow him meekly down an ammoniacal hallway. In the locker room I pull my shorts off quickly, hop into my suit, snag a leg, and crash against the lockers.

"Balance," my father says. "The equitable distribution of mass."

The nylon liner clings to my foot like a fishing net. I grab a pocket and trawl the suit to my waist. Cocking one flamingo leg, I slip through the unoccupied side.

It's crowded in the locker room. Sagging rear ends parade through the showers like sacks of laundry. They smile at me, co-conspirators in their aquatic ceremony. I raise my middle finger like an amulet.

My father hums lightly as he drops a quarter into our locker. He pins the key to the inside of his pocket, next to a fire-resistant ID tag. I grab my towel and follow him into the showers.

Steam rises from the slick floor. Bacteria thrive unencumbered. Small birds and reptiles gyre and gimble in the humidity.

I hack my way through the underbrush with a bar of soap. I scrub the jungle from my face and eyes. I rinse my hair clear of poisonous spiders. When I am clean, I step into the fifty-meter bubonic cauldron.

"Stay off the bottom," my father advises.

He hands me a kickboard and swims away, his arms windmilling through water. I flounder near the tiled edges, battered and bobbing in his wake. My toes curl blue in the icy water. My fingers crack. Amputation will save only my limbs.

Missing children float to the surface of the pool, while their absent-minded parents wait in the Jacuzzi. These are dangerous days; anyone can be hijacked, kidnapped by the SLA, join a cult, a *kibbutz*. Some people will do anything to belong.

It is hours before my father finds me downstream, my body shriveled and wet like one of Grandma's prunes.

"Did you boys have fun?" my mother asks as I haul my shivering carcass upstairs.

I can hear them laughing while I crawl beneath the sheets and cover myself with blankets. The antiseptic smell of chlorine lingers on my skin. My shoulders ache with a pleasurable weight. I think of my father, his skinny arms, his pale thighs. We are cut from the same flesh, our bodies joined at the blade. His lips, his teeth. Whose name?

My nightlight casts a leery glow on the monster in my closet. Next door, David thumps once on the wall. Becca calls for my mother. I curl into the pillows, lazy and warm.

In a dream I am visited by the men of an African tribe. They are impossibly tall with regular scars across their chests, rings through their noses, and circles of paint hollowing their eyes. "*Cha'yim!*" wails the leader, who looks suspiciously like Grandma Miriam. She raises a fork and a huge knife.

I scream.

the
king
is dead

"Go ahead, jump," my father says. "See if I care."

I am standing on the roof of the garage in bare feet and T-shirt after fleeing the dinner table. My mother has pursued me to the window. My advantage. I fit. "Let him kill himself!" she screams through the opening, and my father encourages me to split my head on the gravel below.

Of course I'm not going to jump. I know that; my parents know that. But how do I manage a graceful exit? All escape routes are blocked.

I breathe deeply, concentrate, and then, pressing my arms to my sides, I lift off.

My father's openmouthed pin-shaped head recedes to a geometric point. My mother's screams fade to birdcalls. I skim the trees of our pleasant suburban village. There's Joshua's house, and the skating rink, and the place where my mother gets her nails done. Farther off is the junior high school, where they force you to smoke marijuana in the bathroom, and beyond that, our synagogue and Hebrew school.

"I'm not going, you—" Fumbling for a word, I settled on "fart," but as it emerged from my lips, I discarded it as too silly for a twelve-year-old. Scanning for alternatives, I passed on "fem," "fibber," and "fogy." Finally, I arrived at the *u*'s, and because that damn consonant was tickling my lips, I blurted, "Fuck."

I leaped from my chair, two steps ahead of my fallen-arched mother, and raced for the safety of the upstairs guest room, where I knew, having spied on adults in the yard, that there was roof access.

I increase my propulsion and climb through the clouds. The world dwindles to a map in my geography class. My father is wrong: The earth is flat.

"Stay out all night then," he says. "Freeze to death." He knows he'll be able to use my brain for scientific experiments.

Ignoring him, I sail past Mars and Jupiter; I'd travel as far as Uranus if I could say its name without laughing.

NASA beams my favorite television programs on a coded channel that my mother can't intercept. I have ten years' supply of sugar-coated cereal in my pockets. Antigravity milk keeps it from floating out of the bowl.

They can't force me to go to Hebrew school. There are laws against it. Freedom of religion. Separation of Church and State. I learned about them in my Social Studies textbook. Children have died rather than be subjected to three hours of pasty-faced rabbinical students lecturing on the wonders of *Pesach*. Give me liberty or give me death, they proclaimed. And then they were killed, often by their parents.

"We're doing this for you," their parents said. "We never had a chance to become a *bar-mitzvah* because our father was an anarchosyndicalist."

"Then why don't *you* go to Hebrew school?"

The roof is cold, the slate dark and slippery against my feet. How far would I have to fall to die?

I look for something to hold on to, anything, but the flat black expanse looms perilously. I will lose my footing and slide all the way down. The gutters will snap away ineffectually, trailing my limp body over the edge. Dizzy, and suddenly nauseated, I sit with my back to the window and my heels braked against the slate.

A squirrel scampers along the peak. Its tiny feet click like sharpening knives. It stops, glances at me, then jumps onto an overhanging branch. An acorn bounces after it.

I rest my head on my clattering knees. I do not move. Let me freeze to death; it would serve them right.

The sky glimmers jet and violet. Monstrous shadows move across the moon. Oedipus rubs his head and sniffles.

Overhead, the Furies screech. They will follow us for years until they discover we are Jews, not Greeks.

"Baruch ata adonai, elohainu melech ha'alum."

I race through the prayers, Joshua at my side. We don't know what a single word means, but we can read the transliterations and have most of them memorized anyway.

"Excellent, *Cha'yim*," says Jacob, the fallen *Torah* scholar whose unfortunate fate it is to teach Hebrew school. "But perhaps you'd like to slow down a bit so the rest of us can appreciate your beautiful Hebrew."

"My name is Colin."

"*Cha'yim*. It's a good Hebrew name."

"I'm not a Hebrew. I'm an American."

"You're an American Jew, a Jewish American. In *shul* we use your Hebrew name."

Every name reveals a hidden identity, he tells me. The *Torah* itself is a text of God's names. Each word, each letter, properly understood, illuminate God's true attributes.

"That's a bunch of mystical crap," says Joshua, his apple cheeks speckled yellow, black hair like a shag carpet. "Is that what they teach you guys in *Torah* college?"

Jacob smiles politely. His hippie friends on the Lower East Side warned him not to travel to the suburbs. But he needed the money; work had been scarce since he renounced the *Hasidim* and their illiberal dogma—how far they had come from their spiritual roots! And how bad could it be? he asked himself. The kids were smart; he might even enlighten one or two, teach them their own true history. But he has since given up hope of redemption: We are doomed, dumb creatures bound to share in the bland assimilative pie that passes for culture in the latter half of the twentieth century.

"There are things in this world even you don't know about," Jacob says.

"My father is a scientist," I say.

"Even him," Jacob adds.

"I'm a Marxist," says Joshua.

Last year, in sixth grade, Joshua claimed to be a disciple of Lao-tzu. This year he must have reached the *M*'s in his *World Book* encyclopedia. His intellectual appetite rivaled only by a mouth large enough to feed it.

He unfolds and smooths along the seam of our prayer book a soiled and crumpled piece of paper on which he has painstakingly lettered in slanted lines and small capitals. He reads:

> Man emancipates himself politically from religion by expel-
> ling it from the sphere of public law to that of private law.
> . . . It is no longer the essence of community, but the essence
> of differentiation. It has become what it was at the begin-
> ning, an expression of the fact that man is separated from
> the community, from himself and from other men.

Jacob laughs. "This is just another form of your mysticism," he says. "Fin de siècle German anti-Semitic mysticism."

"Marx was a Jew," Joshua sputters.

"So are you," says Jacob.

I squint at the paper, hoping the letters will reveal their truths. But I am blind; I might as well be reading Hebrew.

"*Cha'yim*," says Jacob, "shall we continue our lesson?"

Joshua sulks in his chair, the speckles on his cheeks expanding into blotches, while I trill through the uvular sputterings of an ancient tongue, dead but for the smallest sliver, a statistical burp from the mouth of the world.

"A real Jew," Jacob says proudly.

Unseeing, uncomprehending, I spit out the words like chunks of earth.

The names of God taste like dirt.

I fly over a barren landscape of cracked pillars and splintered columns. Great men once trod here. Odysseus, Hector, Paris. They slaughtered one another for no reason other than sibling rivalry and a misplaced sense of justice. The gods were crazy. Hundreds of them.

Brother and brother. Friend and lover. Their broken bones littered the countryside.

Nourished by tales of promised glory, poets metering their praise, they left their homes in seafaring vessels, striking out for new lands. On the shoreline their mothers waved good-bye, then returned to typing their dissertations. So many generations had passed; so many to come. But preserved on microfiche, a doctorate is practically immortal.

Assyrians. Babylonians. Israelites. How many more peoples could they conquer? They lay in their blankets at night plotting their strategies. When they fell asleep, they dreamed of city-states and empire. They would return home with gold and women, more lands to add to the family name. Later they would rise up to butcher their fathers and sleep with their mothers, though sometimes inadvertently.

I roll to the cool side of the sheets. It is hours until dawn. I can hear the clash of hooves and the ring of metal against metal. The heroes have fallen. The Greeks have long returned to their islands and coffee shops. The poet has given up the iamb for free verse and stream of consciousness.

I lie in bed and wait for familiar sounds from the ancient homeland: my father making coffee; my mother at the typewriter.

I am the next generation of nothing. A Greek, a Jew, I could be anything. We share dead languages, a Mediterranean view, a soccer match in the stadium. But after school, I learn an *aleph bet* while the streets of Athens fill with boys. No special tutorials or ritual incantations; they are what they were born.

And what was I born?

Behind the Parthenon the gods fight for devotion. They can't pack a crowd into temple as in the old days. They claw each other for crumbs.

The poet, blind and alone, packs up his feet. No reason; no rhyme; life breaks in asymmetrical lines. He slips out the window and disappears in the night.

❖   ❖   ❖

"*Bar-chu-oo ata adonoy-oy elohainu me-eh-eh-lech ha-ah-luh-um*,"
I chant, my prepubescent voice squeaking like my brother's clarinet.

"Screw this indoctrination," says Joshua during recess. "Religion
is the opiate of the masses."

And the fetishism of commodities. Already I have my eye on
potential bar mitzvah presents: a ten-speed bike, an electric guitar,
a Ping-Pong table, a knock-hockey set. Sing, Joshua, sing.

"Where's our integrity? Are we dogs? Lapping at the feet of our
masters?"

For a Ruthless Criticism of Everything Existing. Joshua dictates
and I write:

A spectre is haunting Judaism. . . .

Jacob looks over my shoulder. "This is what you do with your
break? Wouldn't it be more fun to sneak off and smoke a cigarette?"

Joshua scrambles to cover the pages. His shag hair flies out from
under the vacuum cleaner. The polish shines on his ruby cheeks.

"When I was your age, we were interested in girls, not dialectical
materialism," Jacob adds.

Joshua glares at Jacob. "You'll pay for oppressing the lumpen
proletariat."

"You don't qualify." Jacob shakes his head sadly. "Your parents
exceed the income cap."

"Even Marx had a patron," Joshua says.

"But he took time out to screw the maid," says Jacob.

I imagine Marx, whom Joshua has described as brilliant and
hairy, thumping away with the maid in the upstairs bedroom. From
each according to his ability, to each according to his need, Marx
declared. And the maid believed him.

Joshua gathers up his manifesto. "The old order will collapse,"
he says confidently, "and phony religion won't stop it."

"You're a little late," says Jacob sadly, the Fall in his crinkled
eyes. "God's been dead for nearly a century."

"Someone killed God?" I say. I try to picture a knife to His
back. A bullet to His brain. Perhaps He tripped and fell down the
stairs. Or maybe He was pushed. But who would commit such a
dastardly act?

"Some Germans," says Jacob. He rolls a corner of his beard

between forefinger and thumb as if he were preparing to smoke it. Then he looks back up at Joshua and me.

"And the world was silent."

"No girls," I inform my mother. "It isn't that kind of *bar-mitzvah*."

Without girls, she wants to know, what kind of *bar-mitzvah* is it?

I tell her we don't need girls. We can talk about cars and the market and our problematic relationships with our fathers.

"Nell Schwartzman's a girl," offers my mother, suggesting the pale girl in my Hebrew school class with a crush on Jacob.

"She's only half Jewish."

"We'll send her half an invitation."

Convinced that she's addressed my problem, my mother returns to licking stamps. I look down at the growing pile of ivory envelopes, the list of dimly recalled relatives—bald, beady-eyed, with double foreheads—and their husbands.

"Joshua thinks a bar mitzvah should be a solemn ritual," I say. "No girls; no parties."

"I suppose he wouldn't want a ten-speed bike either?"

I catch my breath. "A ten-speed?"

"Joshua," she says.

"No," I say. "He'd make an exception for a ten-speed. He told me."

My mother doesn't blink, but a slight smile turns her mouth, a serpent flicker across her lips.

"Sometimes we do things because they're important to someone else," she says to the envelopes.

"What color ten-speed, do you think?"

"Even though we might not believe in the ritual."

"Blue, I hope."

I am surprised, when her face rises, to see tears in her eyes. For a panic-stricken moment I think I've gone too far, overwhelmed her with my avarice.

"Your grandfather would be very proud," she whispers. Then she reaches across the envelopes and pulls me to her chest.

I can hear her heart thumping and the breath whistling through her lungs. I remember my grandfather telling me that God was a fraud, every rabbi a fool, religion an excuse for the Pope to kill Jews. He sat on the edge of my bed, his hooded eyes blinking rapidly, perspiration like a beaded chain looped around his forehead.

Her fingers press into my neck. She sniffles. Her heart pauses, then resumes beating.

"I'll be sad too," I say, "when you die."

My father will not speak with me. Such hateful words. If I wish him dead, then let him die. My brother and sister, at least, will mourn him.

"You're almost thirteen," he says as he closes my escape window.

"You're speaking to me," I say.

I'm too big for his arms. My legs dangle over his elbows. He carries me like a trussed animal bound for the sacrifice.

"Is this how a boy who's going to be *bar-mitzvahed* behaves?"

"Yes," I say. Since he's never been, how should he know?

"You won't get a lot of presents."

For a man who's sworn off speaking, he's pretty talkative.

He deposits me on my bed. I drop and roll into the blankets, bumping up against the wall. David pounds back on the other side.

"Your mother's making a big party. For you," he adds.

He should fight his own battles, I tell him. Take up the sword, throw down the gauntlet. Let the insults fall where they may.

"It's costing a fortune."

I don't need their gala extravaganza: the bad band with the accordion player; bowls of punch for the kids; the lopsided tables under a slouching tent; chairs sinking into the mud. I am tired, cranky, and worn to the bone. Did I ask for a spiritual coming-out party? Do I look like a debutante? My parents can't pronounce the words, but they expect me to grace the entire family with religion. Why should I enroll in their efforts to regain their lost spiritual footing? They threw it overboard; let them swim after it. I want to be left alone to ride my new bicycle up and down the block every afternoon. To chew bubble gum and collect the trading cards like any normal American kid. They filled their drawers with commemorative pins; why can't I? Instead they hoarded the cards, chewed the gum until the sugar was gone, then stuck the desiccated wad on my forehead. Sing, they said, sing. You be the Jew.

"I suppose we can save the money for your brother and sister," he says when I will not answer.

"David has a bicycle," I protest. "And Becca doesn't need one."

"You'll get your bicycle," says my father, his droopy eyes like watery marbles in a Coke bottle. "I just hope I live long enough to buy it."

At night I fly without instruments, relying on the stars and earth's magnetic field. I dip into the junior high parking lot, strafing the greasers as they hover in an alcove smoking cigarettes.

No one has forced me to smoke pot in the bathroom yet, but I'm taking no chances.

Down the street our rabbi strolls, reading a transliterated version of the Torah. He never learned Hebrew; he doesn't think it's important. It's the spiritual essence that matters.

I circle back for the kill, arm my rabbinical-seeking missiles. What's that? There's something on my tail. I loop the loop, gravity tugging at my cheeks, and come up behind . . .

My mother!

But I don't have time to think; she's gone into a dive, trying to shake me. I follow her down.

We scorch past the supermarket, scattering shoppers. At the luxury car dealership she hooks left. Over the viaduct, around the tennis academy, into the park. A flock of frantic ducks flaps across my path.

When I clear the mess, she's disappeared. I scan the grassy knoll: no sign of the hidden gunman. As I angle warily toward the gazebo, she rises suddenly beside me and yanks at my leg.

We tumble to the ground, teeth clattering on impact; our foreheads explode.

"You're my firstborn," she says. "You split me open. I had no choice but to let you go."

The night air lifts my pajamas with a frozen hand. My bare thighs shiver against the slate hard earth. I drag myself into her lap. "Mama," I cry.

She unbuttons her blouse and presses my head between her

withered breasts. "There's nothing left," she says. "Your brother and sister finished me off."

Someone said that a decomposing body generates more heat than a living one. That a man, buried alive, can freeze to death before he suffocates.

"I don't want to die," I sob. "I don't want anyone to die."

In the tragedies the Greeks fornicate with gods and spend their days on Olympus, sipping apricot juice and ouzo. Their parents forgive them for acting out childhood rebellion. They were young once too and mocked divinity. For a time, everyone thinks he's immortal.

In the comedies, the Jews poke out their eyes.

"Barchu et adonai hamavorach!"

I reel off the prayers like a checklist. The congregation struggles to keep up. Hebrew characters dance at my fingertips, their meaningless squiggles like spilled ink. I skid across parchment anchored only by memory.

The rabbi sweats. The organist pants. Jacob waves me down.

I'm a runaway train. Damn the torpedoes. On this, the most important day of my unformed life, I cannot stop for informed reflection. At 45 rpm, even molasses sounds like blessings.

My parents beam in the front row. My grandmothers emit high-frequency radio signals beside them. Joshua dusts lint from his gold-lapeled smoking jacket. Nell folds and unfolds her invitation. Checks bulge from the pockets of my cousins. Pay to the order of Colin Stone: one million dollars.

I read, in English: *"And it came to pass after these things, that God did tempt Abraham, and said unto him, Abraham: and he said, Behold here I am."*

The assembled multitude stares at me in glazed rapture.

"And he said, Take now thy son, thine only son Isaac, whom thou lovest, and get thee into the land of Moriah; and offer him there for a burnt offering upon one of the mountains which I will tell thee of."

My father stirs in his seat. Something about this tale strikes a familiar forgotten note.

"And they came to the place which God had told him of: and

Abraham built an altar there, and laid the wood in order, and bound Isaac his son, and laid him on the altar upon the wood."

Babies thrown into bulrushes; firstborns slain. Does he know these people?

"And Abraham stretched forth his hand, and took the knife to slay his son."

A little discipline, a spanking, once or twice he urged me off the roof. But murder?

"And the angel of the Lord called unto him out of heaven, and said, Abraham, Abraham: and he said, Here am I.

"And he said, Lay not thine hand upon the lad, neither do thou any thing unto him: for now I know that thou fearest God, seeing thou hast not withheld thy son, thine only son from me."

The congregation heaves a collective sigh; spared my squeaky tremolo.

And what of poor Isaac, trembling on the woodpile? Shall he too forgive his father? Or will the fear of death haunt him until his final days, stalking him like a schizophrenic parent—God's voice urging him to infanticide?

The rabbi snorts, wipes the drool from his cheek, and arises from his nap. Such a long morning; he's been trying for years to shorten the service. At least it's in English.

"Colin," he says. "Today you are a man."

"Thank you, Rabbi," I say, grabbing the microphone from his fishy hands. I've heard too many of his New Age sermons; it's my turn to kindle the inner essence.

I thank the gathered masses, whose trek has brought me wealth and acclaim. I thank my teacher, Jacob Cohen, traffic conductor and truant officer, who has extended my school day to oppressive lengths. I thank my parents, Laius and Jocasta, whom I've had to possess, vanquish, slay, and repudiate, and no doubt will again.

I turn to my prepared remarks, scripted by Jacob, reviewed by my mother. My trembling voice rises over the congregation.

Who are we, I wonder as I read, the blind followers of a vengeful deity, chosen and ignorant? God says jump and so we jump? The Fall goes on forever. We can barely remember it when we land.

Who am I? My parents signed up for the desert tour, complete with box lunch and *bar-mitzvah*. God will provide, they told me when I asked. They didn't say which god, whose god. A little religion goes a long way, spread on some whole wheat, a dry crust. We wash the lumps down with water.

I hear my words like false converts. I promise to grow and learn, to become a better Jew. I will improve on nothing, re-create myself from whole cloth. When the muslin stretches and tears, I'll toss it aside. I can buy a better suit.

In the wasteland, they admire my panache.

"Today I am a man," I conclude. The father of myself. An orphan. The king is dead. Long live the king.

And I didn't even have to poke out my eyes.

I shine down upon the congregation. "Raise your voices," I command. "Sing!"

The synagogue is filled with the rapturous voices of two hundred Jews singing transliterated Hebrew spirituals with organ accompaniment. My father's lucid baritone slices like mountain water through the muck of New Jersey and Long Island accents.

I step off the dais and into the crowd. I am lifted above their heads, borne across the room on linked arms. We spill down the stairs, out of the synagogue, and into the blond light of a fall morning. Past the tables with tiny cakes gathered like tombstones; past the cut flowers and raw vegetable dip; past the tree planted to commemorate the six million.

Around and around and around we spin, faster and faster, the ground whistling by like a last gasp of breath. I close my eyes and rise into the heavens, the newly anointed king. Higher and higher, until the world is a vertiginous plunge down a dark, narrow shaft.

My father's hand, bony and warm, grasps at my wrist.

"Jump," he says.

a
tooth
for an
eye

The metal fence springs against my face, slapping me like a rusty tennis racket.

"Go back to Israel!" shouts Tommy Patrick.

Two weeks into my sophomore year, and I've already made a new friend. He mashes my face into the dirt, shovels grit into my nostrils and gums.

"Kill him! Kill him!" someone shrieks.

Some people can't take a joke. I'd give him back the football if he'd leave me alive long enough to hand it over.

Beaten to death on the playground—how will I explain this to my parents? I wait with neck extended for the final blow, the coup de grace, but it never comes. When I look up, Tommy is flapping like a duck on a clothesline, pinned in the arms of Mr. Lavelle, the playground supervisor.

Kids circle warily, afraid Tommy might bite through his chains as in a Sunday monster movie. His cohorts, skulking at the edge of the circle, flash my life expectancy with rudimentary hand signals.

My friends, erstwhile companions, have vanished.

Lavelle hauls us inside, an arm encircling my waist, the other around Tommy's neck. We stagger down the hall to a glass door stenciled in black and gold: PrinciPAL.

A small, skittery man with a gleaming pate brushes crumbs from his desktop. His eyes dart from corner to corner, as if measuring an escape route.

Lavelle pushes me forward.

"He-he . . . h-h-hit . . . me," I stammer, mucus streaming over my lips. "He-he . . . st-stole our foot-football."

"I didn't hit him! He tripped! He called me a fuck!"

"Language," clucks the principal.

"I've never had any trouble with this one," Lavelle says, pointing to me. Tommy, however, he explains, is a notorious sociopath and virulent anti-Semite. If he's not stopped, he'll grow a small mustache and sing drinking songs about the Fatherland.

"The Jewish people have suffered terribly throughout history," says the principal, his eyes blinking rapidly.

"They're doing okay now," Tommy says. "The Germans gave them all Mercedes."

The principal's head sinks into his neck, and the hard shell of his back rounds off his shoulders. He seems lost in thought, nearly asleep, his fingers resting on his cheekbones. Then he shivers suddenly and pulls at his earlobes. He scampers out from behind his desk. He's nearly as tall as Tommy; eye to eye they stand tooth to tooth. Five feet two inches from the cockroaches.

"And this in our country's bicentennial," he sighs.

I remain in the silent and dimly lit room while Tommy enters the delousing chamber for a special Social Studies tutorial. His screams and cries penetrate the thin walls. Lavelle departs as the first wail rises.

Tommy is sniffling when he emerges. His face streaked with red blotches and his eyelids puffy and raw. For a moment he looks like the child his mother once loved.

"I'm sorry," he sniffles. "I have a foreshortened sense of history."

His right hand trembles as he shakes mine. His eyes cast about the floor. But when he looks up, he is smirking, his left hand balled into a fist.

The principal teeters behind him, grinning at his handiwork; his lips twitch and jump spasmodically over his face. The last thing he needs is a hysterical mother. And the Jews are always the worst.

✼   ✼   ✼

Jacob says young people today lack all spiritual conviction. They must be beaten into submission, tortured with the cattle prods of history, the cement blocks of propaganda tied around their ankles.

"In the suburbs," he says, "religious belief is practiced in malls."

We are watching a Holocaust film, hours of starved and mangled bodies, soldiers saluting Hitler, sober narratives about the "Final Solution." Jacob escapes for a cigarette while the trains rumble toward Auschwitz, Dachau, Buchenwald, Bergen-Belsen, Treblinka. He explains that he has seen the film. "I watch the beginning and hope the ending will change," he says.

I tell Jacob I'm too old for Hebrew school. I've already sung the drinking songs and worn the beanie. My parents have forced me to continue my religious education to get me out of the house on Sunday evenings and occasional overnight trips; they claim it's for my soul, but I know it's for their sanity. "Besides," I add, "I thought God was dead."

"What if He isn't?" Jacob asks.

He looks at me expectantly, as if I've never considered the question, as if he's stumped me with the missing ontological proof.

"I don't believe in a God that wouldn't forgive me for not believing in Him," I say.

"It's sophistry that killed Him."

"You said it was some Germans."

Jacob scratches his beard. Can he explain how Kant's fierce desire to make sense out of a random universe, Hegel's unrelenting search for the Absolute, killed what each had worked so hard to believe? As the tanks pushed into the ghetto and the ovens burned, their countrymen emblazoned their names in glory.

"The infinite exists though we've forgotten to count," Jacob says. "Even the Germans couldn't change that."

"Where was God," I ask, pointing to the movie screen, a white sheet draped across the wall, "while the Germans were trying?"

Jacob's eyes are like two black crystals, coal under pressure, square inches from diamonds.

"He was sleeping," Jacob says. "Their cries woke Him from His dreams."

✿   ✿   ✿

I slink along the corridor connecting the science and language wings, squeezing myself into the bricks. My feet ache. I am hungry. I am tired. I am massed in the hold of a container ship, dressed in labelless jeans and a buttoned-up shirt. My hair is coiffed imperfectly. My speech lacks the proper idioms. In my own country I will become a doctor, a lawyer, a government official. Now I am simply a "tool."

"Flood's over."

"Fag."

It's been two hundred years, but all immigrants are not created equal. The popular patrol sunned in deck chairs rented by their parents while the crew fought for portholes. Once they were ashore, their tans flashed like diamonds. Now they perch on a window ledge, the arbiters of style, denizens of disco cool. I wilt under their cruel gaze.

In the back of the cafeteria my peanut butter sandwich tastes like a shoe washed up on a beach. Through the plate glass I watch new sports cars loop around the parking circle in front of the school. Bleached hair and nose jobs lean from their windows.

"It's Jews like that who give us a bad name," says Joshua.

When everyone's a minority, I tell him, the minorities rule.

"They deserve to be persecuted."

I have stitches over my left eye, a bandage across my nose. My head throbs from being smashed about like a medicine ball. My teeth ache from following it.

"Who's persecuting *them*?" I ask. "They're persecuting *us*. We're being oppressed by our own people."

"Not my people," Joshua snorts. "I'm a Marxist." He tosses the rest of his sandwich in the trash.

I gather my notebooks and pencils and follow Joshua through the maze of cafeteria tables, each populated by a subset of high school species. Geographic isolation, inbreeding. Darwin should have spent an hour with these finches.

In a far corner Tommy Patrick and his friends swill milk from cartons, exploding the containers with a stomp of their heel.

"Hey, Jews!" Tommy calls as we pass near his table. "Have a nice day."

"I'll kick his ass," Joshua says, but softly.

I lower my eyes and shield myself behind Joshua. Under the camouflage of his shag hair and enormous head, I feel safe. His brain will absorb the imminent nuclear explosion and keep on ticking. When the world ends, the last thought will be Joshua's.

Two periods later Tommy saunters from the cafeteria. He careens along the corridor, shoulders rolling and hips swaying. But as he passes the popular patrol on the window ledge, his head suddenly retracts into his neck, and he presses himself against the bricks.

Their wicked laughter trails him down the hall.

I emerge from the bathroom in a mist of hair spray, deodorant, and aftershave.

"Do you know how bad chlorofluorocarbons are for the ozone layer?" asks Becca.

My sister, the vegetarian environmental activist. She prowls our pantry confiscating canned meat products. She ritually sacrifices tofu in the privacy of her bedroom. Her teachers call to complain that she has organized a bologna boycott in the school lunchroom.

"You're seven years old," I say.

"Eleven," she says. "And I know about environmental degradation, thank you."

My mother quizzes me with her own list of vocabulary words. "Halcyon?" she asks as I stop to reorganize my hair by the front door. "Vertigo? Nonchalance? Pneumonoultramicroscopicsilicovolcanoconiosis?" It's never too early to prepare for those standardized exams, she reminds me.

I ignore them both and grab a backpack weighted with library books and rolling papers. "Gottatest," I say as I fly out the door and onto my bicycle for the pitch-black and treacherous ride into town. Oblivious to the possibility of life out of doors, station wagons bomb past me in the darkness.

The alcove behind the library is the perfect spot to light up: invisible from the street, sheltered from the wind. An echo chamber announces each approaching footfall. I meet Joshua by the front steps, and we slip by the quacking ducks to the safety of our hidden niche.

The weed crackles and burns, a raging suburban brushfire. We smoke enough to cripple a small horse. When we have inhaled the contents of Joshua's Baggie, I can barely find my lips.

We stumble back through the Dewey decimal system. Passing patrons tell us to shush. Joshua makes farting noises with his armpit.

"You guys are stoned," says Nell Schwartzman, Hebrew school vixen. Her pale skin looks vampirish in the fluorescent light. Lured by the promise of Joshua's brain, she has walked through the park to meet us.

"Shhhhh," says Joshua.

I collapse in hysterics, my face squashed into the study aids. I'd peel my eye from the page if I could find it.

"This isn't funny," says Nell. "We have a test tomorrow."

"Who's laughing?" says Joshua. They both look at me.

I struggle mightily to regain sobriety. My lack of motor control is extremely juvenile. I am pathetic and weak-willed. I stand no chance of winning the love of the first girl who has shown any interest in me. When she agreed to meet for a study date, phlogiston ignited in my heart.

"You got me stoned," I accuse Joshua.

"It's a capitalist economy," he says. "You demand, I supply."

"Don't start that," says Nell.

Joshua bows his head. For once, he is silent. No clever quips; no cerebral backtalk. He leaves his brain in a vat while his body sinks into the wooden armchair. The transformation leaves me breathless, the tips of my fingers tingling. What magic incantation explains the sudden flush creeping into his scalp like borscht on a carpet?

It was Joshua who invited Nell, I remember, not I.

"Our history," says Jacob as the yellow bus bangs down the expressway toward a weekend of spiritual indoctrination, "is the struggle between assimilation and isolation. In either camp we have suffered. The world doesn't forget you're a Jew."

"Because we keep reminding them," says Joshua.

"The holidays reflect this conflict," Jacob continues, ignoring Joshua. "*Purim* warns about isolation; Esther saved her people because she married the king. *Hanukkah*, with its story of the destruction of the Temple, warns about the impossibility of assimilation."

"That's no reason to be a Jew—because the world won't let you be anything else."

"Be what you want. You're always a Jew."

I fall asleep somewhere beyond the ideology exit. I've already discarded my baggage.

When I awake, I see lights flickering around a campsite. We park near another bus with *St. Mary's* stenciled on the side and lug our duffel bags into the wooden cabin. It is cold and dank; the smell of clogged toilets wafts through the bedrooms.

I unload my bag on a mattress stained with the residue of unspeakable acts. On the wall next to my bunk bed, in dark ink, someone has scrawled: "Steve + Mary 2/1/77." Whatever Steve and Mary equal, I don't want to sleep on it.

In the gloomy kitchen Nell and two younger girls light the Sabbath candles. Enormous shadows flicker across the paneled walls. Ghosts of Christmas past. Jews? they ask. Who invited the Jews?

Jacob prepares dinner. His is a *Shabbat* of spiritual renewal, he explains, not dogmatic regulations. Let the *Hasidim* starve themselves with rules; he will eat.

"Secret East Side recipe," he says as he dumps four jars of spaghetti sauce into a pot.

Soon the kitchen fogs with steam and salt. Plastic silverware glimmers in the candlelight. Paper cups blush with red wine.

"Let's chow," says Joshua, smacking his hands.

"Let's bless," says Jacob, smacking Joshua's bottom.

"*Baruch ata adonai, elohainu melech ha'alum, ha'motzi lechem min ha'aretz*," we recite. Bless this *challa*, baked at the supermarket, which looks like a braided hot-dog bun.

"The Sabbath is a taste of the world to come," says Jacob.

Salty spaghetti. And burned garlic bread. The Messiah will order Chinese food.

Later the campground drones with the sounds of guitars, earnest voices, and crackling fires. Joshua and I pick our way along a dark trail, tripping over roots and beer bottles. We emerge near a lake where water slaps against a gazebo. Our feet clomp up the mossy stairs.

Inside, the gazebo smells like damp blankets. A slight wind rattles loose shingles. Joshua perches gargoyle-like on a decaying bench.

"Colin," he says solemnly. "Please recite the blessing over the marijuana."

"Blessed be thou, O Lord our God, king of the universe, who has bidden us inhale the wacky weed."

We smoke late into the night, our tongues like rope in mouths of wool.

When we return to the cabin, Jacob waves us over to a small gathering by a moth-eaten couch. A younger boy is talking eagerly about the perils of adolescence and sexual awakening. Several of his friends nod in serious agreement. Joshua sneezes.

"Any more spaghetti?" I ask.

Jacob gestures at the sagging, dented refrigerator. I unstick myself from the floor and wander into the kitchen.

Dense white objects, like food for a space voyage, line the refrigerator shelves: packages of marshmallows; milk; blocks of cheese; cooked spaghetti. Fluorescent light bathes them in an unearthly glow. Tucked behind four dozen eggs, I find the pot of sauce.

My face is propped between door and shelf, a telltale red mustache evidence of my nighttime foraging, a finger in my mouth as if measuring for a fever, when I hear her voice.

"You guys are stoned."

I bump my head swiveling out from the spaceship. "No, no," I insist as I exhale bits of spaghetti.

"You left me with the baby-sitter," she says.

I focus on Nell's pale face, her brown eyes so black that her pupils are invisible.

"We didn't," I say. "I didn't."

She inhales; her collarbone pokes above the top of her scoop-necked shirt.

"I don't think he likes me," she says.

"Of course he does," I say, folding my arms in front of the spaghetti sauce sprinkled across my belt line. "He likes everybody. He's dumb that way."

"Joshua, I mean."

I feel my mouth lose its elasticity, my smile slip into an alien grimace.

Before I can construct an elaborate and bejeweled lie that will save the princess and banish the evil magician, Joshua alights like a buzzard on the butcher block.

"Jews," he says, by way of greeting, his hair bristling like a toilet brush.

"Joshua," says Nell.

"There's a gazebo."

"Show me?"

Without another word, they glide, sloe-eyed and slack-jawed, out the back door and into the night.

I gaze around the mildewed kitchen. The wood floor is cracked and pitted, years of accumulated dirt between the boards. The cabinets are lopsided and droopy, likely to crash from their perch without warning. Rust chips stain the sink. Plaster flakes from the walls.

I scrape my sneakers along the floor. The sound they make is not unlike a sob.

In the living room Jacob sings the joys of figs and oranges. He inclines his head beside the curve of his guitar, indicating that I should join him.

"Where's Professor Marx?" he asks between verses.

If I knew, I would tell him. But by now he could be anywhere. T-shirt; brassiere; panties. Young people can't be trusted to keep their clothes on.

"Bedfellows make strange politics," he says sagely.

"They're not," I say defensively.

"Even stranger are the geometric shapes—triangles, for example."

I scrutinize him closely: the fine hairs sprouting next to his eyes where his beard doesn't grow; the deep lines creasing his mouth; his white teeth, flat and even as filed stone. He strums lightly on his guitar.

"I predict a long life," he says. "Many children, many loves. Your heart will be broken; your heart will be strong. You'll wander through the desert and emerge in the Promised Land."

"She's just a girl," I say.

"Lovesongs are always about girls."

His empty bed at dawn.

Unslept, unwashed, where has he spent the night?

"Incredible," he says as he plunks down on my bunk.

"Did you?" I manage.

He squints at me as if I've desecrated an ancient temple. "It's not an Olympic event," he says.

But then he tells all: the passion; the intertwined limbs; the sighs; the confessions; the lack of adequate birth control.

"You should always carry one in your wallet," I say.

"I forgot my wallet," he says mournfully.

A loud snore punctuates the early-morning stillness. A bed creaks; someone mutters in his sleep.

Joshua lowers his voice. "I left it in my pants."

I am too dazed to speak. He's suddenly older, having drunk from the fountain of Eros and bathed in Thanatos's shadow. *Woman* is no longer an abstraction. She lives; she breathes; she sticks her tongue in his ear. He pities my impoverished adolescence, my inadequate schooling. From this day forward he will have to tutor me like some half-witted cousin whose parents have foisted him upon his bright and shining relative in the hope that some of the gloss will rub off.

"I'm exhausted," he yawns. He swings his legs off my bunk and climbs the wooden ladder to his. I watch the mattress undulate as he finds a comfortable spot.

"You know who's responsible for all this?" he asks when he's settled down.

"Who?"

"Hitler," he says.

"Hitler?" I repeat, incredulous.

"If it weren't for him, I wouldn't be here."

His reasoning, I tell him, is twisted sideways and backwards. "Hitler wanted to kill you," I say.

A wave rolls over my head. "The only reason my parents sent me to Hebrew school was Hitler," he says. "They don't even believe in God."

If he hadn't gone to Hebrew school, he explains, he wouldn't have met Nell, and if he hadn't met Nell, the night would never have happened.

"Thanks, Adolf," he concludes.

I have never heard a more perverted version of the Great Man theory of history. "You're cracked," I say.

A voice at the back of the bedroom tells us to shut up. The sea calms. All is still.

"Joshua?" I ask.

"Mmmmm," he says, already asleep.

"You don't mean that about Hitler."

He doesn't answer. A soft whistling noise echoes from the ceiling. The roof beams sigh. I am left alone to ponder the great spheres: sex, death, love, birth. Each contains, within its perfectly rounded self, a longing for the absent infinite.

I flop about the lumpy mattress, my hormones raging, my face smooth and unshaven. I have been beaten up, humiliated, and lost the girl. I can't throw a punch; I can't dress myself; I think Sodom is merely a town in ancient Palestine.

When Moses led the people from Pharaoh's iron grip, they danced on the muddy flats of a giant empty sea. Bread rained from the sky, and water sprang from rocks. He promised them a land of peace, overflowing with milk and honey. They sang for joy and praised His name.

Later, because they walked too slowly, God sped them there in cattle cars. Some drove their own convertibles, waving to their friends as they roared down the autobahn, oblivious to history and the anguished cries of those pressed to the walls of the holy city.

And God threw up His hands, leaving His throne and the fate of His people to other minor deities.

He hasn't been heard from since.

❖   ❖   ❖

"Maccabees!" commands Jacob. "To the field of honor!"

I struggle awake, sandbags stacked against my eyes to keep them from flooding. It's only noon; can't he let me sleep?

In the true communal spirit, Jacob has arranged a volleyball game with our religious competitors. Now he buzzes around the camp, arming us with nuggets of volleyball wisdom: Don't spike till you see the whites of their eyes; peace through superior ball handling.

"Kill the *goyim*," adds Joshua.

We trudge outdoors into a bright and burning sun. The air smells like burned pine needles. A bird screeches tunelessly.

The court is a barefaced patch of hard sand and scrubgrass. Eight boys and a girl regard us skeptically from the other side. Their counselor, a freckled woman in a sundress, encourages them to engage us in benevolent recreation. We toss a ball around tentatively, as unsure of our skills as of the proper mode of interfaith intercourse.

Someone suggests a game. Jacob claps his hands as if the idea is an epiphany. "Winners get the kingdom of heaven," he proposes. "Losers admit they were wrong about the Messiah."

"I'll keep score," says the freckled counselor.

We form three haphazard rows of three. Joshua heads for the server's box. I stay up front, where I hope balls will arc harmlessly beyond my reach. We win the coin toss, and Joshua's first serve loops into the back corner untouched.

"Way to go, Josh!" shouts Nell from the sidelines, her hands around a mug of cocoa.

He serves again, traps, sets, and spikes. Soaring above the court, he rewrites Newtonian physics. He's an example for millions of schoolchildren. Cereal boxes clamor for his picture.

"Two serving zero," says freckles.

On the other side of the court a thick-faced blond boy menaces the front row. On Joshua's third serve the blond leaps high above the net and slams the serve back at my head. I duck, and the ball bounces inbounds behind me.

"Save yourself," Jacob advises. Nell laughs.

We switch servers. The blond doesn't move.

"Rotate!" Joshua says. "You got to rotate."

The kid glares at Joshua but steps back a row.

I flip the ball to their server. He wins three points before sending his fourth serve into a tree.

"Good block," says Jacob.

We creep up the point ladder. Two for us, one for them. Three for them, two for us. Each time Joshua breathes, Nell cheers.

"Eleven serving thirteen," announces freckles as she tosses me the ball.

The vagaries of rotation have placed Joshua and the blond facing each other in the front row as I shuffle into the server's box. The ball is surprisingly light, almost weightless, its taut skin like a grimace.

I blow on one hand, rub my fingers into my palm, then slap the ball into the air.

"Net!" bellows the blond. "Our serve."

"Take two," says Joshua, ducking under the net and retrieving the ball from its unsuspecting holder.

"Our serve!" says the blond.

Joshua tosses me the ball.

"Give me the ball," the blond grunts.

"Take two," says Joshua.

"Come on, guys," Jacob says halfheartedly.

"Fucking cheat," the blond says. He takes one step to the middle of the court and pushes Joshua.

"Hey!" says Jacob. "Quit that talk."

Joshua staggers backward, grabs the net, then regains his balance. The blond crosses the center line and advances toward him. Jacob and Nell shriek. Joshua dips into a crouch, a perfect boxer's parody. The blond approaches, his fists like two cabbages. Joshua feints left, and the blond follows, countering with a right and exposing his chin. Joshua drops into the empty space between bodies, shifting his weight and uncoiling a massive uppercut that slams the blond beside his ear. There's a crack, and a pop, and the kid goes down, a tiny squirt of blood trailing from his nose.

"Some punch," says Jacob into the silence.

I look at the boy on the ground, his mouth pressed to the dirt, tiny flecks of sand along his lip. The volleyball bounces nearby.

"He pushed you," I hear Nell say.

The woman in the sundress draws the boy's head onto her lap. She dabs at the blood on his cheek. His eyes open, blink. He spits a tooth into her hand. She inspects the white and red globule on her palm, then begins to wail, a soft moan without end, a cry that sounds as if it will never stop, as if it will carry the birds to their winter homes.

A cry of vengeance.

"Violence," Grandma Esther says, wiping the remnants of cheesecake from the table, "only brings more violence. Look at your uncle Asher. After he shot those two coloreds, he never had anything but trouble. A streetcar ran him down in Florida."

Pay heed, Joshua, and look both ways before crossing. Remember Tommy Patrick, dead by his own hand when he was only seventeen.

god's eye,
the devil's
mouth

Marjorie, not the Morningstar but the evening one. The one whose black hair shines like the beginning of time from a chair perched at the edge of the Big Bang.

Olive-eyed, dark-complected, anorectic Jewess.

I bump through the hallways like a blind astronomer trailing a comet. The pull of gravity lures me heavenward.

I crash into the library doors. I collide with my homeroom supervisor. I stumble into class. It's difficult navigating with a thin gauze of Vaseline coating your lenses. Soft focus distorts the vision.

Her radiance washes all other light from the sky. From this distance, if there were other life, it would be extinguished by nuclear fusion and gamma waves.

"Wouk's is the world of postwar assimilation," says Mr. Lavelle, our senior AP–English teacher. "The beginning of the era when Americans believed anything was possible through self-creation and fashion. Marjorie's demise illustrates the emptiness of those beliefs."

"She dumped a real jerk for a better life in the suburbs," says Marjorie.

"She sacrificed love for convenience and was blinded by vanity to true happiness."

I wash the windows of the observatory, open the sliding panel doors. Let her extraterrestrial glow wash over me.

"Lavelle is wrong," she says as I lap behind her down the hallway. "Marjorie found happiness in the suburbs."

I imagine Lavelle choosing the books for his honors English class. Here's Shakespeare, and here's Tolstoy, and here's one the kids can relate to. Was it anti-Semitism or simply an error in judgment?

"Lavelle doesn't know anything about love." She slams her locker.

"Give you a ride home?" I squeak.

We find my car in a potholed corner of the student parking lot. It rattles and coughs as I coax it onto the road. I nearly sideswipe a neighborhood security van, a truck loaded with gardening implements, an expensive European import. Marjorie shrieks with pleasure.

"You'll kill us!" she shouts.

"Sure!" I say, joining in the fun.

We sputter past tiny stores with faux aged lettering, their windows cluttered with inconceivable items of no apparent use. We pass Nell's house, climb a small hill overlooking the duck pond, then spin through a residential section of white houses with Georgian columns and perfect lawns.

She directs me down a treeless street, as flat and wide as an interstate highway. A thin wire of muscle cords along her forearm.

Two Mercedes, license plates "I DOC 1" and "I DOC 2," hunker like sumo wrestlers in a circular driveway.

"My dad's an ophthalmologist," she explains.

"Mine's a scientist," I say stupidly.

She looks out the window at the manicured grass. Her hand alights on the door handle.

"My grandfather was an anarchist," I add, anything to keep her in the car.

"Mine's a jeweler."

"He was arrested once for disturbing the peace and distributing leaflets."

"Did he go to jail?"

I shake my head, mildly disappointed with my grandfather. "My grandmother bailed him out."

If she is impressed with my dangerous family history, she doesn't let on. Instead, she opens the door. Her left hand rests on the space between our seats.

"You should be careful," she says, her eyebrows knitting together like a scarf. "They keep records."

"No," I say, "there are none." When he died, they couldn't even find his birth certificate. Only the memory, vague at best.

"You're lucky."

"I guess."

"Well, see you Monday," she says.

"Monday," I repeat, as if to prove I have the intelligence of a parrot.

And then she is gone, her palm outlined in the fine vinyl dust, her fingers like ghostly trails across a blue prairie.

"Ask her out," says Joshua. "She digs you."

I tell him that dating would ruin a beautiful platonic relationship.

He chews carefully on my grandmother's cheesecake. The last piece he ate nearly broke his jaw. "There are still three virgins in our class," he says. "I think you'll get an award at graduation."

In addition to art, science, literature, economics, history, and politics, Joshua is now an expert on love. For a year he has been sleeping with Nell, a 365-day head start. She wears his shirts to class, rolls up and belts his jeans around her waist. The bliss of the newly sexually awakened on both their faces like acne.

I reach for the telephone. I hesitate for only a moment, imagining rejection, embarrassment, death. Then her numbers spin off my fingers with the practiced skill of many late-night hours hunched over the dial.

"Hello?" says her voice.

"Bbbbbbbbbbbb movie bbbbbbbbbbbb," I say.

"I'd love to," she says.

My arms shake with exhaustion when I hang up the phone. My right ear is permanently embossed with tiny dots from the receiver. Somewhere near my kidneys, my heart twitches.

Joshua has fallen asleep at the kitchen table. I gently move his face out of the cheesecake and onto his plate.

"Did you get the trophy?" he asks groggily.

I drop his face back into the cheese. True love admits no clever quips from lard-filled Marxists.

Our foreheads thud; our teeth clack; my lips find hers.

I'm kissing Marjorie Kaplan! Girl of my dreams. Boyhood fantasy made real. Film at eleven.

She swishes her tongue inside my mouth, searching for lost coins, cleaning under the seat, bumping my tonsils like a small fish.

Alarm bells ring. Technicians rush to the telescope. The sky is falling! Sound the klaxon!

"Colin?" she says into my mouth. "There's a siren going off in your house."

In my fervent pursuit of a kiss I have kneed the "panic button" in my mother's car, igniting the house with a suburban symphony of whistles, lights, and bells. We should have parked in her driveway; ours was darker, until now.

I leap from the car, catch my foot on the seat belt, and plunge into the driveway. "No problem, no problem!" I scream, plucking gravel from my palms. "I'm home!"

Inside, despite the shrieking alarm, it is eerily silent. "I'm home!" I shout again. The code box blinks its unruly welcome. 6544? 6455? 6554? 6445? I can't remember the combination.

My brother creeps into the hallway holding a large butcher knife. "Is it safe?" he asks.

"David! I forgot the fucking code!"

He sheathes the knife in a belt loop and expertly punches a sequence of sixteen digits onto the number pad. "You have to override central command," he explains.

One by one, like animals off the ark, my family gathers in the kitchen.

"You told me to wake you . . ." I begin sheepishly.

Four pair of eyes dart past me to the front door.

"It was open?" Marjorie says, her voice rising into a question.

I scurry to her side. "Everyone, this is Marjorie. A friend," I add.

"Did you borrow her lipstick?" asks Rebecca.

My father coughs nervously. My mother chatters gaily. I wipe my lips with the back of my hand.

In two minutes my mother has assigned seats at the kitchen table and coaxed the Kaplan genealogy from Marjorie. Our families go back a long way, to the gates of Ellis Island, practically. They once shared a thin strip of block in a row of tenements on an island off the Hudson.

"I thought the ringing was in my ears," my mother coos sympathetically. "If your brother hadn't woken me with that knife, I might not have gotten up."

"I'm glad I got to meet you," says Marjorie.

"Hungry?" asks my mother, wrapping an arm around her.

Marjorie says she could nibble on a few bones.

"Cannibal," growls Becca.

"Isn't it past your bedtime?" says my mother, shooing Rebecca from the kitchen.

The women sit at table, their hands and elbows locked around steaming cups of tea, their foreheads pressed together. My father, brother, and I gaze dopily across the stove, too tired to sleep, too dumb to move. We follow the Ping-Pong of conversation with lolling heads and drifting eyes.

When I awake, they are still chattering. I lift my head off the gas burner. My brother has curled onto the floor near the dishwasher. My father snores on the couch. The first tendrils of light seep through the skylights.

"Tomorrow's a school day," I say.

"Already?" Marjorie sighs, twisting a ring around her left index finger.

She and my mother share reluctant farewells. They have so much to talk about and so little time! But what a pleasure it was finally to meet. They look forward to many more hours huddled around the hearth.

I fish for the car keys in my jacket pocket. My mother picks them up from the table and hands them to Marjorie. They giggle like schoolgirls on a first date.

"Drive carefully," my mother says.

"I don't have a license," says Marjorie.

They collapse into jiggling fits of laughter, their whoops and screeches like sirens heralding doom, untimely death, and the full eclipse of the moon.

Graphic representations of grades as a function of SAT scores cover the east wall of my bedroom. Multicolored charts listing deadlines and admissions requirements plaster the west wing. Maps with triangles indicating primary targets and circles and rectangles for secondary and tertiary sites clutter my desk. Computers run worst-case scenarios, highlighting casualty figures and collateral damage. Reams of data spit from dot matrix printers:

> Nestled in the quiet heart of America's rugged beauty, Deep Thoughts College nurtures serious minds, dedicated to the pursuit of intellectual rigor and masculine companionship. Twenty men live in a monastic environment, reading seminal works of Eastern and Western civilization, while raising organic vegetables and living holistically with small animals.

> *Located in the pulsing heart of America's urban center, Intense Competition University drives overachievers to unimagined extremes. Undergraduates share cramped living space with medical and/or law students, developing and cultivating their own neurotic tendencies. Large vats of coffee located strategically about the campus allow students to take advantage of the combination twenty-four-hour library and suicide prevention center.*

In a rented Winnebago, with a support crew of twenty, my father and I make the college tour.

"Who's your favorite author?" he preps me. "The last book you read? The most important issue facing the earth? The person you most admire? Your favorite method of transportation?"

I tell him to leave me alone. No one would ask such stupid questions. I stare back out the window at a pastoral landscape imported from Iowa at great cost for the happy, hippie undergraduates at one of America's most overpriced private colleges, leaving a great rent of mud and rock through a significant section of the Midwest.

At my first interview I am stumped by the transportation question.

"Public transportation," my father admonishes me. "Intelligent urban systems transport more people more efficiently than conventional carbon-based limited-passenger-capacity models."

For my next interview I buy my father a toupee and a pair of sneakers and spend the afternoon at the movies while he wows the admissions committee. On my way back to campus I am mugged by two boys wearing university sweatshirts and caps.

"Do you know how much tuition costs?" one of them says.

"Financial aid," explains the other as he relieves me of my watch.

My father tells me not to cry; he thinks I'll be accepted early admission. "Look at the bright side," he says. "At least you got to meet some students."

Up the coast, our bus rumbling, my father in the back humming show tunes and fryin' up a mess o' catfish. The roadies love him, call him doc, beg over and over for the story about mitosis.

"What's so great about college?" I ask after my fifteenth interview. "Boring old professors droning about a bunch of dead guys."

My sixteenth interviewer has the most perfect teeth I've ever seen. In her office overlooking the hills of western Massachusetts, reflected light illuminates her flawless smile. The former captain of women's cross-country, she's staying on campus an extra year to work in the admissions office.

"They have a great science department!" I tell my father excitedly over a plate of fried eggs. "Great facilities! Great resources! Great . . . great!"

My newfound enthusiasm heartens my father, who's growing weary of singing songs and regaling the roadies with tall tales of brave deeds by mitochondria and Golgi apparatus. He has a friend in the chemistry department; maybe he could make some phone calls.

"Nuclear chemistry!" I say. "Neurochemistry! Human chemistry! Tell him I love all the chemistries!"

He swirls the broken yolk around his plate. He's always thought of his eldest son as his mother's child, their tastes pitched toward books and theater. He had pinned his ambitions on his inquisitive and dexterous second son. But now he dares to hope that both boys will follow their father's lead, finding the same calm precision in the axioms of science and the balance of chemical reactions.

He smiles warmly at me, his future collaborator. Perhaps they will name a research wing after our family.

"There's only one thing," I add. "Do you think they'll make me *study* chemistry?"

"We're a little concerned about our grades," Marjorie's parents confide.

"And we don't test very well."

"But we have good extracurriculars."

"And strong recommendations."

Their bleached living room shimmers like a mirage. I sit in a sunken oasis shaped like a grand piano. They offer me coffee, pastries, sandwiches, ignoring my every word while maintaining a facade of interest and delirium. A small animal, probably a dog, yaps at my feet.

Marjorie nibbles on a cookie, then excuses herself for the bathroom.

"What do you think about our chances?" whispers Mrs. Kaplan. Her stockings sigh as she crosses and uncrosses her legs.

I squint at a framed print of obscure religious lettering. E. F P. T O Z. L P E D. Vague words of encouragement roll from my mouth.

In the bathroom Marjorie pokes at her tonsils with a toothbrush, dribbling saliva into the toilet bowl. Her gag reflex isn't what it used to be. She finally manages a thin trickle of bile—lunch.

She returns to the oasis smelling of toothpaste and lavender soap.

"Feeling okay, sweetie?" asks Dr. Kaplan, silver-haired and gold-plated.

"Fine, Daddy," says Marjorie.

Mrs. Kaplan smooths her dress and crosses one nyloned leg over the other. Her remarkable bosom rises like a hoisted flag. "We're worried about our figure," she says.

"We have a tremendous figure," says Dr. Kaplan, kissing his wife's cheek.

Marjorie turns away while I nod in overenthusiastic agreement. Dr. Kaplan fixes me with a baleful glare.

"Have you ever looked closely at the human eye?" he asks.

When I don't answer, he continues anyway.

"Doctors used to believe that every image you'd ever seen was imprinted in your eyes," he continues.

I look at my toes. They are hidden inside my shoes.

"What is the eye? Just a mass of tissue and blood vessels and fluid. If I removed your eye from its socket, where would those images be imprinted? Could I find them? Where would I look?"

"Daddy, don't be disgusting," says Marjorie, her fingers twisting her ring.

"Obviously the images aren't *in* your eye or *on* your eye. They're in your brain somewhere, stored in cells as chemicals. Even then they can't be viewed like a film or a photograph. The cells don't have tiny microscopic movie screens. *No single representation exists, yet the images persist.*"

He wipes a tiny fleck of spittle from the corner of his mouth.

"You tell me you still believe in evolution."

Mrs. Kaplan's stockings punctuate the silence. Marjorie's fingers dismantle another cookie. The dog growls at my socks.

Natural selection operates by whimsy and caprice. A casual glance, a haphazard motion, and suddenly you're a chosen trait.

I smile at Dr. Kaplan. He doesn't frighten me with his faith in teleology. God or Darwin, neither made it into the twentieth century.

My mother's dissertation, dense as a slab of granite, on the living room bookshelf. In a fit of fecundity, she has dashed through 354 pages and bloodied her sword in its defense. *Laughing in the Devil's*

Mouth: The Jewish Humorous Anecdote in Eastern Europe, 1930–1945. Now she awaits, head bowed, for the final honor.

Grandma Esther, listing like a sinking boat, slumps on Becca's armrest.

"Grandma?" says Becca, digging her elbow into my ribs.

Mom steps to the podium, shakes the dean's hand, receives the hallowed parchment. Her new adviser, barely old enough to remember the old adviser, slips the crimson hood around her neck.

In the Brighton Beach walk-up Grandpa Isaac wipes the flour from his palms and swings her into the air. Every night with a book in her hand, the dimming light from the street illuminating the pages; his pamphlets extolling the virtues of the working classes lay unopened next to dog-eared copies of Dickens and Twain.

His only daughter. His only child.

"*Yitzchak*," says Grandma, "you want she should break her neck?"

I nudge my father. There's a guy sitting next to Grandma with a scythe. Big black robe and a hood. Bony hands. Refuses to introduce himself.

My father switches seats with Becca while the newly crowned and unemployed parade up the aisle and into the dwindling years of a fading millennium.

"Dad?" asks Becca.

But my father isn't listening. He's talking to the man in black. How did he get here? Does he have an invitation? We can't permit gate-crashers at this celebratory occasion.

The man smiles politely. He's only passing through, surveying the territory. The place seems familiar, though maybe it's the faces that remind him. After a while one tragedy looks like any other. He loses count.

He rises from his seat and joins the black-robed procession as they march toward the exit, his round head bobbing in a sea of squares. When he reaches the door, he turns and tips his scythe. His teeth shine like skeletons in his mouth.

My father tightens his grip around Becca's shoulders. His long fingers like dinosaur talons. "She'll be fine," he says.

But Rebecca has seen enough. White knuckles near her neck. A ghoulish imprint on her skin.

When she howls, she raises the dead.

Grandma Esther makes a wig from her hair. It hangs like a scalp over the bed.

The room smells of soap, perfume, baby powder, urine. Rebecca refuses to enter. David holds his breath when he delivers Grandma's newspaper. Why couldn't she pass silently in her sleep like Grandma Miriam, her body discovered by anxious neighbors? My parents left us at home for the funeral.

My mother cleans the bed, carries her to the bathroom, props her head up in the tub. Her mother's wasted body, naked, breasts drooping like bananas; the skin stretched and folded where fat no longer supports it; a shock of pubic hair, veined with gray. Grandma lifts her arms to soap her neck, but the muscles betray her, and the soap slips into the water. She cries, soundlessly. What is happening to me? she asks. Her daughter turns away as she fishes for the soap.

Downstairs my parents discuss *what is to be done*. No one says the word, but everyone knows what word they mean. Oncologists offer their diagnoses, lowering their voices to conspiratorial whispers. If there's anything we need, they say, letting their voices trail off into implication; they've known my father for many years.

"She's got cancer," I tell Marjorie, feeling the word bump against my teeth.

"My grandfather died of cancer," says Marjorie. "He went crazy at the end," she adds.

I imagine Grandma Esther, her brain invaded by marauding cells, struggling to identify familiar shapes in a confused landscape. If it's Hungary 1930, why does that boy look like her grandson? Perhaps it's her brother, beaten to death in prison by Nazi collaborators. Why didn't he get out, run away, fight back?

"She's taking chemotherapy," I say. "They said she's got a good chance."

"They have to say that. Otherwise they get sued."

"No." I slam my locker door shut. "You don't know my grandmother. When my grandfather had a heart attack, she carried him downstairs to a taxi. She never even cried. My mother told me."

Marjorie lays a hand on my arm. "Colin," she says, her voice flat as paint. "Nobody lives forever."

Music blares from the living room; the house vibrates in an uneven pitch.

I sit on the couch wedged between my best friend and my best friend's girlfriend, who was never mine. A beer between my legs, a bourbon in my fist, listening to Dr. Kaplan tell us that the big money is in neurology.

Nell's hand alights on my knee. She inclines her head, and I can smell cucumbers in her hair. One more drink and I will chew on it like a fantastic fruit.

The party careens into the night, all screeches and peals, the nearest runaway truck ramp miles behind.

At midnight Marjorie emerges from the bathroom, her lips swollen, her eyes red and puffy. She glares at me as she passes the couch.

"Sweetie," says Dr. Kaplan, "these are the best years of your life."

"You're drunk, Daddy," she says.

"My girl's a high school graduate. Don't I have the right to a drink?" he asks us.

Joshua, Nell, and I agree. Praise to the adults who buy us beer and drink with us in their house. Why can't all parents be like Dr. Kaplan? Cheers to Dr. Kaplan. May his hand always be steady as he wields the laser. May his license never be revoked for operating under the influence.

"Can I talk to you?" Marjorie commands.

I rise from the couch, leaving my major organ systems in my shoes.

"Go easy on him, honey," slurs Dr. Kaplan.

"Daddy," warns Marjorie.

"She's a killer," he says proudly.

I tail Marjorie across the living room, down into the oasis, and up toward the bedroom suite. I lose her in a knot of people smoking near the bottom of the staircase. When I emerge from the clouds, she's vanished.

I follow a cold trail of uneaten bits of food and pop songs. The detritus of a suburban adolescence.

At the top of the stairs Mrs. Kaplan steps from the exercise room, a pink towel around her neck, her impossible body sheathed in Lycra. She grips my arm as I pass. "We're so proud of all you young people," she says, waving a cigarette at me.

My first clue, that familiar smell, like burning perspiration.

I reach for the joint, and my fingertips brush her wrist. She leans into me, the warmth of her heavy breasts, her moist heart beating the air between us.

"Colin!" Marjorie calls.

I jump, stung by a dragonfly.

"Honey," says Mrs. Kaplan, "this is your night."

Marjorie hisses at her mother and yanks the joint from my mouth. She hauls me into her bedroom and kicks the door shut; the narrow point of her heel leaves a horseshoe indentation in the paint. We dive into the bed, ricocheting against the pillows. Our bodies buried in down.

"Get a grip on your libido," she says when the dust has settled.

My head is a feather, filled with fluff and bourbon. It swims about the room, carried on the warm currents of an overactive endocrine system.

"Here," I say, unbuttoning my trousers. "Show me how."

The phone call in the middle of the night. The hushed voices and whispered cries. A morning of anxious relatives and neighbors rushing to make coffee, drink coffee, refill coffee.

The pine coffin, the barren parlor, the rent garments. I stand near the pallbearers tugging at the sleeves of my new suit. Too short, too tight. I wanted a blue one.

Rebecca, her dark hair swept back off her forehead, her lips lightly painted, holds forth before a coterie of cousins, their Adam's apples like swallowed birdcages. David sticks close to my mother, circling behind her as she moves through clots of well-wishers. Tides well in his moon-shaped eyes.

We shuffle into the waiting limousine. My father sits up front, his ostrich legs folded across his sparrow chest. He twists awkwardly in his seat to reach back for my mother's hand. She leans forward, her head pressed to the divider. When we hit a bump, she leaves a makeup smear on the Plexiglas.

Along the highway the dead are spread like loam across sun-scorched fields. Headstones peer from yellowed grass as the road dips into mirage. A soft dust falls faintly, coating everything with a thin layer of soot, residue from the town incinerator. Ashes to ashes.

"Ben," my mother commands as the limo rumbles to a stop on loose gravel. "Fix Colin's tie."

My father fiddles with the knot around my neck. His fingers smell like coffee. He presses my cheeks with his palms. "It looks fine," he whispers.

The air rushes out. We step into the light.

A tumbling path leads down a battered hill. The sun beats fiercely by the open grave. A circle of mourners stand clear of the edge.

The rabbi wipes sweat from his brow with a stained handkerchief. A failed novelist with a captive audience, he tells us the short story of Esther Newman's life. The eldest of six girls. Her only brother killed by fascists. An immigrant's life of hard work and sacrifice. The love of husband, daughter, son-in-law, and grandchildren.

"*Yitgadal v'yitgadash sh'mei raba,*" he intones, reading from his mimeographed and transliterated copy of the mourner's *Kaddish.*

David chokes back a sob. My mother pulls him close, burying his dark head in a black crease.

"*Yitbarach v'yishtabach v'yitpa'ar v'yitroman v'yitnasei, v'yithadar v'yitaleh v'yit-halal shmei d'kdusha, b'rich Hu.*"

May He who creates the harmony of the spheres create peace for us and for all Israel.

My mother tosses a handful of earth. Tiny rocks clatter against wood. She teeters on a lip of grass, swaying slightly to an internal rhythm. Then she turns and clutches Becca with one hand, David with the other; together they retreat toward the limousine.

I watch the gravediggers shovel dirt into the hole. The rasp of sand on metal. A dull whistle. The muffled thump.

ESTHER NEWMAN

BELOVED MOTHER, WIFE, GRANDMOTHER

✡

"Colin!" my father calls.

I turn and run from the grave.

Our house is a cornucopia of pastries, cakes, cookies, and fruit salads. Cousins whom I've never met spew crumbs into my face. Relatives who have aged grotesquely, faces curdled with brown spots, hands mottled with white spots, tell me how much I've grown.

David mopes from room to room while Becca stands imperiously near the food, touching nothing, surveying all. My mother searches for extra silverware, glasses, chairs, while the synagogue's calamity auxiliary implores her to mourn. My father follows behind them, opening chairs and rearranging the forks.

"Let's get away from all this food," Marjorie whispers.

She slips her hand into mine and tows me from the living room. We climb the stairs, navigate the hallway, and moor in the still waters of my bedroom.

Her hands on my neck; her mouth in my hair.

"It's okay," she says. "Everything will be okay."

I know I should bear the loss like a rusted anchor cast over my shoulder, but I am far out at sea, bobbing on the waves of bottled desire.

I tilt my face, and then she is kissing me, tiny minnows darting between the rocks. She kicks the door shut. Her bare toes grip my shins.

"Is there a way to lock this?" she asks as she fiddles with the knob.

I break the latch, trapping us in the room. In case of fire they will find our naked and charred bodies humped in a corner.

The X of her arms as she lifts her shirt. Her bra falling away like a white flag.

"Do you have something?" she asks.

A rainbow assortment of condoms, a veritable PX of contraception, each unit carefully weighed and inspected, rubbed once for good luck, packed in a brown, unmarked package, and mailed to me.

She reaches behind her, finds the drawer and then the condoms.

"My parents," I say.

"Can they hear?"

I shake my head.

"Do you love me?"

I am eighteen years old. My last grandparent has just died, the final link to a past I never knew or troubled to discover. My family is in mourning nine feet below me. In two months I will leave this house forever and spend the next ten years searching for my home. Like any orphan in history, I crawl toward the clean, well-lighted place.

"Yes," I say.

She presses my palm to the hollow between her breasts, the hard plate of her ribs. I can feel the steady thumping of her heart: one-two, one-two, one-two. Each stroke an affirmation. Every pump a promise. The blood rushes to her muscles, her organs, her brain; her lungs breathe new life into wearying cells.

Renewal and decay. Redemption and loss. In five thousand years certain themes tend to repeat. We wake; we rise; we renovate. We build oases in our living rooms. If we cannot exclude the infinite, at least we can draw blueprints for the measurable.

My name in Marjorie's mouth. Her hands in my bones. I am inside the circle. I am returning to the spheres.

Here I come.

freedom

find

the

jew

Clifton Reed Lancaster III.

"Call me Dirk," he says, thrusting out a hand like a pot roast, a jaw like a nutcracker. His hair a dusty cotton boll.

Hail the college on the hill. Praise to our founder: the patron saint of biological warfare, seller of smallpox-infected blankets to the Indians. And greetings to our future alumni, those bright young men and women who have had every advantage life can offer and even some it can't.

Our microscopic room, a bare cell; its semipermeable walls leak outside noise. Drunken arguments, desperate pleas, the late-night supplications of forlorn freshmen.

"Top or bottom?" he asks, his southern accent like a wandering eye: Now you see it, now you don't.

A door clangs. The toilet flushes. Beer cans rattle down the hallway.

Above me two hundred pounds bounce and sag against wires thin as paper clips. He snores. And talks in his sleep. Centuries of land ownership have made him proprietary and insular, oblivious to the biological needs of his fellow beings. It is hours until, with a pillow shoved into my ears, I fall asleep.

At the gates of the ghetto my family waves good-bye. The firstborn has been slain. Lamb's blood marks the door. It's too late to return; silent armies pursue me to the sea. There's been a terrible mistake, I cry, don't let me go. But I am driven from my home, with nothing but crumbled flat bread in my pocket, farther and farther into the desert.

"You don't look like you're from a ghetto," says Dirk.

Master of phrenology, he unpacks his compass and measuring tools. Hmm, he mutters, that sloped brow, those heavy eyelids.

"My mother has blue eyes," I explain quickly. "My grandmother had blond hair."

"My grandmother has blue hair."

I laugh too loudly, pound him on the back. "Blue hair!" I gasp with relief. "She has blue hair!"

"To go with her blue blood."

"Blue blood!" I shriek. "Blue blood!"

We walk to the dining hall. Two preppies, tall and fair, our collars up against the light breeze.

I square my shoulders, pinch my nostrils, inhale. It's no good, I'm spotted. They've seen the movie.

"How are Jew?"

"What would Jew like?"

"Jew get enough to eat?"

At a table of student organizations a dark-haired woman calls to me.

"Join the Hillel Club?"

I look away, scan for Dirk.

"Leave me alone," I snarl.

Dirk sits at a large table circled with beefy athletes: Tex, Rex, Max, Chex. Next to them, he looks almost of normal dimensions.

They grunt into their plates.

"My roommate, Colin," Dirk says, introducing me to his prep school classmates.

We play a game. It's called Find the Jew. Those sneaky Jews, they change their names, change their clothes, attend college in the hills of Massachusetts. You can't even spot one in the shower anymore because crafty Jewish doctors circumcise everybody. But now, with JewFinder, your worries are over. Simply set the dial to "Semite" and point. A green light tells you that you've found the Jew!

"Football," say Tex, Rex, Max, Chex, lifting their heads out of their food. A fluorescent orange disk at the bottom of their plates indicates where to stop eating. They push back from the table like tugboats in a haze of methane. Big scrimmage tomorrow; they have to shield their brains from the rigors of speech.

"Charmers," says Dirk to their trash can rear ends.

A tiny muscle, I notice, twitching below his eye.

I roll off the bunk, crash against the doorframe, plunge headfirst into a bean bag.

My mother's voice on the telephone, like water underwater.

"Did you get our letter?" she asks.

Unfortunately I've already spent the money on beer and other food groups. I'd like to come home for *Yom Kippur*, but it's hard to hitchhike on the holy days. When you're weighed down by prayer books and musical supplements, the trucks won't stop to bear the extra load.

She hands the phone to my father. Perhaps he can rattle my religion bone.

"No one is leaving school for the *Jewish holidays*," I plead.

"We'll pick you up," he offers, a simple domestic transportation matter.

I can't waltz off campus for some atavistic atonement ritual. Though half my professors have canceled classes, there are parties to attend and mixers to mix.

"We never celebrate the holidays," I claim.

"We're getting older," he says.

I tell him not to include me in his mortality research. At my age I defy the laws of entropy, skewing his results.

"It would mean a lot to your mother," he whispers conspiratorially, as if she weren't listening on the other line.

"She has other children."

"They'll be there."

"They live there," I remind him.

"She misses you."

My parents placed me in this rocket and aimed me at the moon. They encouraged me to live among aliens. They believed the advertisements, the glossy brochures: to boldly go beyond the boundary that separates the second generation from an American elite. Don't forget to visit, they pleaded as my hatch was latched.

"Will you come home?" he asks.

I'm in a hardened silo, three thousand tons of concrete on top of my head.

I'm buried in a mountainside, shielded in lead.

I'm orbiting the earth, seven times every second.

Find me.

The facade has collapsed, laying bare my true scaffolding.

"I knew you were Jewish the first day we met," says Dirk. "Half my prep school was bar-mitzvahed."

"The half that's not here."

"The half that graduated."

Saturday afternoon. Frisbee on the quad. A dog with a bandanna tied 'round its head. It's difficult to imagine my grandparents in this landscape of green, bouquets of marijuana, manure, and patchouli.

Grandma Esther saunters past, pleated skirt and denim jacket, hair freshly washed and clipped in a barrette, running shoes slung over her shoulder. "Dudes." She waves.

Grandpa Isaac, his beard sporting three days' growth, sails by on a banged-up ten-speed. "Chi Phi, party!" he calls.

"Alan's grandfather died at Auschwitz," Dirk says about the asthmatic sophomore down the hall.

"My grandmother died in a nursing home."

"In Germany?"

"Far Rockaway."

Disappointed, he butters his white bread. He wants tragedy. A long history of sorrow. Mere death will not satisfy him.

"So how'd you get the name Colin anyway?"

I tell him about the surgical instruments, the mumbled incantations, the drop of wine, the drop of blood. In the morning, my parents awoke thick-tongued with a son whose name sounds like an intestinal disorder. Colin Stone.

He parks his shoulders on the curb. His legs stretch across the green valley. "I'll call you Portnoy," he says, pleased with his multicultural education. "I think your parents would approve."

"Go home," says Marjorie. "What's the big deal?"

My head in her lap. Her roommate on the floor.

Her bare legs dangle off the side of the bed. Underwear and bras peek from her drawers like unruly flowers. French movie posters gloss the stippled walls like café windows.

I've hitchhiked to Providence, the most mislabeled of cities, to see her. In penance for the town's laughable hyperbole, the college has tied the hairshirt of simplicity around its name: Brown.

Her door opens on a dormitory of women who play in rock and roll bands and the men who love them. An entire population of reinvented suburbanites. They don black clothing, pierce body parts, shade their hair with radioactive isotopes. In case of fallout, their health service stocks suicide pills.

"For one day you'll be bored and hungry."

Marjorie believes that *Yom Kippur* is the dull-witted cousin of Christmas. Slower, sorrowful, with a limited culinary range.

"Ritual's cool," says the roommate. "All those candles."

I tell Marjorie that I have strongly held philosophical beliefs about theology. If God is omnipotent, free to do whatever He chooses, how can He be omniscient? Choice requires freedom, but omniscience means that He knows everything that will happen. If the outcome of every choice is already known, He can't be free.

"God is free and not free," she says, unconcerned. "That's why He's God." She brushes my lips with her blouse. "I'm on the pill," she whispers.

Her roommate has not moved. Outside, in the hallway, the tinny sounds of an acoustic guitar, two women harmonizing about hunger in Latin America, a smoke detector buzzing.

"Are you okay?" asks Marjorie, her hand on my forehead.

One a day, for the prevention of birth.

Two men bang into the room, a shave and haircut on the open door. "Rodney! Simon!" squeaks the roommate.

Rodney kisses the roommate on the mouth while Simon stands

coolly to the side, eyeing me through slit eyes. Marjorie introduces me, explaining that Simon is her theater TA, as if his unwanted presence were simply a dramatic entrance.

Simon smirks, his dark-shadowed cheeks dimpling like an underwear model.

How pleased I am to meet them, I lie.

"Your friend could use a suntan," Simon says in a perfectly awful British accent.

"Rather," says Rodney.

"He's on medication," contributes the roommate.

"Who isn't?" says Simon.

"Come for an outing?" Rodney asks.

The roommate jumps to her feet. What could be more fun than a ride down the interstate with the cast of *HMS Pinafore*?

"We can't," says Marjorie. "Colin gets carsick."

"Bad luck," says Rodney.

"Strap a bucket 'round his head," suggests Simon.

"I do not," I protest.

Marjorie glares at me. "The pills?" she says pregnantly.

My medical condition, I nod somberly. An overproduction of reproductive fluids leading to irritability and a proclivity for excessive jealousy. The doctors have advised plenty of bed rest.

The British Americans sweep from the room in a fanfare of theatrical gestures and pompous articulations. They'll be back, they warn, after they have a great deal of fun.

Marjorie turns; the door clicks locked behind her. A predatory gleam in her eyes. An unfamiliar taste in her mouth.

Could God make a pill so large that He couldn't swallow it?

In the library bathroom, graffiti:

> God is dead.—*Nietzsche*
> Nietzsche is dead.—*God*

"Nietzsche isn't happy that God is dead," says Joshua. "Everything we've believed in has collapsed."

Another day, another road trip. The truckers have become familiar with my skinny arm, thumb extended like a swollen Popsicle. Like a mobile missile, I am carted from site to site on a flatbed. It makes for a difficult target.

"We live in the ruins between secular and religious life," he continues. "We think of ourselves as Americans, but then something, like anti-Semitism, reminds us that we're Jews, too. Who can blame us for being confused?"

They've polished his cheeks at Harvard and buzzed his Eraserhead hair. He's read some new books; their shiny spines poke from his coat pocket like pet beetles. He fingers them gently as we stroll through the gates.

"I'm Portnoy," I say.

"I can't believe he calls you that," Joshua says.

"It's a joke."

"First they make a joke; then they stick you in the ovens."

"I think you're leaving out a couple of intermediate steps."

Leaves crunch beneath Joshua's boots. Traffic roars past the river. Two women with a boat over their heads jog across the bridge.

"Collapsing economy, fervent nationalism. The signs are everywhere," says Joshua.

"This from a guy who thinks Hitler was the best thing that ever happened to him."

"Sure, Hitler was great. Without Hitler there'd be no Jewish state. There'd probably be no Jews. We'd all be Americans by now."

"We are Americans," I remind him.

"That's what you think," he says.

We stand over the river, looking down into its muddy, paper-swirled depths.

"I don't understand," I say. "You read Nietzsche, you study German, you think Adolf Hitler was a Jewish hero; but Dirk is an anti-Semite because he calls me Portnoy."

"I'm a Jew," says Joshua. "He's not."

A few short weeks in the castle and Joshua has become a Semitic prince. Raven-haired beauties serenade him, cooing secret songs about the homeland. How easily swayed by music, the talk of politics and art. He slips into a dark overcoat, head bent, lips muttering, while I toss a football in the blond light off the hills.

Downriver, the skyline is filled with mirrors. Buildings reflect buildings reflecting themselves.

"You're about as Jewish as Dirk," I say.

"*Baruch ata adonai*," he intones, a magic incantation to conjure his identity. "*Shmata, shmata, shmata.*"

I kick a loose piece of dirt through the railing. "It worked," I say. "Now you're Portnoy."

"Wrong generation," says Joshua. "I'm the son of Portnoy."

"Revenge of Portnoy."

"Portnoy strikes back."

"Bride of Portnoy."

Joshua grips me around the shoulder as if he's afraid we may tumble off the bridge. His cheeks glitter like candied apples. "Portnoy is dead," he declares. He raises my arm with his other hand. "Let us bury him."

We toss the body into the brackish slime. It sinks without a trace.

They are coming to get me. It's a short drive. They don't mind.

I array my defenses: gasoline-filled trenches, concrete barricades topped with razor wire, antipersonnel mines. My flamethrower spits old wounds, perceived slights, forgotten treacheries.

"I don't believe in God," I say. "I don't believe in the Jewish religion—or in any religion! They're all lies!"

In a corner Dirk sweeps dust off petrified dust. Each layer of silt, a fossil record. The history of the college buried beneath the anthropologist's hands.

"You're both hypocrites! You wouldn't know a Jew if he smacked you on the head with the Torah!"

Dirk opens the window, and a breeze swirls the dirt into attractive new configurations. He lays down his broom and watches the dust settle.

"Happy New Year to you, too!" I bang down the phone.

The handset rattles in its cradle. Tiny vibrations assume an enormous clarity in the still air.

I look down, scuff my shoes along the floor.

"I told them I wasn't coming home," I say.

"I heard you," says Dirk.

The Book of Life rests on God's massive desk, a desk so large He cannot move it. In the book He's printed the names of those who will survive the New Year. The pages smudged with additions and obliterations. God squints in the twilight, His vision no longer keen. He thanks Himself for spectacles. Now if only He could find His pen.

"It won't kill them," I say.

A thin mist of furniture polish glistens on Dirk's fingertips. He rubs the sides of his perfect nose. "Maybe not," he says, leaving a grease slick up his brow. "But do you want to take that chance?"

Caravans of women swarm Highway 9. Horns blaring welcome. They bang at their windows, kick at the doors. Let them at us.

Chi Phi's annual *Yom Kippur* party.

In honor of our Jewish friends, reads the invitation, who can't eat or drink on this holiest of holy days, we, their Gentile brethren, will imbibe for them.

I remind Dirk about our signal: A ribbon around the doorknob means do not disturb; no ribbon means please make up the room now. I hand him a red ribbon.

"I don't think I'll need it," he says.

"Better safe than sorry."

"Not with this. Unless I use it as a tourniquet."

I sit at my desk and blow-dry my hair. Tiny puffs of smoke wisp from my head. Dirk rifles through his closet and then mine, tossing brightly colored shirts onto the bed.

"No plants or animals were injured making these clothes," he says.

The telephone rings, but we ignore it. We have both spoken to my mother too many times.

"I don't feel guilty," I say.

"Your hair is burning," says Dirk.

The plug sparks as I yank it from the socket. The room plunges into darkness. I can hear other voices down the hallway complaining about the sudden loss of power. The eerie glow of emergency lights seeps under the door.

We sneak out of the dorm and trudge across the semi-darkened campus. In the distance, sirens.

The power outage has not reached Chi Phi, although lights flicker in the basement as the floor heaves with people dancing above.

God could bury me in a pile of heathens and agnostics, I think, but first He'd have to find me, hidden in the bowels of the Greek alphabet. A handshake so secret that even He doesn't know it.

I inch toward the bar. Dirk vanishes in my wake, swallowed by a tide of ponytails and polo shirts. I grab the wooden railing, holding on to splinters lest I drown.

Dirk's schoolmate, Rex or Max, tends bar. Though he has been at college for less than a semester, he draws like a pro, angling beer against the side of the cup, skimming foam from the top, sloshing it on the counter with the perfect blend of aggressive nonchalance.

"Beer?" he manages when he sees me.

I hold up two fingers and jerk my thumb in what I hope is Dirk's direction.

"Shouldn't you be in church?" he says as he fills two cups simultaneously from one tap.

"I'm fasting," I say. "Between beers."

"Can you do that?"

"Special dispensation," I explain.

He shrugs and hands me the beer. A woman, her elbow in my waist, knocks half down my leg.

"Sorry," she says. Her blouse scoops as she leans into me, revealing the black lace of her bra and two white crescents of skin.

She wipes at my leg with her hand, pushing the liquid into my socks. Her head bobs below my waist.

"Please," I say. "Don't. Stop." She stands up. I give her the half beer. She says she'd rather have the full one. "As long as you're offering," she adds.

She tells me she's visiting her boyfriend, a senior bio major. He collapsed with a sudden and mysterious virus, something to do with his thesis. She came to the party with his roommates instead.

"What was I supposed to do," she says, "nurse him back to health?"

I glance around furtively for her boyfriend's roommates, but no one seems particularly interested in me.

"Florence Nightingale," she says. "No, thank you."

I weigh my empty cup in my palm.

"Anyway," she adds, "he doesn't know I'm here; he's in a coma."

The strains of the *Kol Nidre* fill the taproom, blending with beer and sweat. Three times the cantor raises his voice; three times the congregation chants its response. *Avenu malchainu.* The long-suffering violence and humiliation of the Jewish people resound in the melody:

All vows, obligations, oaths, anathemas, which we may vow or swear or pledge from this Day of Atonement until the next we do repent. May they be deemed to be forgiven, absolved, annulled or void—and made of no effect. They shall not bind us nor have power over us and the vows shall not be considered vows, nor the obligations obligatory, nor the oaths oaths.

I place my fists against my ears. I renounce the renouncing.

"I hate this music," she says as she directs me away from the bar.

We wend our way upstairs to the sticky and cup-ladened dance floor. We jerk and hop spasmodically in a room of epileptics. I try to match her bounce for bounce. Her hair curls damp with perspiration. Her elbows knock together like knees. When she smiles, her mouth moves through the flashing blackness like a fish.

She asks if I want to get some air. If she's offering, how can I refuse? I snuffle in my jacket for a pocket. Stale wrappers and bits of nitrogen. Marjorie's phone number.

Outside, a crumpled drunk beneath the porch. A man urinating above him. A couple locked together at the mouth. All is quiet on the western front; Massachusetts welcomes you.

She takes my hand as we approach the War Memorial. Her fingers tuck into my palm. I slip against her knuckles.

Down the hill the bird sanctuary gleams with a dull glow. Physics experiments run amuck. Lights from the gym shadow soccer fields and tennis courts. The air crackles like voltage.

A shock when our lips touch, the faintest trace of blue dancing between our teeth.

"I live over there," I manage.

"Come on," she says.

A crowd has gathered in front of my dormitory. An entire congregation. Their heads bent in prayer; their voices echo across the quad.

Shema Yisrael, Adonai Elohainu, Adonai ehad. Hear, O Israel, the Lord is our God, the Lord is one.

I elbow through the masses, their evil eye upon me. Their tongues trailing like bloodhounds. At the edge of the crowd, my mother, dressed in black. Marjorie at her side.

I duck into the entryway.

"You're shaking," she says, her hand on my neck.

I fumble with the lock, unable to slip the key into the hole. Finally the door opens, and we tumble into the darkness.

A single candle burns on the windowsill.

I flip the light switch. Nothing.

She gasps, a gulp I mistake for pleasure.

I follow her gaze through the open bedroom door, the sagging mattress, springs stretched taut. I'm about to tell her that maybe this is a mistake: I have a girlfriend; she has a boyfriend; the lights don't work.

He looks up. His face planed in the candlelight. A dark face. Curly black hair.

Then I see, cheek pressed to the pillow, Dirk.

"Colin," he says. "The ribbon."

From outside, the *shofar*, its plaintive cry like sobbing.

Tekiah! Awake and repent. For the sin we have committed before Thee, O God of forgiveness, forgive us, pardon us, and grant us remission.

The sky bursts into flames; a thunderclap splits the walls. I turn my head, shield my eyes. When I look back, I am a pillar of salt.

dial "o" for oppression

"I can't marry, have sex, or join the army," says Dirk.

"But no one ever killed six million of you."

"That was two generations ago. Today Jews are white, straight, and American."

"What about gay Jews?" I ask.

"They face discrimination. But not because they're Jewish."

"What about grape Jews?"

"They leave a purple mustache."

Sophomore year. A new game sweeps through campus. *Dial "O" for Oppression*. Dirk scores ten points for growing up gay in the South. I lose a turn for being raised among the highest concentration of Jews west of Tel Aviv.

"I should write a book," says Dirk as he waters our nearly departed plants. "The multigenerational saga of a southern family gone bad with miscegenation, incest, and autism."

It's been written, I tell him, like a warning to Lawrence heading into Arabia. There are only fourteen stories, or nine. There's no reason to bother.

"I don't hate the South," Dirk intones as he sprinkles a brown cactus. *"I don't hate it. I don't."*

"You have to suffer for art," I say.

Dirk shakes the remaining drops into the flooded cactus, then flops onto our fourthhand couch with his biology textbook. A puff of dust rises like volcanic ash from the pillows.

"I'm not suffering for anyone," Dirk says, his shoulders hunched like a grazing buffalo. "Especially a guy named Art."

"Homoeroticism in antebellum literature," I explain to my parents.

"Wonderful," says my mother. "How's biology?"

"I dropped it."

A crash on the other end of the line. My mother's voice, again, measured. "Don't we have to sign something?"

I explain that I'm not in high school anymore. The only thing they have to sign are the checks.

My mother thinks I should read some classics before I dive into obscurity and deviance. "Ignorance," she claims, "leads to intolerance and fascism."

Why should I worry about the growth of National Socialism when I can live in the sheltered academic grove? The tree-lined warmth. The singing birds. I'll sit naked on the quad reading lyrics from plantation songs while the windows are shattered and the lawns lit by crosses.

"These are the years to accumulate knowledge, to hoard for the future."

I tell her I'm not a squirrel. I can't hold the periodic table in my cheek. Bury it for the winter in the frozen earth.

"It took fifteen years to complete my dissertation," she says. "I had to work, raise a family. But I had the education before I began."

"Eighteen years," I say.

"There was a lot of research. My adviser died."

I pull the book over my eyes. It smells like a musty closet.

"And now that I have a dissertation, I can't even find a job."

"You don't want a job."

"I've worked hard for forty-five years. I'm not getting any younger."

"I think the first fifteen were probably pretty easy."

My mother doesn't want to hear my rationalizations. If I want to be ignorant and despised and lacking in any employable skill, that's my prerogative. She and my father, however, will not condone my idleness.

She puts him on the telephone.

"Your mother majored in English," he says, his voice a thin wire of weariness. "Look how happy it made her."

"Why would anyone read this stuff?" asks Marjorie.

We sit in her parents' oasis, our stomachs churning Thanksgiving turkey, volatile gases building. The summer of love has faded, our tip jars emptied of baubles and sentiment.

"They don't have a choice," I say. "It's assigned."

She turns the pages over, as if she's missed something on the other side. "Who cares if a bunch of queers were oppressed before the Civil War?"

"Gays."

"Whatever they're calling themselves now."

We stare hatefully at each other for a moment. Absence has made the heart grow thorns, wild and woolly like an unkempt lawn. Was it just puppy love, turned foul like an old dog's breath?

"Have you always been this narrow-minded?" I ask.

Marjorie forces a laugh. An explosive snort. "Please," she says. "You don't know the first thing about the world."

In the last year Marjorie has aged ten and I've lost two. I dare not compare my youth with her ripened, wizened maturity.

The ceiling creaks. Hairline fissures appear in the white stucco. An old song leaks through the plaster.

"I know about anorexia," I say.

Marjorie's hands grapple with the ring on her finger, turning, tugging, sliding. I have thrown down the gauntlet, and she regards it like a dirty leather glove. She'd pick it up if it wouldn't make her nails dirty.

"Bulimia," she says finally. "And you don't know anything about *that* either."

"You think I didn't hear you in the bathroom?"

"I had problems," she says. "I was going through a difficult time. All you could do was listen at the bathroom door?"

"I wasn't listening."

"That's disgusting."

"So is sticking a toothbrush down your throat."

"Oh, I despise you!" she says theatrically.

Bits of plaster sprinkle into my lap. The ceiling threatens collapse. Marjorie's face locks into a grim mask. Ruin is everywhere.

"Does this mean we're not going out anymore?" I ask.

Her face unlocks; the sky falls. But when I brush the stars from my mouth, I am still clinging to the earth by a fingernail.

"Beneath the blond veneer," says Dirk, "who knows what demons lurk?"

Incense burns on the radiator; shrunken heads hang from exposed piping. Dirk reads from a revised medical recipe book. Two eyes of newt, two wings of bat. He's concocting a potion to score me points; he hates to win without a contest.

I tell him that's no veneer, that's my real hair.

"In the closet," he says, "everything appears blond."

"I'm not in the closet," I say.

"Trust me. I know closet."

Where did Dirk learn the colorist's art? Though we spread our branches over the same ground, I never let him see my roots. I washed, bleached, and conditioned in private, careful to avoid the public shower.

"Come out," he continues. "It's cold here by myself."

"I don't know what you're talking about," I say. "I'm as Jewish as anyone I grew up with."

"The first sign of oppression," he claims, "is not knowing you're oppressed."

I was oppressed by my own people, as Joshua never forgot to remind me. But here I've never felt more free. Blonds, and nearly blonds, and the almost blond. Together we constitute a happy invented community. I didn't even have to trawl down a muddy river, braving mosquitoes and black flies. Instead I drove a rutted highway from the gold coast of Long Island to the green hills of western Massachusetts. At the end of the road a fraternity of secret sharers welcomed me with an armful of beer.

"This is my home," I say. "I like being blond."

Dirk shakes his head sadly. Clearly the dye has gone to my head. "There's no hope," he says, dumping his recipe in the trash. "You're suffering from veneer disease."

My parents refuse to acknowledge I've switched majors. Denial before Guilt, then Anger and Despair.

"They've discovered organisms that are neither living nor dead," says my father.

"A lung disease caused by the inhalation of very fine silica dust?" quizzes my mother.

I stare off through the window at a circle of freshmen kicking a small leather ball. Each attempts a more outrageous maneuver as the ball goes around. One catches it behind her knee and flips it across the circle with her heel. Another somersaults and kicks just as his head skims the ground. A third sails into the air, bounces the ball off his chest, and knocks it back to the center of the circle with his forehead.

"Colin?" My mother's reedy voice through the tiny speaker.

"Your mother's calling," says Dirk, without looking up from the couch. He has lost interest in my case.

The world is lit by mystery and miracle, unfathomable events that flicker like fireflies. Why study science when its laws explain only observable phenomena? The inner life of *Drosphilia* remains as unknowable as God.

"Did you see that?" I say.

The kickers have joined hands. The ball zips between them, darting and ricocheting, a cornered animal. Their feet jump and dance. Their bodies rise above the ground. They gather speed, and soon the entire circle is hovering several inches off the earth.

"They're playing hacky-sack," Dirk says indifferently.

The somersaulter trips, and the ball falls to the ground. The players look at the dirty leather sack lying at their feet.

I open my eyes and turn away.

"Hello?" says my mother. "Are you still there?"

I'm floating above the earth. The entire planet a blue-green disk. Flip it into the air; sail it across space.

Kick. Kick hard.

❁   ❁   ❁

"I'm coming up," I say. "We can't do this over the phone."

"Don't come down," says Marjorie. "There's nothing to talk about." She has brought our dog to the vet, she tells me, and put it out of its misery.

I borrow Dirk's car. Drive on the wrong side of the road, against one-way traffic, over pedestrians. I outrun red lights and bump speed bumps.

Don't Even Think of Parking Here, a sign says. Your Girlfriend Doesn't Want to See You. I scrape against the sign and slip out through the hatchback.

Marjorie's apartment overlooks the busy street. The third floor of a three-family house. From her window one could jump, or fall, directly into traffic.

"What are you doing here?" She greets me by the door.

Her hair is piled high off her neck, held together with a pencil. Loose strands tumble down her forehead. She's gained weight. Her skin glows with secret oils and salts.

"You look great," I say.

"I told you not to come," she says, blocking my entrance.

"Jorie?" A man's voice, British accent, from inside the apartment.

"It's just a friend, Simon. I'm going out for a minute. Ta." She pushes me from the door and toward the stairs.

"Ta?" I say. "Jorie?"

She glares at me, a needle through my eye.

We walk silently along the crowded street. College students, their faces dumb with learning, chatter idiotically about the Semiotics of Deconstruction and the Deconstruction of Semiotics. Lives lived under erasure. Their brains placeholders for absent texts.

Marjorie guides me into a bookstore café, a place where the Presence of Literature gives the illusion of meaning to inane conversation.

"What are you doing here?" she asks again, after we've ordered expensive frothed flavored milk drinks.

"You're living with *him*?" I say.

"He's an actor," she explains. "I'm an actress."

Since when did Marjorie become an actress? Was there a TV special I missed? A B movie? I tell her she's an ophthalmologist's daughter. She can mate only within the species: radiologist, dermatologist, gynecologist.

"Funny, funny," she says. "You're so clever." She presses the back of a spoon against her cheek. "You'll be cracking jokes over your dying patients."

"I dropped my premed classes."

She releases the spoon. "Too bad for your patients."

I growl at her until the warm milk arrives.

Her voice softens. "Go home, Colin," she says. "We're not in high school anymore."

I look around at the tables of bearded men, brassiereless women—suicide pills in their pockets, the troubles of mother earth on their shoulders.

"It's a brave new world," I say.

"Whatever that means."

"It's from a book. That you didn't read."

"You're such an intellectual," she sneers. "You and Joshua. Printing up those ridiculous pamphlets."

"You're sleeping with your drama professor."

"He's not my professor. He was my TA."

"Lumpy British wannabe."

"He's from London."

"Via Pittsburgh."

"He lived eight years in London."

"Ha!" I conclude triumphantly.

"But he was born in Surrey."

"Slumming with the working class. What would Daddy say?"

"His father is an earl."

I am silenced by the American craving for all things titular. He will inherit an estate with a basement full of corpses while I acquire a propensity to fall asleep on the couch.

"He's not interested in all that," Marjorie continues. "His brother runs the houses. Simon lives off a very small income."

Pity the poor aristocracy, succumbing to incest, hemophilia, and feeblemindedness. Their pockets lined with the blood of peasants, tenant farmers who till their own graves. At least in America the destitute live freely on street corners and subway grates.

"Don't look so smug," says Marjorie, catching my smug look. "You think it's any different when your parents pay for college?"

"I didn't bring my valet to college."

"Simon doesn't have a valet."

"He needs one."

Marjorie laughs. A woman's laugh. A cigarette-tinged chortle from the back of her throat. "I think you're jealous," she says.

The British royal family has set up housekeeping in my girl-friend's bedroom. The Queen's jewels on display every night. Murderous might be a better word.

"Do you love him?" I ask.

"I do," she says.

"Then why should I be jealous?"

I back out of my parking space, across the frozen yard, and directly into Marjorie's porch.

"Jorie," croons the downstairs neighbor, "I think you've got a visitor."

I pry the steering wheel from my sternum.

"How did you get here?" asks Marjorie, false concern and innocence.

"Took a left," I manage.

"Had a bit of an accident, have we?" says Simon, the smashed windshield like cobwebs across his face.

I am airlifted to the University Health Services, where they diagnose me with mononucleosis, strep throat, and chlamydia. Nothing a triple dose of antibiotics can't cure. I slowly bleed to death internally while an ancient and disbarred physician depresses my tongue and takes my temperature repeatedly from the ear. He asks whether I've had these symptoms before. I tell him this is the first time my heart has been broken.

I detail the damage to my parents from my hospital room: two cracked ribs, a ruptured spleen, a broken nose, and they don't accept my health insurance. "They want to give me a nose job," I add gleefully, thrilled like all hypochondriacs by actual injury.

"They are not touching your nose," my mother says. "Your father will find a plastic surgeon."

"Better hurry," I say. "They're training interns."

Marjorie appears at my bedside, a vision in white. "I don't feel bad for you," she says. "You wrecked a perfectly good porch."

I hang my head in shame.

"To say nothing of your friend's car."

I wince. If I survive, Dirk will kill me.

"How's your nose?"

"Crooked."

She touches my IV. "Does it hurt?"

"Only when I breathe."

The bed sags when she sits, twisting the needle deeper into my arm.

"Colin, I'm sorry," she says. "I didn't want things to end this way."

Out in the hallway, the coroner has arrived for the autopsy. They've cleared space in the morgue. He scribbles the cause of death on a rusty clipboard: acute embarrassment following attack of self-pity.

"I still love you," Marjorie says. "But you have to admit we're leagues apart."

She has ascended into the ranks of dissipated British aristocracy while I wade in the mongrel American waters.

"Leagues?" I say.

"Feel better." She kisses my forehead. "I'll call you." She crooks her little finger as she waves good-bye.

I look at the bottle the doctor has left. *Take one in case of extreme pain. May cause severe and irreversible drowsiness. Do not operate machinery while taking this medication.*

Suicide pills.

My nose will heal, but the dull ache between my eyes lingers. Insurance agents and lawyers call me daily. Do I want to sue the owner of the car? Do I want to sue the owner of the porch? (How dare they build that porch in front of the building!) For destroying Dirk's only possession I stand to reap a small fortune.

Dirk, at least, approaches his impending indigence with good cheer. He has tithed my income for the next twenty years and extracted a sacrifice of the firstborn.

"I loved that car," he says.

"You shouldn't become attached to material objects. It isn't healthy."

"I'll remember you said that when someone sets fire to your clothes . . . while you're wearing them."

My parents arrive, bearing bread and bandages. Dirk excuses himself for the lab. Experiments have gone awry; life arises from particles of dirt and forgotten shoes.

"Such a handsome young man," declares my mother. "Does he have a girlfriend?"

"He's not interested in girls," I say.

"There's plenty of time for that," she agrees. "He has a lot of schooling ahead of him."

"Internship, residency," my father contributes.

"I'm not going to medical school," I say.

My parents exchange a guilty look.

"You should do what interests you," my father says.

"You have so many options," says my mother. "There's no reason to rush through your life."

Do I look that bad? Sure, my eyes are a little black and blue, and I can't take a deep breath. But I feel okay. I do.

"We only want you to be happy," my mother adds slyly.

I smile weakly. Like all happy families, we suffer from the unrelenting banality of our resemblance to other happy families.

After they leave, I wander the narrow streets from storefront to alcove, mooning at the saccharine lyrics of hackneyed folksingers. If the heart is a muscle, you gave me a charley horse.

Life must be more than respiration, circulation, and waste management. The brain scoops ice cream. Kidneys relax by the pool. The human body is capable of fantastic feats: generation, propagation, miscegenation. Love, however, is a mutation.

An old pawnbroker leers at me as I crawl past her store. Someone's landlady lurks at the bottom of the stairs. "Need a room?" she offers. I shrug and thrust my hands deeper into my jeans. I hurry into the fog.

It is dark when I return to my square yard of space. Dirk snores fitfully in his room. The open door an undated invitation. I leave the lights off and crawl into bed.

I dream of Raskolnikov. He has borrowed a car and driven to K in search of Sonya. My name is Sophia, she says when he finds her; I'm going to be an actress. He drives from the house in a mad rage, embracing her porch with his car.

Later, nurses shove needles behind his gums and into the roof of his mouth. His nostrils are corked with wads of cotton. A wrench is clamped to his nose. The doctor bears down, breath stinking of garlic, and cracks the bones back into place.

But the face, my face, will not be restored by surgeons' tools. A hairline fracture cleaves it into dueling hemispheres: half a world against the other half.

Sometimes, from the edge of the abyss, spring will shed a little light.

A woman smiles as she passes; her eyes follow me down the street.

Is it my new haircut, the one that camouflages my suddenly advancing hairline? Does she sense intelligence and sensitivity beneath my wolfish exterior?

I look back. She has stopped in the middle of the sidewalk. I crash into a telephone pole.

"Colin!" she calls.

I shuffle dazedly toward her. The street spins on its axis while the world whirls around it.

"It's Nell," she claims. "From high school?"

I open the yearbook and insert a photo of this sleek woman with her spiked jet hair above the pale-faced girl with long brown locks.

"No," I say.

"Hebrew school? Jacob? I went out with your best friend?"

I've lapsed into a sudden immobility, a rare case of second-chance fever. I hear words but am unable to respond. "Transferred." "Taking a class." "Blink your eyes once if you can hear me."

My lips are frozen to my teeth. I smile, and my gums come unglued, flapping loosely in the breeze. How can I speak when my mouth is unraveling like a flag?

She asks if I'd like to get some breakfast. I wave my face in agreement. She doesn't notice the threads spooling down the sidewalk as we walk into town.

We sit near the back of a diner at a funnel-shaped table that acts as a conduit for cigarette smoke. She tells me the story of her misery in Boston, her transfer to the women's college down the road, and the anthropology class she takes on Tuesdays and Thursdays, while I tear and sniffle fiercely. "I'm much happier now," she says, laying her hand on my forearm as if to reassure me.

I feel the weight of her entire body resting on my tendon.

"Do you still see Marjorie?" she asks, lifting her hand.

"Jorie?" I say, and launch into a ten-minute diatribe on betrayal, revenge, and near-fatal injury.

"Trevor would kill me if I were unfaithful," she says when I'm finished.

"Your dog?"

"My boyfriend."

I glance at the fire exits. Bang Head Against Door in Case of Emergency.

"He's crazy that way."

She met him at the opening of a friend's Soho art gallery. He bought a nude painting of her friend.

"He's the first man with money I've met who hasn't been an ass."

"Money does that to people," I commiserate. "They buy naked pictures of anyone they want."

"Like all the boys we grew up with," she says.

I agree, then quickly change my mind. My father gave his life to science, I tell her, in exchange for a free, but incomplete, DNA map and coffee mug. "We weren't rich," I say. "Not like Marjorie's family."

"You had to have money in that town," she says, ignoring my Nobel plea, as a pink flush like rosewater creeps up her neck. "If you didn't, you were a pariah."

Did Nell's family have money? I can't remember. It didn't seem to affect her social status, however. She still dated Joshua, voted Most Likely to Renounce Socialist Theory and Oppress the Masses.

"No one feels like they belonged in high school," I say. "Being poor has nothing to do with it."

"Really? You ever ask Tommy Patrick how he felt?"

"Before he killed himself?"

"You think he liked sitting alone in the cafeteria with his friends?"

"I sat alone in the cafeteria with Joshua."

"Being poor in that school was like being black."

"I think there were three of each," I say.

"When my father lost his job, Joshua's parents wouldn't speak to me," she says grimly.

I push the grease around my plate, absorbing this new information.

"It was bad enough my mother was Catholic. Poor and Catholic, that was practically immoral. I think the rabbi threatened to excommunicate them."

Now I'm certain she's exaggerating. Joshua's parents didn't even know what a rabbi was. Joshua's father called him a "priest" at Joshua's *bar-mitzvah*. And the rabbi, if he noticed, couldn't care: He thought Catholics were Jews with a different songbook.

"Fuck them," she continues. "I was dating Trevor by then anyway. Joshua was screwing anything that moved."

She signals to the waitress for the check. I try to pay, but she slips the waitress a twenty without looking at the bill. "Next time," she says to me. And I, desperately hoping for a next time, agree.

She drives me back to campus in a bright red convertible. It purrs and growls while she shifts effortlessly through the gears. The leather seats squeak; the brushed chrome dashboard glints in the afternoon sun. When we hit the speed bumps, it feels as if we will never touch ground.

She leaves me at the steps of my dormitory. I wave good-bye until she is a blur on the horizon, a barely visible dot. And then she disappears entirely.

❊ ❊ ❊

"Who's coming to the beach?" Nell asks.

She's dressed for cricket: long white pants, shirt, and hat. Her black hair a shock of punctuation atop her head. It's been two years, or two days, depending on how time is measured and whether space is curved, but she moves with the ease of someone traveling the speed of light.

Dirk claims he's allergic to sand. No amount of coaxing can squeeze him into Nell's two-seater. "You kids go without me," he says. "Send a postcard."

There's not a class I wouldn't cut for a day trip with Nell. Even if we can't go back in time, there's always forward. I leave Foucault in the toilet and grab a towel.

The beach is three hours distant. Nell makes it in two. The whine of police sirens has faded to a pleasant buzz by the time we arrive at the shoreline.

She pulls the car onto a gravel strip. Rose hip bushes and scrubby pines edge the road. She switches off the engine, and for a moment the only sound is the distant rumble of ocean. The sea breeze blows a salty breath into my mouth.

"I love this place," she says. "So peaceful. Trevor and I come here all the time."

She points across the dunes to his house. Four stilts hold it high above the surf. In a strong wind it will be carried aloft like a broomstick.

She opens her door and steps from the car. I climb out and follow her past the scraggly vegetation and onto the sand.

"Careful of the dunes," she warns. "They're eroding."

I look down at the water below, white ribbons curling away from the coastline. Across the steely green I can almost see Portugal, wavering like an island kingdom. If I jump, I might reach it. I tuck my head between my legs, lock my arms over my head, and somersault down the dunes. A spray of sand trails me like smoke, coating my lips with grit and sticking to the corners of my eyes.

Nell tumbles after me, shrieking.

"That was fun," she says. "Let's do it again."

"Does he own the beach?" I ask.

"No one owns the beach," she says. "They just have access rights."

The ocean crashes against the shore. Tiny animals struggle against the tide. The moon rises; the sea heaves. Carapaces in its wake.

"Could he buy it?"

"Not for all the money in the world."

She stands up and brushes sand off her brown forearms. "Can you do this?" she says, and spins into a series of perfect cartwheels on the hard sand along the water's edge.

I run after her, marking her sea creature footprints with my toes. She laughs when I catch her, breathless and wild with expectation. Her hair twisted in the wind like meringue.

"It's like falling," she says, straightening, her left arm raised as if to hold a platter, right arm petting a dog.

I stand beside her, poised in tense mimicry.

"Teach me," I say.

white
lies

Dirk licks his finger and scrapes it across the mirror. "Is that all there is?" he sings, squeaking the finger over his gums.

"Gone, gone," I lament.

My mother warned that smoking marijuana would lead to a life of drug dependency. Perhaps I should take my junior year at the Betty Ford clinic.

"How could something so good be so bad?" I ask.

"Cocaine isn't bad," says Dirk; "it just costs too much."

"I meant bad in the economic sense."

Our dealer's cupboards are bare. Market demands have run his stock, and his supplier has fled to safer jurisdictions. We scour the countryside for alternative production sources but are forced to settle for beers in the basement of a fraternity.

"Without drugs," says Dirk through a jaw clamped tight as a vise, "life is a desolate and wretched affair."

My throat swells with bitter mucus. I drink quickly, hoping to fight the crash. When it comes, I am as unprepared as always. My forehead slumps to the tabletop, skidding into a beer slick.

"I need a girlfriend," I moan.

"What about me?" says Dirk.

"It's not the same."

"In the long run," he says, sweeping the dank room and its dull-eyed denizens into his forty-gallon hands, "all this will seem oddly dated."

I stare at him through glazed eyes. My dilated pupils refuse to focus. The advancing tsunami gathers force, smashing through the beachfront, tumbling into my Pabst Blue Ribbon with a swirl of foam and seaweed.

"In the long run," I say, advancing a famous economic theory, "we'll all be dead."

If it's Tuesday, it must be Holes and Poles.

"Human Sexuality," says Nell. "They don't offer it at Smith. Besides, I like to take one class with boys. It gives me an excuse to wear lipstick."

We flip through magazines in the campus bookstore. Nell sticks to fashion. I peruse the classifieds. *Help wanted*, I read. *Must love travel, adventure, sudden and inexplicable head injuries.*

I tell her the course is a notorious "gut," populated by football players and the symbiotic creatures who lodge in their hides.

"I can use the easy grade. I missed too many classes last semester."

Couriers needed, I read. *Transport expensive and discreet cargo. Large body cavities a plus.*

"I catch up on sleep during the films," she adds.

"How can you sleep?" Most students take the class for the movies, it's cheaper and less embarrassing than renting them.

"I'm tired."

I worry about her, I tell Nell. She's wasting tuition and time on a lightweight course. Worse, she's not taking advantage of the free movies. What would her parents say?

"You worry? I'm touched. I didn't think you cared."

I set the magazine back in the rack behind *Speeding Slugs*, *Death Traps*, and *Big, Bad Knives*. "I'm serious," I say. "Take an English class with me."

"I can read English. I don't need extra help."

"You need help with human sexuality?"

"That's for me to know and you to find out."

"When?"

"Are you hungry?" she asks. "I'm hungry. Let's get some breakfast."

I look at my watch. It's eleven-thirty. "Breakfast was three hours
ago," I say.

"Come along for fun then," Nell says.

"You didn't answer my question," I say as we emerge into sunlight.

"I hate mornings," says Nell as she covers her eyes with one
hand. "Trevor and I sleep until noon."

Like vampires, they avoid the dawn. They forage for food on the
necks of the guileless and unsuspecting.

"Who's Trevor?" I ask.

She laughs. She has answered my question.

Two gaping, ciliated, woolly caves stare up at me. I bend closer and
vacuum a white canal into my nose.

"Always nice to see you," says Dirk, taking the rolled bill from
my quivering hands.

"The pleasure is mine," says Nell, her hair shaking like porcu-
pine quills, a silver necklace dangling at her pale throat.

My body parts jingle and tap. Dirk leaps up to change the music,
changes his mind, then changes it anyway. The needle scrapes across
the record: fingernails on a blackboard.

"Ayyyyyyeeeeeeowwwww," he wails.

I buzz around the room like a children's toy, reversing direction
when I bang into the walls. My eyes collect grit in the back of my
head. My teeth ache.

"I feel pretty!" Dirk sings.

Each grain burns a small crater in my mucous membranes. Red
blood cells, like teenagers at a rock concert, rush into the gap. They
wrap the foreigner in their overcoats and spirit him to warmer
climes, where a Latin beat pulsates from the street and the avenues
are jammed with neurons in silly hats and noisemakers.

Dance! Dance! Dance!

We rumba across the living room, sparks flying from the carpet.

Nell takes Dirk's hand and fox-trots into a corner. I perform a solo tango.

"You're lovely boys," says Nell, kissing Dirk.

"Change partners," says Dirk.

He whisks me into a frenzied Charleston while Nell two-steps around the couch. My knees knock together like maracas. My hips crack and pop. Dirk pulls my arm from its socket and waves it over his head like a flag. I drop, exhausted, to the floor.

"Medic!" calls Dirk. "Medication!"

Nell's cool hand against my neck. Her breath across my cheek. "Coke gives me . . ." she says, her voice trailing off like a string of loosed pearls. I struggle to catch the missing word.

Dirk labors above us, his body moving in jerky rhythm to an invented beat.

Nell presses her lips to my ear. I can feel her teeth. "Life," she whispers.

"Ugly," says Dirk. "I'm growing uglier by the minute."

Nell lays out another line on the cracked mirror. I watch as she painstakingly chops, dices, and slices with an expert's panache. The razor blade glitters between her fingers.

"We've tapped the source," says Dirk.

"He's not the source," says Nell. "He just has connections."

"Miami?"

"Tampa."

I drum my fingers anxiously against my chin. I grind my teeth down to the nubs. I wait my turn at the line and snort like a water buffalo. The oasis, however, is shrinking. Soon the weight of the dunes will bury us.

"Baby powder," says Dirk. "We need more baby powder."

Nell sniffs deeply; her nostrils vibrate. She runs a lonely finger over the unfolded and empty edges of paper. "He cuts it with laxative," she says.

"*Je suis finis*," moans Dirk, in his best southern-fried French.

The music has stopped. Nell creeps toward the sagging sofa. I follow her onto the pillows and collapse into foam.

"Who will love me?" Dirk asks the empty room.

❂   ❂   ❂

"You were my best friend's girlfriend," I say. "How could I tell you?"

The earth has moved, but we have not. I am propped against the sofa's edge; Nell reclines against me, my comforter tossed across her ankles. Her skin smells of cucumber. In the twilight she is paler than humanly possible, her lips blue as a corpse's.

"It's better this way," she says. "I like being friends."

"Me too," I lie.

"I was never attracted to you," she adds. "If that helps."

"Thanks," I grimace.

"I mean, it's not like you're unattractive. You're just not my type."

"Wealthy, older, with artistic pretensions."

"Exactly."

She shifts; her backbone rubs against my ribs.

"I'm an expensive date," she continues. "You wouldn't want to make my car payments."

What happened to the girl who weathered Joshua's Marxist mania while Jacob sang of socialist collectives? Have the grubby fingers of the decade of greed rubbed the shine from her idealistic forehead?

"People with money pretend money doesn't matter," she says. "At least I'm honest. I know what I want."

"A car. A house on the Cape."

"The same things you had."

"I never had a house on the Cape." I was a fashion victim, I remind her. The popular patrol tormented me from their perch on the window ledge.

"But to people like your friend Tommy, you were sitting on that ledge."

"He wasn't my friend."

"To him, you were another wealthy Jew."

"It's my fault he killed himself," I conclude. "Because I reminded him he wasn't a wealthy Jew."

"He killed himself because he was gay."

"Tommy Patrick was gay?" I say incredulously.

She rises from my chest; the comforter slips to her feet. "He shot himself in the mouth," she says, amazed at my density.

Many famous writers have shot themselves in the mouth, I tell her; that doesn't mean they were all homosexual.

"Colin," she says, her necklace climbing her throat. "Tommy. Was. Gay. Everybody knew it."

In the farewell letter I wrote for him, Tommy apologized for smashing my head into the fence. Suicide, he explained, was his best chance at repentance. He hoped I could forgive him.

"Physical violence is always a manifestation of latent homosexuality," Nell says. She hasn't slept through all her classes. "You shouldn't be surprised."

Death is a surprise. Sexuality arrives like a train on the wrong track with a different schedule to a strange destination when you're waiting for a taxi. Who can explain it? Climb aboard.

"I'm not surprised," I say. "But I can't forgive him."

"Because he was gay?"

"Because he's dead."

She lifts the blanket and stretches her legs onto the orange crate that passes for our coffee table.

"I wish I had stood up to him," I say. "Joshua would have."

Nell snorts. "Joshua couldn't even stand up to his parents."

Her black eyes darken. The necklace drops into a deep hole in her collarbone.

"You were sleeping with Trevor," I say.

"Did he tell you that?"

"You did."

"And that justifies his behavior?"

"You were cheating on him."

"Too bad we didn't live in Louisiana. He could've shot me."

No need to go to extremes, I protest. Suicide, murder, the things we do for love.

"Believe me, your best friend was no damsel in distress," Nell continues. "He gave me about six different diseases before I even met Trevor."

Should I be surprised by the perils of human intercourse? Sex and death walk hand in hand; black-robed figures with their unclad brethren. Sleep through class and miss the warning labels.

"Thank God for penicillin," she adds. "And doxycycline. And streptomycin."

I raise my hands to ward off the onslaught of antibiotics.

"It's all right," she says. "I'm cured."

Generations of bacteria, exposed to hostile conditions, develop a resistance and thrive. Mutation or adaptation, accident or design? It's crowded here in this petri dish.

"He loved you," I say.

"No," she says. "He loved the sound of his own voice."

"Where does he get the drugs?" Dirk asks at dinner. "Did you ever think about that? Armies of peasants are oppressed, judges are murdered, just so these drug lords can satisfy our cravings."

"He's not a drug lord," says Nell. "He's not even Colombian."

She has emerged from a sea of silver spoons and sequins. Pale and wan, her eyes squinting and restless under the fluorescent lights.

"You look like shit," says Dirk.

"Just because he sells drugs," says Nell, "doesn't make him a drug dealer."

I squeeze her knee reassuringly beneath the table.

"He's an art dealer," she adds.

"Who sells drugs for a living."

"We support it," I say. "Without the buyer there'd be no seller."

"Exactly my point."

"It is?"

Dirk leans on the table, his giant forearms like downed sequoias. "How can we treat the illness if we suffer from it?"

What explains this sudden swing of Dirk's moral compass? Last month he was the happy inhaler of the crystallized product of the coca plant; today he's plugged his nostrils with goody gumdrops.

"Drugs are our friends," says Nell. "They keep us alive."

"They anesthesize us," says Dirk.

"That's why the government wants you to say 'no,' " says Nell. "Say 'no' to imagination, to art, to fun."

"They alienate your friends."

"Ah," says Nell, kicking my ankle beneath the table.

"We're your friends," I say to Dirk.

"I had one friend," he says. "Now I have two." He gathers his tray and pushes back from the table. He has an exam tomorrow, he announces. When we overload our dopamine receptors, he will dissect our brains. Until then he's headed for the library with an IV drip of coffee.

His eighteen-wheeler back sways down the meal lanes.

"He's in love with you," says Nell after he's gone.

"Dirk?" I say.

"Don't play the ingenue."

I bat my eyelashes and avert my blushing face.

"It's jealousy," she continues. "He thinks I'm stealing you from him."

I thank her for her scholarly observations, but my train runs along a straight track, no deviations permitted. Uphill, downhill, into the tunnel. Be careful of the caboose.

"We read about this. It's called transference, or something."

"You missed a few classes," I say.

"One or two."

"You're failing a gut."

She fixes me with a steady stare, her pupils like ink dots on black paper. "I was late to the makeup exam," she says.

"It's the easiest class at the college."

"Are you my father?"

"You show up, you get an A."

"A is for 'ass,' which is what you're acting like."

"You could learn something."

"Good-bye." She stands abruptly, leaving her tray on the table. Does she expect me to bus it? "Call me when you want some more coke," she says.

"Nell," I say.

Her black head a fading dot in the sea of white.

A sleepless night. Dirk's snores rolling from his bedroom, rumbling around the furniture like large animals, bumping against my bookshelves. I toss and turn so often I feel like a short-order cook. Tiny sounds—footsteps on the path below my window, a poster flapping against a bulletin board—conspire to amplify my unhappiness.

I knew she had a boyfriend, a man friend, a sugar daddy. He's violent and ruthless and collects late-nineteenth-century impressionist landscapes. Drugs and wild abandon brought us together. Sobriety will tear us apart.

"How can you sleep with someone you don't love?" I asked.

"It's easy," she said. "I close my eyes and concentrate on the road."

Everything has been cut and chopped and lined on a mirror. The brain is teased through the nose into sharp focus. When the drugs wear off, the epiphanies dissolve like hard candy.

He sits on the window ledge and laughs at my clothes. He squeals from the parking lot in a black sports car. He doesn't invite me to his parties.

I slink along the hallway, hugging the walls. I am the walls.

She only wanted what everyone had: bread; water; a cool spot on the sand. To share the feast as if she belonged, and to believe it. The new gods are the same as the old, no less forgiving. It's the temples that have changed.

Night. The spheres in discord. I roll around in sheets like a cat's tongue. A sharp pain cuts into my backside. I reach into the blanket, and my hand brushes a row of razors.

I lift her silver necklace from the tangled comforter. It snares the fabric like a hook. I will wear it around my head like a mortal coil. Shuffle it off when I sleep.

A sleep that ends dreaming.

"She hates me," I say to Dirk. "She hates you."

"She's gone downtown," he says. "She'll be back on Monday."

"Tuesday," I say.

"It's her life," says Dirk. "Let her ruin it."

How can he be so indifferent to suffering? She doesn't want the expensive car, the house on the beach, the drug pipeline. It's a winsome ploy to regain the childish pleasures, to belong to the club that wouldn't have her as a member. She used to be such a diligent student, when diligence was a scarlet letter. I understand, I tell him. I was young once too.

"You fool," says Dirk.

I ring her answering machine until the tape spools over with an endless loop of garbled messages. Call me, I plead, I've given up yeast and legumes; I'm surviving on a diet of water and paste. Religion is a poor substitute for mass opiates.

The woman who answers the hall telephone is an unfamiliar voice. She asks for my credentials, my pool affiliation. I am patron saint of the tardy, I tell her, friend to the delinquent. She has avoided me for days. Ignored my entreaties. Reduced me to sniveling to a stranger on a dormitory phone.

"What, don't you know?" says the stranger.

Pity the ones who bear the sorrow, brunt the pain, break the news. They never imagined the stillness of a quiet heart. The weight of inorganic matter. They never dreamed that loss could be so tactile, like sticks snapping in a hard wind.

"I don't know anything," I say.

And then she tells me:

The red convertible roars into an explosive ignition. She coaxes the engine back into an idle, then eases out of the garage. Main Street is gray and abandoned. The stores zip past in a haze of blue exhaust. The city is three hours distant; every minute matters.

On the highway the earliest hints of a long winter slip through the ill-fitting windows. She turns on the radio to mask the cold, but the news is filled with stories of grisly deaths, wars, and famine, and the only music she can find is somber and funereal. She would rather be chilled than listen to a catalog of horrors.

Trevor had said, Come down, we can't talk about it over the phone, and she had agreed, as if talking were all that was needed. But now she wishes she had stayed in her room, turned off the phone, shut the lights, drawn the curtains. A tragic heroine, she thinks.

The familiar road blurs past tumbling cities and denuded fields torn apart by gigantic machines. The promise of the future swallowing the present. Gaping holes where something once flourished. She drives fast.

She loops off the bridge for the clanking and pothole-ladened ride down the east side. With each jarring bump, the suspension seems to give way, until the car is nothing more than a metal sled scraping dirt on a denuded hill months past the last snowfall.

It's not love, she had said, and instantly she regretted both her honesty and the duplicity. It had never been love. Now would come the months of agonizing unpleasantries, angry quips attributed to bad moods and chemicals, until one of them would finally admit it wasn't working, it couldn't work: the age difference, the distance. The lie had been easier.

She parks across from the homeless shelter, leaving the car like an act of faith, and zigzags the garbage-strewn sidewalk to his building. She buzzes once, a warning, then slips his key into the lock. The key doesn't fit right, it was made on the wrong blank, and she jiggles it in the lock the way he showed her. If only he had replaced it, she will think later, if only he weren't too cheap to replace an eighty-nine-cent key.

She feels the gun first. She's never felt a gun before, but there's no mistaking it: the perfect roundness in her back, the weight, the hollow center of the barrel. Move, is all he says. There are two of them. Two white men, which surprises her, and then she is surprised by her racism. They make no effort to disguise themselves, and this, more than anything, frightens her. She avoids looking at their faces, as if to reassure them that she can be trusted. She won't betray them.

They force her into the elevator. When they press his floor, she thinks for the first time that they won't rape her; if they wanted to, they would have done it already. And this, too, frightens her.

He is waiting by his open door when they get out. His

face, its movement from happiness to fear to recognition, tells her how serious it is. He mouths her name, and one of them says, Shit, it's his girlfriend. The other laughs and says, That's his problem.

The apartment is clean and well lit. A new series of landscapes hangs along the living room wall. She can see his account books lying open on the drafting table, his glasses resting on their frames, a cup by their side.

I've got money, says Trevor, there's plenty of money. He brandishes his wallet.

Fuck your money, the one with the gun says. Can't snort your money.

Oh, Trevor, she thinks. Oh, Trevor. That's what this is all about.

Trevor raises his hands. Apologetically, she thinks. I'm out, he says.

Do you think I'm fucking around? says the gun. He spins to her, a ballet dancer in jeans and a hooded sweatshirt, a smudge of dirt on one cheek, a cracked tooth, one eye a different color.

She feels the bullet before she hears the shot. A sharp pain like a hanger through her abdomen. She can't breathe; someone has knocked the wind out. Her hands grab the air, gathering it like a trunkful of cotton dresses, burying her face in its fragile weave.

He's killing me, she screams, but the sound that emerges is a gurgle, like water from the bidet in their hotel in Paris. Look at that, he had said, the toilet is leaking. You're a barbarian, she said; who let you out of your cave?

And then there is another shot, and this time she doesn't feel anything at all.

Nell's parents live in town, across from the duck pond and library, in a house with a wraparound porch, dormer windows, and a picket fence. An anachronism in a town of developed cul-de-sacs, houses that bristle with faux Georgian columns and circular driveways.

Christmas morning my father and I drive by on our way from

the twenty-four-hour store for pancake mix. There's a single light shining in an upstairs bedroom. A trail of smoke from the chimney. A tree in the living room.

It's early. No one's awake. Half the Jews in our town are celebrating Christmas, dreaming of new bicycles, chemistry sets, tennis rackets. Kids get what they want here; the *Hanukkah* man sees to that.

"Did you know her well?" my father asks.

"No," I say.

"It's a tragedy."

"Yes," I say. Birth. Love. Death. Which is the comedy? I wonder.

We continue down the empty road. Snow falls in flawless white crystals, smoothing the irregular landscape. My father's fingers drum the steering wheel as he hums a show tune.

She has reinvented herself. It's the life we imagined. Endless opportunity, freedom from history, a fashionable wardrobe. We live in an era when anything is possible, when Jews sing for Jesus, and no god makes distinctions. Straight through the door and out of history.

In the rear window I watch the house fade to gray. The tires cut four black lines, negative images across a blanket of white. New crystals quickly cover the scars.

I turn back to my father. Wipers brush snow from the windshield. The headlights suspend each flake as it floats toward us.

Home, Dad, I breathe. *Home*.

all
men are
socrates

"You will learn the syllogism," says the Law School Admissions Test instructor. "You will learn the fallacies."

His bald pate gleams with perspiration and fluorescent light. He whacks a ruler across his palm, emphasizing major and minor premises. When my attention drifts, he whacks the ruler across my knuckles.

I recite: "All fools are mortal. Socrates is mortal. Socrates is a fool."

"Sophist!" he exclaims, breaking the ruler across my skull. "Philistine! Goat!"

I stagger from the classroom, my head cracked and bleeding.

"Maybe you should take one of those normal courses," suggests Dirk.

I wear a bicycle helmet, a hockey mask, lacrosse gloves. He trades in his ruler for a baseball bat, pounding me across the room until I am soft and lumpy like a medicine ball.

"Have you no respect for the greatest philosopher in history?" he shrieks.

I throw myself at his feet and beg for mercy. "All men are mortal," I say. "I am a man. I am mortal."

He will spare me, but for how long? The clock is ticking on my career bomb. Life arises from first principles and deductive logic. I think, therefore there are thoughts. But the self remains elusive and unformed, a shadow being of incantations and false hopes.

"Should I go to law school?" I ask Dirk.

"You like to argue," he says as he stuffs medical school applications into a postal bag.

"I do not," I say.

I walk across campus to another session of beanball. The hills are balding. A chill wind blows. The standard propositions are advanced: Keep your options open; work within the system.

Can the son of a scientist fall far from the tree? Galileo, Kepler, and Newton predict his elliptical orbit around the familiar. The law is the Law. But what would happen if he swerved slightly like Lucretius's atoms? An apple might knock him unconscious, upset all the familiar principles. Even deductive logic requires an inductive kick start. First principles don't grow on trees.

After class I meet Dirk for the deadly nightshade. We sit in a damp basement where sullen waitresses take poetry instead of orders. Dirk stows his stethoscope and tongue depressor beneath the table.

"I like rules," I admit. "I like finding the answer."

"You'll be a good lawyer," he says.

"But what if I make the wrong choice?"

"It's too late," he says, a sugar cube decaying in his teeth. "The future is in litigation."

I hum along the twisting road in Dirk's new car. An early graduation present from parents with nothing but money. It smells green.

I have left him my inheritance as collateral. "No offense," he says as he makes an imprint of my credit card, "I'd hate to lose it if you don't die."

The college on the hill disappears over the crest like a redbrick Oz. Take off your magic glasses. Forget the happy songs. The woods have burned. Trees block the forest. No ones listens when they crash to the ground.

I've done my time in the English fields. Bad weather, a poor harvest, these are the perils of the profession. It's fine for my mother to sit at the kitchen table reading her novels, but you've got to eat. How many starving English majors can dance on the head of a pin? After a while they collapse from malnutrition, their mouths making the sound of one hand clapping. Interpretation piled atop interpretation, it's enough to drive anyone to hunger.

The road opens onto a six-lane highway. I pay the toll and accelerate into the passing lanes. From the hills to the ocean, all paths lead to the ivory tower. I don't ask for much: truth; beauty; a six-figure starting salary. In a world where everyone has a theory, unity is another hypothesis.

Sixty, seventy miles per hour. I move relative to objects outside my field of motion. Or I'm standing still. Who's measuring? So many laws: one for relativity; one for entropy; another to justify murder in the name of the state. No wonder my grandfather pledged his allegiance to anarchy. The people of the book had the book thrown at them. You want law, they were told, here's law: Thou shalt not mingle; thou shalt not marry; thou shalt not pray; thou shalt not live. Their eyes went blind from the fine print, their teeth pulled for the gold.

In the distance, the dwarf city of the north. Stunted buildings rise along the river like weeds in a shady lot. Children scamper through the narrow doorways holding their books aloft. At every lamppost, a decree.

When all are dwarfs, even the dwarfs are giants.

"It's the corporate sellout," says Joshua.

"I don't see you leading any revolutions," I say.

We are huddled in David's room on a hopelessly cold New England night. Wind rattles a broken pane, buffets against an old T-shirt that billows like a spinnaker. David's roommate has moved to a hotel.

"This is ridiculous," says David. "Let's go to Joshua's apartment."

"Revolution begins here," says Joshua, motioning to his head.

"Yeah, and evolution begins here," I say, grabbing my crotch. "So what?"

"You don't ask the fox to lead a hen rebellion."

"Cambridge to Cambridge is not a radical movement."

"Oxford."

"Guys, it's freezing."

David watches in horror as our voices become raspier, our movements slower, our skin frozen with droplets of our own perspiration. Soon he will have to eat us in order to survive.

"Follow your genes," says Joshua. "The secular version of the *Torah* scholar."

"*Talmud.*" It's my turn to correct him.

He waves his hands in the air; he can't be bothered by trivialities.

"When our parents told us we could be anything we wanted," he says, "they meant any kind of doctor or lawyer we wanted."

"You think getting a Ph.D. in English literature confounds their expectations?"

"A Rhodes scholarship," explains Joshua. "It doesn't necessarily lead to a Ph.D."

How Joshua convinced the Rhodes committee that carrying marijuana in a backpack was a sport, in order to qualify for the scholarship, remains one of the great unsolved mysteries of the twentieth century.

"There are little children starving in Africa," I say. "Isn't that what our parents said? Reading Milton doesn't do anything for them."

"Neither does making a ton of money."

"I'll mail it to them."

"What's wrong with trying to help people?" asks David.

"Which people?"

"The sick. The needy. People who are less fortunate than us."

"Have you ever met them?" asks Joshua. "They're drug dealers and drug users and child beaters. They hate Jews. They hate blacks. We don't want to help those people. We just want to talk about it."

"I do," David says quietly, hugging his knees to his chest.

"You want to tear open their chests and rip out their hearts," Joshua says.

"You're full of shit," I say. "You know that, Joshua."

"Sure I am. But at least it's my own shit."

He beams with delight like a child who's smeared his feces against the wall. Look what I made, Mom. It came out my ass. Or was it my mouth? He can't remember. It's one end or another.

"All your pretty arguments," I say. "I wonder what Nell would think."

We sit silently in the cold.

"It's fucking freezing," says Joshua finally. "Let's get out of here."

The big chill has lowered one leaden foot. Sculls choke the Charles River like frozen dragonflies. Their hapless crews scramble up the icy banks.

We stroll briskly toward campus, Joshua pontificating, David and I trailing in his wake. All roads lead to the tower. From the tower, however, there is only the road.

"If truth, then beauty," Joshua says, describing his Rhodes proposal. "If beauty, then truth. Which is the fallacy?"

"Too many axioms," I agree.

We struggle against the tide of bodies floating out to sea. The students look impossibly young, raised on Milk-Bone and suet, barely out of diapers, cloned from pedigreed nurseries. David details the soap opera of freshman life while I attempt to catch the eyes of attractive women who ignore me and stare at David instead.

My baby brother! The boy who kept my mother busy with ontogeny while I was recapitulating phylogeny. The history of the race is a tale of disfavored older brothers: Cain, Esau, Aaron. Murder, betrayal, rebellion.

At the gates to the castle we dismount our camels. The gatekeeper snarls at our passports. He's let too many of us into the hallowed halls.

"Someday," says Joshua, "all this will be yours."

"They've got to accept me first," I say.

"Piece of cheesecake," he says.

"You'll be a great lawyer," says David.

"What if I don't want to?"

"Then you won't."

But staring into the mouth of the fortress, I know what I want, as if some deep genetic spring were urging me into the water. Here is the palace of law, high on the mountaintop. Its vaulted ceilings, the gilded dome. Here is tradition, generations of fealty, a nobler purpose. The men who passed before me linked in a timeless knot. It's the new religion, a spiritual calling. Nature or nurture, this band around my heart?

The vandals have departed; there are no barbarians at the gate. May peace and prosperity reign.

We return to the Square, my head in a fog of admissions. At a blacktop lot Joshua reclaims his car. I kick the edges of a pothole while a man in tattered clothes with an unkempt beard and dirty hands asks if we want our windows washed. Joshua gives him a dollar. When the car arrives, the man pulls a spray bottle from beneath his jacket, a squeegee from his trouser leg.

The parking attendant steps from the idling car. "Get out," he yells, his vowels tinkling with a foreign accent. "Go home!" He's short, but compact, while the squeegee man, in his baggy clothes, is a woolly bear.

"Joshua," I say, in the frozen moment before conflict, when a simple explanation will defuse.

The attendant grabs the squeegee from the man's hand. It somersaults across the lot, a ballet of water and wood.

The squeegee man straightens. His hand glints in the dwindling sunlight. A knife? Keys? He swings too quickly to be certain. A red bloom blossoms on the attendant's cheek. His hand rises to pluck the astonishing flower. His eyes dilate—anger to horror to fear—as his fingers discover the sticky bouquet. He steps backward as the squeegee man advances, raising one arm to shield the blow.

"Joshua!" I scream.

"Hey," says David.

The squeegee man lumbers unhurriedly toward the attendant. I circle the perimeter of combatants and approach from behind, lunging at the squeegee man's shoulders as the circle collapses. My hands slip on his loose jacket. He turns, and for one paralyzing instant I anticipate the blow across my face. Instead he twists his shoulders and shrugs me off.

The attendant, safely out of range in his booth, gingerly cradles the telephone. The squeegee man makes a quick calculation, retrieves his squeegee, and fades back into the alleyway. In the distance, sirens.

My heart thrums in my chest like a hummingbird's. Bile rises in the back of my throat.

Joshua picks up his keys where the attendant has dropped them. He blows the dust off and shoves them in his pocket.

"He had a knife," says David. He rests his hand on my trembling arm.

I run my tongue along the inside of my gums. No blood, no cracked molars. I am not sure whether I am relieved or disappointed.

The attendant comes out of his booth, a red rag pressed to his face, a crowbar in his other hand.

"I kill the nigger motherfucker," he says.

I've chewed enough graphite to slide through a keyhole. Black dots zigzag across my answer sheet like drunken insects. In front of me a woman in a tight ponytail vomits into a paper bag, then folds the bag neatly and returns to her exam. A man spontaneously combusts, his hair a halo of fire. No one looks as he runs screaming from the room.

My pencil moves toward (b), but the tiny microchip embedded behind my ear buzzes softly. I switch to infrared, and the correct response is highlighted from an orbiting satellite.

An enormous clock peals off seconds like banana rinds. The proctor fires a burst from her machine gun over our heads. Guards scurry down the aisles, separating us from our booklets, dislocating the fingers of those who are too slow.

"Did you get aabddaccdaeeacbbcadc for the last twenty?" asks the vomiting woman.

"No," her neighbor panics. "I got aabddadcdaeeacbbcadc."

I stumble down the steps of the gymnasium, my brain a pastiche of caffeine and sugar. Number two pencils dance like Sugarplum Fairies, their pliés deep and graceful. They giggle as I walk past, tiny eraserheads wiggling with glee.

At the top of the hill, near the War Memorial, I stop and survey the green expanse of peaks and valleys. A bird hops past, a chunk of bread clenched in its beak. Overhead the sun shines warmly. The air smells of pine.

I step up onto the circle of granite. The names of the dead are etched in stone. The battles where they lay a forgotten geography lesson: Argonne; Verdun; the Marne.

No German philosophers for them! Only Russell and Whitehead, big men who believed in the power of reason and logic. Then the other war came, and their tidy systems were blown apart by French collaborators and Nazi apologists. First principles be damned. But after a while the philosophers found they didn't mind. They played backgammon until they were drunk on it, cheating ferociously and wagering their life savings. Without the burden of *being* and *reason* and *knowledge* they were truly free. They were in-the-world, as Heidegger had promised. Another German! But they didn't care. They were too far gone. Besides, at least he made the trains run on time. Or was that Mussolini? No one could remember.

I follow the bird, which is hopping absurdly, the bread as large as its head. It sets the meal down, and in that instant another bird, larger and swifter, snaps the morsel from its feet. The small bird screeches, its plaintive cry like a sketch of crying.

After a moment it looks at me and, no longer burdened with food, soars off the hill and into the sky.

The fat envelope bears no return address.

"You open it," commands Dirk. He scurries behind the sofa. When the bomb explodes, he will be safe from shrapnel and flying body parts.

"You're a doctor," I tell him.

He grabs my wrist and pirouettes around the living room, dragging my limp body like a rag doll behind him.

"Sixteen down," he says. "Four more years to go."

"Seven," I say.

"Five," he compromises.

He opens a bottle of champagne. He has chilled it for this mo-

ment, or another. A half-dozen bottles jam our minifridge in anticipation of life's small celebrations.

"To the boys in green," he says, and drinks.

I watch the bubbles skitter to the surface.

"And the girls in white," he adds, motioning with his empty glass
to my full glass.

I toss back the champagne. The bubbles burn my throat like a
thousand pinpricks. I feel hot, then suddenly cold. Sweat tickles my
forehead and the back of my neck. My eyes refuse to focus. The
bubbles have invaded my brain like a colony of red ants.

"Is it something I said?" asks Dirk.

I should be happy for him; he has labored in the dark recesses
of the library, inhaled vats of formaldehyde, and poisoned his mind
with the chemical formula. But like any well-meaning roommate, I
despise his hard-earned fortune. Let him wallow in rejection while
I ascend the tower.

"What will become of me?" I whine.

"The American dream," Dirk reassures me. "Two point two children. One point five automobiles. Three chickens in every two pots."

"My parents mortgaged my chickens."

Dirk tightens his nutcracker jaw. I insist on spoiling his parade.
"Rice and beans in a federal penitentiary," he says, grinding his
teeth.

I am vaguely encouraged by the prospect of definite vocation.
"Money laundering?" I ask, hoping for a white-collar crime.

"Grand larceny, auto." He pours a second glass. "To the future,"
he says, "or five to seven. Whichever comes first."

The bubbles dart up my nose. I drink quickly, my eyes stinging
with tears.

Why, I wonder, do we never drink to the past?

Good news travels in pairs like shoes.

I tear from the post office, cross campus, breaking every college
sprint record on the way. I fly through the dining hall, upending the
salad bar, ramming the sneeze guard into the dairy dispenser.

I race to the War Memorial. The fields are half filled with

winter-heavy athletes, chugging through the motions of practice. Weeds peek through cracks in the tennis courts. In the distance the hills are spotted with bare trees like liver spots.

"Hello!" I call.

"Lo, lo, lo." My voice echoes like Humbert Humbert calling his love.

"I got into law school!"

"Fool, fool, fool," comes the echo.

The lacrosse team, scalps hanging from their belts, glare up at me. Most have found jobs with investment banks and brokerage houses. Five years from now half the team will be under indictment. They do not like lawyers.

Someone shouts, and the team charges up the hill.

I am slow and easily winded. My loafers slip on the grass. Soon I will be stretched into webbing for lacrosse sticks.

A silver sedan screeches to a stop inches from my face. A man in an Italian suit and calfskin shoes, his hair gleaming black, steps out. He lifts me to my feet and deposits me in the front seat. The doors lock, and the windows shade dark gray.

"Comfortable," he says. He's not asking.

I twist in my seat. It adjusts automatically to my new posture like a hand squeezing my bottom. Who is this sartorial stranger?

He pulls a business card from a stack tucked into a retractable dashboard tray.

ELIJAH ROSENKRANTZ
COVERT OPERATIONS

"Call me Eli," he says. "Everyone does." The car thrums along the road. "Seat belts." He clucks, waving at the loop behind my shoulder.

I strap myself down. Objects in the Mirror Are Closer Than They Appear. "How did you get here?" I ask.

He checks his watch. "Shuttle," he says. "Picked up the car at the airport." He looks at me for the first time. "Mercedes," he continues, his voice trailing off the *s*. "Not my first choice, but . . .

"Don't worry," he adds, misinterpreting my look of alarm. "It's on the client."

Foreign governments. Wealthy bankers. Shadowy Zionist conspirators. The list of possible suspects is endless.

"Sorry," he says when I ask. "Attorney-client privilege. Work-product. Immunity."

We drive in silence for several minutes. Through the heavily tinted glass I can see the signs of spring: mud; broken twigs; manure.

If he's come to give me a message, he seems in no hurry to deliver it. We meander over the road as it dips into the valley, out past the malls, and into the surrounding farmland.

"Cozy locale," he says. "Nice place to visit."

"But you wouldn't want to live here." I finish his sentence.

"Too quiet. Too many cows. In the old days, sure. But we live in the city now."

"You're married?" I say, prodding for information.

He smiles. His teeth are capped. His skin is taut and shiny, stretched to fit his face.

"We bought our own place." He ignores my question. "But the payments are killing us."

Has he kidnapped me to discuss his mortgage?

"Renovations. Expansions. Plumbing problems. It's been a terrible headache."

We pass a lone runner jogging steadily into oblivion.

"But enough about *my* problems." He raises both hands from the steering wheel. "What do *you* think about my problems?" He laughs, a short, whooping, hyenalike yelp.

I have fallen into the clutches of a bad-joke–telling, foppish, myopic guardian angel. If he doesn't drive us into a ditch, he'll kill me with household anecdotes.

"What are you doing here?" I finally ask, exasperated. "What am I doing here?"

"What are any of us doing here? You think I know the answers?" He shakes his head. "Life isn't a syllogism. Plug in the premises and QED. Life meanders. It's fluid. Doesn't obey the simple rules you and I have postulated."

My luck to be driving with a mystic. Someone for whom cause

and effect is an interesting theory. Turn the wheel to the left, go straight. Press on the gas, the car stops.

"Keep your eyes on the road, please," I implore him.

"A lot of crazy drivers in the boonies," he agrees.

He zigs and zags through increasingly unfamiliar territory. Dark forests. High desert. Exotic animals peer at us through the underbrush. Zebras. Pronghorn antelope. Squid. Nothing unnerves him. He turns on the radio, the high beams, the windshield wipers. He fiddles with the cigarette lighter. "Damn rental cars," he says as he tries to light a cigarette with the radar detector.

I help him shove the wires back under the dashboard. He makes a sudden sharp turn and knocks me against the door. My seat belt locks, pinning my neck to the window. When it releases me from a chokehold, we are gliding to a stop in front of my dorm.

"Home again, home again," he says, and unlocks the doors. "Watch your step."

And then he is gone. One taillight blinking like a lunatic uncle.

"You'll never believe this," I say when I enter the living room.

"You got into law school!" says Dirk, grabbing the letter from my hand. He whisks me around the room like an electric beater.

I try to warn him that there's a prophet on the loose, covertly battling the pagan foes of Israel. But it's too late; I'm butter.

Hail the college on the hill. Four years and untold millions of dollars, only a small percentage of which has been invested in repressive regimes, and we are better men. The ethnic have been sanitized, the race purified, gender eliminated. Now we march forth in lock-step to the drums of a benevolent capitalism. Let us not forget, as we attain positions of power and oppress the unfortunate, that without us the world would be a nicer place.

"Quite a moving speech," says my mother.

"The guy's always hated diversity," agrees Dirk.

We eat soggy chicken and lumpy bread beneath a sweltering tent. Swirls of relatives eddy into cooler pockets, seeking ice cream, soda, watermelon. Small children scream with boredom.

"Why would such a nice young man go with other men?" asks my mother, intent on keeping the players straight.

Dirk's parents, fortunately, are not blessed with her keen sense of observation. They chatter politely about this year's tobacco crop, oblivious to my mother's stage whispers. Dirk has trotted them out like show horses, ready for the pasture. I stare at Mrs. Lancaster's remarkable hair, stiff as an ice-cream cone, and Mr. Lancaster's boll weevil face. How did such bizarre individuals produce a son like Dirk? What genetic information was misread, sparing Dirk from a life spent cowering under a shopping bag, two holes cut out for his eyes? A slight kink in his DNA, a subtle swerve of the chain, and the long train of snout-nosed progenitors skips a station.

Nearby, my father stands birdlike, weight on one leg, amid a knot of fathers, their voices pitched to mass hysteria as they discuss the recent run on the market. His eyes, bobbing behind his glasses, search desperately for the exit ramp.

At a rectangular picnic table David quizzes the premed adviser. The adviser hands David a pile of brochures and flees for the keg.

Rebecca affects a bored insouciance, her pale face tilted toward the sun while she ignores the entreaties of half my friends who buzz round her like bees.

O chosen one, O Jewess, they sing, grace us with a glimpse of your olive skin.

The land overflows, but not with milk or honey. Shellac oozes from the green hills, coating the valley in a pristine veneer.

"We're so proud of you," my mother says.

I struggle to breathe through the amber. Each step draws me closer. Soon I will be assimilated into the translucent mass.

"You're your grandfather's dream," she adds.

"The anarchist?" I say.

"My father? He was a baker."

"But he went to jail," I say hopefully.

"Did he? I don't think so."

The first generation goes to prison. The second generation forgets. The third generation invents the memory. We lie because truth is a cave in our hearts.

Dirk interrupts my revisionist musings by grasping me around the chest and squeezing whatever air remains from my lungs. He holds up a bottle of hemlock.

"To the best five years of our lives," he says, pouring me a cup.
"Seven," I remind him.

We drink. My eyes burn with poison. With two thick fingers I brush at the tears. They etch in acid their crooked lines down my face.

My pupils, my pupils, I cry. I gather them around me. Their beatific faces. Their golden limbs. The false knowledge I have taught them will corrupt the ages.

All men are fools.

Socrates is a fool.

All men are Socrates.

QED.

false
idols

law
of the
jungle

Look to the right, advises the dean. Look to the left. In a year one of you won't be here.

Hail the law school on the mountain. Breathe that rarefied air. Clamber over the backs of your classmates.

In the gloomy stained glass amphitheater the dean tells us a bedtime story:

Two law students are camping when suddenly they hear a bear pawing at their tent. "Let's get out of here," says one.

"Okay," says the other, "but first let me tie my running shoes."

"Don't be stupid," says the first law student, "running shoes won't help you outrun a bear."

"I don't have to outrun the bear," says the second. "I only have to outrun you."

I twist in my seat to meet my right-hand neighbor. His gold teeth gleam cruelly, the points of his incisors flashing like dueling pistols.

"Nathan," he says. "Nathan Weiss." His last name escapes like steam from a radiator.

Knee-high to a gnome. A gargoyle made flesh. When he smiles, his mouth expands across the width of his face, threatening the collapse of ears and nose into that yawning chasm until only the grin remains. His chest and arms are monstrous, freakishly muscled, the result of hours at the gym in an attempt to gain in latitude what he lacks in altitude.

"Pleased to meet you," I say naïvely, as if I could charm the bear into docility.

"Is that your stomach growling?" he asks. He bends down to tie his shoes.

I turn to the hapless victim on my left. He smiles dumbly as if he had nothing to worry about. Within a year they'll find his mangled and half-devoured body at the base of the mountain.

Two number two pencils, three colored markers, two felt-tips, four spiral notebooks, an eraser, and an Erector set. The first day of kindergarten.

My assigned seat is the exact midpoint of the room, the cruel joke of a heartless computer. I am dead center for professors' potshots, a walking bull's-eye tattooed on my forehead. I sit unswerving through four classes while all manner of rotted fruit comes my way. My clothing is stained with foul torts and breached contracts. I have committed every crime in the book and succumbed to procedural weakness. I am an error of fact and of law. I am an eggshell plaintiff. I am a reasonable man foreseeably present in the stream of commerce when a soda bottle explodes in my hand, steering pins fail on my Buick, firecrackers cause a stampede on a railway platform toppling giant scales onto my head.

"Miss-tah Stone," a shrill voice whinnies.

I look into the merciless eyes of a man who recently argued before the Supreme Court that sterilization was an appropriate punishment for mental retardation.

"I'm sorry, sir," I squeak. "I don't speak Latin."

"Ah, a comedian," he says. His long fingers threaten to curl into my eyeballs, tearing away the flesh and scooping out the vile jelly.

I stare back down at the page. *Assumpsit*, I read. *Quantum meruit. Illegitimatati non carborundet.*

"Don't let the bastards grind you down?" I venture.

A nervous twitter runs through the row. I can smell someone's body odor.

"A sense of humor is a wonderful thing," he says. "I used to have one too."

I smile pathetically, a small domesticated animal who has lost the instinct for fight.

He circles my face on his seating chart. Draws a crosshair on my nose. When he sets his pen down, I realize that he has dedicated himself to ruining my life.

If I live that long.

"Bad luck," booms Nathan after class. "You did okay, though." His voice rumbles through the earth's mantle, shifting tectonic plates and causing minor structural damage halfway across the continent.

We amble toward the Square, buffeted on the winds of Nathan's vocal cords. Tie-dyed neohippies and blackened punks observe our progress with a mixture of awe and glee.

"Jack and his Beanstalk!" I hear someone shriek.

We elbow into a crowded pizzeria. Nathan orders a pie and eats three quarters of it. He vacuums cheese off the top, leaving the denuded crust lying like a bloody battlefield on the soggy plate. He returns to the counter for another slice as an afterthought.

"Eat," he says, patting his washboard belly, "or be eaten."

Clotted milk roils about my stomach. Methane brews in my intestines. "The pizza didn't really stand a chance," I say.

"Law of the jungle." He rubs the smooth muscle along his forearm. "There are only two food groups: you and them."

I tell him there are certain things I won't eat.

"You've never had to go hungry," he says. "You took all that land from the Indians."

"Me?" I say.

"Your ancestors. The ones on the *Mayflower*."

"Not mine," I say. "Unless they brought their rabbi."

"Their rabbi?" He stops. "You're a Jew?"

"*Baruch ata adonai*," I declare.

"A Jew named Colin?"

"After my grandfather, *Cha'yim*. My parents picked the name from a book."

"You're a Jew?" he repeats, his voice a thin reed of disappointment.

"Sorry."

He shrugs. "It's not your fault." His clawed fingers pick at the shriveled crust.

"An accident of birth," I agree.

"Could you sue?"

I feign a laugh, anything for my new friend. But when I open my eyes, I see that he isn't smiling.

He's eating.

Wiry tendrils of black hair sprout from my palms.

"What measure of damages, Miss-tah Stone, for this freakish misfortune?"

My underwear is soaked. My head throbs. My fingernails are swollen and bloody. How many days can I bear this torture? I am prepared to surrender, to reveal any secret, to betray my country, my people, my sense of humor. I promise never to make another joke if only he will withdraw those interminable digits from my optic nerves.

From across the room, a voice booms.

"A reasonable man in the plaintiff's condition should be grateful for the operation that saved his hands. The slight malfeasance of grafting chest hair onto the palms constitutes partial performance and not a breach of the entire contract because the hands were saved. Therefore, the proper measure of damages should be compensatory, i.e., the cost of a lifetime supply of depilatories or other hair removal products, not the indeterminate and speculative value of two hands in perfect condition."

Stunned silence. The bear swipes at an empty tent. Nathan has tied his own shoes, then lifted me onto his back and sprinted to safety.

"Yes, well," coughs my persecutor. "Very good. Ahem." He looks at his seating chart, trying to connect the joker in the center with the gargoyle perched in the upper rows. What happened to menace and intimidation? he wonders. Students would quake in their seats. Now everything's fairness and affirmative action, as if life were a whipped dessert topping. Perhaps it's time to return to the Justice Department, where he can pervert the civil rights laws and authorize wiretaps of leftist agitators.

He sighs and wipes his glasses along his bow tie. It's the inequity of equity that really bothers him. In a perfect world the lion would eat the lamb, not lie with her. Vegetarians, pacifists, and a liberal judiciary have perverted the natural state of affairs. Life should be poor, nasty, brutish, and short.

He, the son of parents who fled Europe in 1938, knows from what he is saying.

"I decided it's okay you're a Jew. We can still be friends."

His smile caverns across the living room, swallowing my futon couch, the kitchen table, two chairs. I cling to the doorframe but feel myself slipping into the vortex.

"I've never really had a Jewish friend," he continues. "I don't date Jewish women. I just don't like them. I'm an anti-Semite, I guess."

It's been five years since I set foot in a synagogue. I mix milk with meat on Yom Kippur. I eat pizza and beer on Passover. If God watches, He's disgusted with my dining habits. How many planks can be replaced in the ship of Theseus before the boat loses its identity entirely?

"But I *am* a Zionist," Nathan insists. "My parents are big supporters of Israel. They have a fund-raiser every year. It's important that there's a place where people who want to be Jews can live."

"Like a Jewish reservation."

"Except it's their own country. And they have the Bomb."

If the Sioux had placed a few spies at Los Alamos, they could have carved out a small strip of desert for themselves. Hostile neighbors to the east and west. Strategic alliances with foreign powers. Airlifts and aid bonds. Their own F-16's to strike nuclear power plants deep inside California.

His smile floats in the center of my apartment. Light bends toward him. He is an infinitesimal dot: massively dense, impossibly small.

"We take care of our own," he says. "The Indians don't do that. Or the blacks."

"We have an intact social structure," I say, repeating something I heard my mother say years ago.

"The Asians do, though," he continues, ignoring me. "They're the Jews today."

If the Asians are today's Jews, I wonder, tomorrow will they be yesterday's WASPs?

"Especially the Koreans. They work hard. Nobody wants to work hard anymore."

"I don't think every Korean works hard," I say.

"Have you seen them? Clipping the brown part off a green bean? It's incredible!"

"Some Koreans are lazy."

He frowns. As deep and wide as a gash in the earth. "Are you a racist?" he asks.

"Some Jews are lazy," I say. "Not all of them are doctors."

"They're not?" The grin returns. Like a cat stalking a bird.

"No," I say. "They're lawyers."

If it's Tuesday, that must be the president of Nicaragua.

The Yard overflows with journalists and tourists. In one corner a former revolutionary lectures on investment strategies. On the steps of the library a leading unannounced presidential candidate, his mistress by his side, distributes free copies of his book, *Piling It On and Taking It Off*. At the gate two members of a religious sect sell crash pads for levitation accidents.

Not a student in sight.

In the Square every doorway is occupied by a scraggly wretch of indeterminate sex clutching a guitar and caterwauling about love, betrayal, and patricide. They are from Iowa or Germany, self-fulfilling hippie prophets of the liberal northeastern university town; their parents have paid for their tickets.

"Get a job," Nathan growls.

We turn a corner and nearly run into David, head tilted, engaged in rapturous dialogue with a raven-haired classmate. He blushes, then introduces us to Alexandra.

"We're having lunch," says Nathan, in a tone used to command ancient sailing ships. No one disobeys.

Soon we are sitting in Nathan's favorite spot, hunkered next to tins of tomato sauce and a white mountain of mozzarella. Slice after slice vanishes behind his teeth. Strings of cheese dangle like power lines in Godzilla's mouth.

Alexandra seems enraptured, enthralled by the awesome display of eating pyrotechnics. Even David watches with stunned amazement. The conversation dwindles while we all observe Nathan eat.

"I've never seen such an appetite," says Alexandra.

"Keep up the fighting weight," says Nathan, slowing only to spray bits of food across the table.

"Are you a boxer?"

"A law student." He lays down his crust. "Did you know you can stop a charging bear by punching it in the nose?"

Alexandra shakes her head. Black curls coil down her neck like pencil shavings.

"It's a question of timing rather than strength. One good pop."

"Really?"

Nathan flexes the muscle on the back of his forearm. Large as a loaf of bread. "Of course you've got to be strong too."

David leans into me. "She has a boyfriend," he whispers.

"Not anymore," I say.

"He loves her," David protests.

I race back through the years, attempting to summon a female face from my brother's past. There was a Julie or Cindy something, his prom date, but according to Rebecca, whose finely tuned ears miss little, they never kissed. Once he mentioned a woman in his biology class, but it turned out he was talking about the professor. Has he loved and lost, or just never loved?

Something small and surreptitious passes between Nathan and Alexandra when we part. I ask for details, but his smile is like the Chinese brother who swallowed the ocean.

Later I remember David's face: a moon stripped of its atmosphere by a larger body, two eyes peering from its bleak and wind-swept surface.

A solitary man behind the eyes.

I wake at night to the sound of heavy breathing outside my tent.

I can't escape, I tell my parents. Christmas is a mere study break before the final onslaught of exams.

They understand. Hard work. Commitment to one's career. Fear of the bear. They'll ship a first-aid kit and a St. Bernard back with David.

I arrange my notes in color-coded categories. I buy file folders, organizers, sticky tabs, index cards. I tape a study schedule to the refrigerator. I sweep the dust off my desk. I brew multiple pots of coffee.

I go out for lunch.

"Legal reasoning encompasses four paradigmatic argumentative modes," explains Nathan. "Each can be manipulated to necessitate a particular result."

My forehead feels tight and prickly, a snare drum of anxiety. My eyes glaze like eggs in a kiln.

"The regime of legal rules is mere foliage for distributive and/or paternalist motives," he continues as he reaches for my pizza, "a smoke screen for judges' social and economic agendas." He chomps at the dry crusts and clotted cheese.

"Oooooooooaaaaaahhhh," I wail.

"Sorry," he says, pulling the crust from his mouth. "I thought you were done."

I wave him off. I cannot eat. Bile rises in my throat. I am being devoured in a pizzeria by a grotesque ornamental figure designed to divert rainwater.

"Are you all right? You look green."

"Fine," I sputter. "Lots on my mind."

He snaps his fingers. They crack like trees in a hurricane. "Sensory overload," he concludes. "The mind can't absorb a constant barrage of information. I know the perfect solution."

My parents, I protest vaguely. Exams.

"Tell them it's a fund-raiser," he says. "For a good cause."

"On Christmas?"

"Christ was a Jew," he says. "Look at the loot he got."

"We're so glad you could come," coos Mrs. Weiss.

"We've heard so much about you," adds Mr. Weiss.

"No, we haven't."

"Yes, we have."

"Objection."

"Overruled."

"They're alumni," Nathan explains. "My mom was one of the first women on law review."

Dueling bulldogs. They're the same height, same color, same growl. I tower above them like Livingstone among the Pygmies.

"How was the trip?"

"How's school?"

My head flips from one to the other, a Ping-Pong of queries.

Is that crazy man still teaching torts? Does the dean give the speech about the bear? Is that cute little bakery still run by Arabs?

"Nathan says your parents are academics."

"He says they're very well known."

I mumble something about Nobel prizes and MacArthur grants.

"They sound like our kind of people."

"Let's have them for dinner."

I nod ambiguously as the maid passes a platter of cakes and coffee.

"Clothilde," says Mrs. Weiss, "this is Colin. He's Nathan's new friend from the law school."

Clothilde eyes me with a jaded suspicion.

"Isn't she lovely?" says Mrs. Weiss when Clothilde has left. "Such a poor girl. She has a Ph.D. in mathematics. We recovered her during a human rights tour."

"Terrible repression," clucks Mr. Weiss.

Nathan explains that we don't care about human rights; we have exams in three weeks.

"Absolutely," Mrs. Weiss agrees. "I took my first exam in the midst of the Cuban missile crisis. I didn't understand what all the fuss was about."

"Claire could have studied through the Holocaust," says Mr. Weiss.

I say that Anne Frank studied through the Holocaust as a way of maintaining her sanity.

"Poor girl," says Mrs. Weiss. "Did she manage to finish her schooling?"

"Unfortunately, no," I say.

"So many were forced to give up their culture. It's really a tragedy."

The tragedy, I tell her, is not having a culture to give up.

Mrs. Weiss clucks in agreement. "But enough gloom and doom." She brightens. "Let's eat!"

Table manners, I learn, are hereditary.

In the middle of the night the door creaks open and a figure drifts into the room. She floats silently to the window, her naked body backlit by streetlight.

"Come." She motions to me.

"Who are you?" I ask. "What do you want?"

"I am the ghost of Christmas future," she says. "I have much to show you."

"Go away," I say. "I'm a Jew. I don't believe in Christmas ghosts."

She draws a piece of paper from a flesh-colored satchel around her belly and unfolds it. "Did I get the wrong address?" she asks.

"I barely know these people," I protest.

"But you've forsaken your own family, a mere sixteen miles toward the east, to celebrate Christmas with them."

"My family doesn't celebrate Christmas."

"*Hanukkah*, Christmas, same thing."

"No, it's not," I say. I explain that *Hanukkah* celebrates the deliverance of the Jews from the oppression of the Syrian-Greeks who had attempted to impose heathen practices on the Jewish population. The Maccabees defeated the Syrians, cleansed and rededicated the Temple, and lit the Temple *menorah*. Though there was only enough oil to burn for one day, miraculously the candles burned for eight. Thus do we celebrate *Hanukkah*, the Festival of Lights, for eight days.

"If you had listened in Hebrew school," I conclude, "you might have learned something."

"Never mind that," she says. She slips between the sheets. Her hands are cool and dry as they press against my back. Her skin smells like cucumber.

"Nell?" I say to the still air.

But the room is empty and dark. From the avenue come the early-morning sounds of garbage trucks and buses. I snuffle into the pillow, seeking a deeper solace.

The door clicks quietly behind me.

Clothilde lingers over my coffee, pouring until the cup overflows. I catch her hand, and her fingers quicken around mine. When I look up, she smiles strangely, half grin, half grimace, the chipped front of a tooth exposed.

Broken china and glass have been swept into a neat pile at one end of the table. An accident, explains Nathan, his father dropped a plate. Clothilde's smile twists downward.

In the living room a Christmas tree tilts awkwardly toward the wall, a single ornament dangling from a branch, hung as if by accident or afterthought. I look closer and discover that the ornament is a sesame bagel, still warm.

"It is no good," says Clothilde. "It is, how do you say, against God."

"God made bagels," says Nathan.

"No," says Clothilde. "A Jewish man did."

"God made Jewish men."

Clothilde spits on the carpet, turns, and bangs into the kitchen.

"No wonder the death squads tried to kill her," says Nathan.

We finish our breakfast in relative peace, disrupted only by the sound of Nathan's molars. No sign of the Weisses, Esq.'s. Nathan leaves his dishes lined up on the table like a shooting gallery.

Outside, hordes of shoppers jam the avenues. Adorned in animal skins and pelts, they bludgeon one another to within inches of their credit limit. Dazed and dying for a bargain, survivors stagger into department stores.

I follow Nathan's gold card. He aims to boost the gross national product to record highs, single-handedly to lift the economy from the doldrums. Thank you, Mr. Weiss, chimes the chairman of the Federal Reserve. Bless you, Mr. Weiss, echoes the Secretary of Commerce.

At every corner I see a woman who looks like my mother, a man posing as my father. Sibling impostors follow me down the street, tormenting me with guilt, plaguing me with their commitment to family. They don't believe in Christmas fund-raisers.

I've had a tragic accident, I explain to these ersatz kin. My mind floats in the basement of a law library, sucking on a nutrient fluid of statutory enactments. My body exists only as a neurochemical projection into temporal space. I think therefore I think.

"Remember the lonely this holiday season," cries a man holding a placard.

"Pity the parents whose children have forsaken them," laments another.

"Repent, repent," cries a third. "The end is near!"

It's the night before Christmas and two law students, C and N, who are Jewish, are wrapping presents beneath the Christmas tree. C has had too much to drink and little practice wrapping Christmas gifts. N, observing C's problem with a particularly large gift, leans over to hold the box while C staples it shut. In his vigor, C staples N's hand instead, causing N to howl in pain. The family cat, shocked by N's howl, leaps off the couch and into the Christmas tree. C tries to grab the cat as it rebounds off the tree but knocks over the tree instead. The tree falls on N, surprising him but leaving him uninjured. However, the Christmas lights, which were clumsily assembled by N's father, are twisted around a lamp, and when the tree falls, the lamp crashes onto the floor. The sudden surge of power overloads the circuit breakers, causing them to short. N finds the fuse box and switches back on all the breakers except for the one that powers the refrigerator. In the morning N's mother awakes to find that her Christmas ham has gone rancid. Normally a ham should stay fresh if left at room temperature for eight hours, but this ham was improperly cured by the local butcher. She bakes it anyway, hoping heat will kill the bacteria, and serves it to her guests at a fund-raising dinner for Israeli sovereignty. Two guests, who keep kosher at home but knowingly ate the ham, become violently ill with trichinosis.

American society being as it is, all parties intend to sue. Discuss every possible action and all available defenses.

"Merry Christmas," says Nathan.

The book falls from my lap. I'm late for my final exam, and I'm dressed in pajamas. "What time is it?" I ask in a panic, leaping to my feet.

"Six in the morning. I thought you'd want to open your present."

In the living room the tree still stands; there is no cat. The refrigerator hums quietly in the kitchen. I smooth my wrinkled shirt and hair.

"But I didn't get anything for your parents."

"That's all right. You're Jewish."

We wade into the boxes, boots hiked to our hips. Ribbons and string twine around our heels like seaweed. Nathan fishes a box from the depths of red and green and hands it to me.

A chemistry set? The incredible visible woman? I tear the slippery paper from its spine.

A legal dictionary complete with common Latin phrases.

"I told them you could use one," says Nathan.

"Thanks," I lie.

Nathan spears a large box, weighing it in both hands before carefully removing the wrapping paper. He extracts the staples from the top flaps with thumb and forefinger, laying them on the paper. He shakes the box.

"Feels like bronze," he says.

He withdraws enough tissue paper to fill a case of Kleenex,

smoothing each piece and setting it beside the paper and staples. His hands reach deep into the box.

"Looks like gold."

Perched on the cathedral gutter, mouth stretched in a salacious smile, he counts his Krugerrands like Scrooge. One a day, to sew into the lining of his clothes.

The radio plays a Christmas carol. Brightly dressed children dance across the television screen. A nation rises to celebrate the birth of its Lord.

At the base of the mountain lie the smashed and shattered tablets. A few words, nothing more, are visible in the dust.

What did this people unto thee, asks the lawgiver, *that thou hast brought so great a sin upon them?*

They will not live to see the Promised Land.

territorial
waters

"Damn foreigners," says Nathan.

May I present Eduardo Razores, folksinger, politician, Don Juan.

"What's wrong with their law schools? They have to come up here and jabber their way through ours?"

Eduardo, I explain, is already a lawyer and a man of some renown in his country. He wishes to be educated in the ways of the Anglo-American system of jurisprudence.

"They're just a bunch of aristocrats on a two-year vacation in the United States."

"You must come to my flat," says Eduardo. "We are having a fiesta. Please, bring your friends. Especially the beautiful women." His dark eyes glitter hallucinogenically.

We are no longer neophytes, the newly proselytized. We sit in the back of the classroom, shunning our assigned seats. Professors beg us to do the reading, to pay attention, to come to class. Why should we? Aren't we 2Ls? Hazed by fire, rigorous in intellect, zealous, ambitious, indolent. Employers are queued outside our doors, their résumés in hand, fistfuls of cash, promising summers of extravagant lunches, cruises along the river, cocktails, concerts, theater in the park.

"I've got too much work," says Nathan.

He sits in our shoebox kitchen. The dregs of a coffeepot in front of him. A cheap mystery novel splayed open on its spine.

"We promised Eduardo."

"Don't these L.L.M. students ever work?"

"They don't have to. They're rich."

"I'm rich and I work."

I nod at the novel.

"Criminal procedure," he says.

But when Alexandra calls to invite him to dinner, he begs off for Eduardo's party.

As he slithers across the carpet he leaves a trail of slime.

Two bars drown the ground floor in tequila and triple sec. A salsa band percolates upstairs. I undulate through the crowd, reaching back for Nathan as if for a flotation device. But he's already submerged in a sea of brunettes. I fire my flare gun and collapse onto a life raft dehydrated, exposed, mutinous.

"Colin!" calls a voice. "How good of you to arrive." Eduardo smiles warmly. "Where is your very short friend?"

I say that he is working the crowd, which Eduardo acknowledges with a concerned frown.

"I hope he will not be hurt," he says.

He introduces me to the very tall, very blond woman by his side. Elisabet, he explains, has just arrived from Norway, some trouble with her visa, studying for the L.L.M.

"I. Am. Pleased. To. Meet. You," I say, my mouth moving over the words like cud.

"My English is fine, thank you," she says, with a trace of a British accent.

Eduardo roars, as if he's been stabbed through the diaphragm with a poker. "She is very funny," he gasps. "She is like Ibsen."

"Ibsen is not funny," says Elisabet.

"Bergman, then."

"Bergman is Swedish."

"Have another drink," Eduardo says to the room.

We are drinking something "authentic," Eduardo tells us. Drunk in sufficient quantities, it causes hallucinations. Elisabet sips hers. I drain my glass.

Soon Munchkins are dancing the flamenco with bejeweled Gypsies. I rub my eyes and Nathan appears, twirling his partner across the floor.

"Your short friend is an excellent dancer," says Eduardo. His hand settles on Elisabet's shoulder, then eases to the back of her neck. She stiffens and turns to me.

"Dance," she instructs.

She grabs my elbow. Eduardo grabs my arm. Beseechingly his eyes drill into mine. Then I am yanked onto the dance floor.

"The worm," growls Elisabet.

"It causes delusions," I say.

Nathan bumps up against us, his eyes glazed and sweaty, his mouth fixed on the neck of his dance partner like a giant leech or a miniature vampire.

Elisabet's joints snap in and out of place to the backbeat. One shoulder rotates forward, then the other, like oil derricks positioned high above the North Sea. A frozen wind blows across the platform; I pray for warmth inside.

Eduardo's forlorn gaze stalks us across the floor. I swallow the contents of an abandoned bottle. The music shifts, the beat changes, and still we are dancing. Elisabet's long form sways like the shadow of a shadow. Drink me, calls another bottle. And I do. Then, like Alice through the looking glass, I disappear.

We are kissing in a closet somewhere. The heaves and thumps of a party filter through the door. The smell of laundered shirts and wool surrounds us. Elisabet's palm is on my collarbone, her hand on my neck; I can feel my pulse in her fingers. I struggle to my feet, but I am already standing. Then I fall down.

We are lying on the floor in a closet. My head is wedged in a corner. Elisabet moves above me. She does not wear a bra, but she does wear underwear. I know that if I don't breathe soon, I will die. But if I die, I won't need to breathe.

A stiletto slices my eye as the door cracks open.

"But my coat's in there," someone giggles.

"Call a cab," comes the perfectly reasonable reply.

"What are you doing?" whispers Elisabet.

I look down to see that I'm unbuttoning my jeans.

"Oh, no," she says as she snaps her shirt closed. "Don't make a mistake."

I reach out for her but miss and embrace my own head instead.

She stands crookedly, bamboo in a hothouse. "It's late. You're drunk," she keenly observes.

"Tomorrow's Sunday," I explain.

"Put on your clothes," she says.

I wriggle back into my sweater while Elisabet combs her hair with her fingers. When we open the door, I realize I am wearing someone else's sweater, backward. It's black, cashmere. I leave it on.

The band has taken a break, and Eduardo sits alone on the makeshift stage, a single light trained on his guitar.

"Old men in the streets talk of justice," he sings, "their gums shine bright in the night / years have left their feet aching / and their breath smells like a dog's."

Elisabet says she is going home. I say that I will walk her. I wait while she gets her coat.

"Do not leave me / alone in the streets / the men with their gums / are waiting for me."

Two songs later she appears near the top of the staircase clutching her coat. I wave from the back of the crowd. She looks at me, then at the stairs, the slightest hesitation as she measures the distance.

"Aaayyyyyyyyy," sings Eduardo.

Then she is gone.

She has the advantage of surprise and a head start. But what I lack in speed I make up in resourcefulness. I hurdle a kissing couple, flatten a wallflower, and skid down the banister. I alight directly into a tray of champagne glasses, shattering them in an explosion of flutes.

"Monsieur!" screams the wretched waiter.

I slalom around the broken glass, a manic skier on a speed buzz, and dive at the front door. The doorknob pulls away in my hand. I can hear someone shouting for Eduardo. In a last desperate effort to escape, as crack Finnish troops pursue me through the snow, I lunge through an open window and land in a small concrete birdbath.

When I come to, a little bird is perched on my shoulder. "Twit, twit," it says.

Two sets of feet patter through the kitchen. A woman's voice, lilting and low, roils my dreams. In my semiconscious state I roll over, expecting to find Elisabet beside me. Instead I find a pool of saliva.

I wake and clump to the bathroom in the apartment I share with Nathan. When I open the door, a woman screams.

"Have you met Gretchen?" asks Nathan.

"Hallo," says Gretchen, a positively enormous woman in a tiny bathrobe.

I moan and flee for the back porch, where, like Gulliver in Lilliput, I render obsolete the local fire department.

"Where's your Swedish friend?" asks Nathan when I return.

My hangover, a dull and dreary Sunday, the loss of motor control. I tell him the truth.

"This is a mistake," says Gretchen. "You are a handsome man."

"Forget about her," says Nathan. "There're plenty of birds in the sea."

As if to punctuate his remarks, the phone rings.

"If that's Alexandra," he says, "I'm not here."

He seeks shelter in his bedroom, battening the shutters and nailing closed the door. Gretchen lashes herself to the mattress. Their high-pitched squeals whistle through cracks in the walls.

On the other end of the receiver, her cries the gathering storm, sobs Alexandra.

We're a large firm with the camaraderie of a small firm.

We're a small firm with the resources of a large firm.

We're a medium-sized firm with the resources of a large firm and the camaraderie of a small firm.

We're not as large as a large firm, but we have all its resources.

We're not as small as a small firm, but we have all its camaraderie.

We're not as medium as a medium-size firm, but we have all the resources of a large firm that you would expect from a medium-size firm and all the camaraderie of a small firm that a medium-size firm would have.

I stack the interviewers on top of each other, shuffle, and cut the deck. The same gray suits look out from their suites.

They'll fly me to New York, San Francisco, L.A. They'll open an office in Paris, London, Bombay. Bring my wife, if I have one, or my fiancée. They'll pay me a bonus just for breathing, and another bonus for leaving. They have a free dining room, a health club, their own weight trainer. On weekends I can play on their courts in the country. Golf too, if I'd rather, or a quick game of polo. And of course, remember, the weekly payola.

Just sign here, says the man with the forked tongue and tail.

"Take the money and run," says Nathan.

But what about my ideals, my commitment to the public interest? I ask, as if I were Atticus Finch instead of Tommy Killian.

"Find a new hobby," says Nathan.

What they're looking for, the gray suit explains to me, is someone who's willing to stand up for the beleaguered megacorporation with its stable of attorneys and its silos of cash against the crippled, cancer-ridden, brain-damaged, birth-defected, illiterate, impoverished plaintiff.

"Goddammit," says a lawyer who represents the American Producers of Carcinogens, Inc. "We're in a war, and we need the best!"

Everyone is entitled to the best defense, I explain to Joshua, Rebecca, and all the other unbelievers. It's easy to criticize corporate lawyers, but corporations have rights too, and someone needs to protect them.

"Who protects us from the protectors?" asks my sister, the vegetarian poet/actress.

"These firms do a lot of pro bono work," I say, falling back on my second defense.

Rebecca, her mind honed by the first month at a university whose president will resign to fulfill his lifelong dream of playing with baseballs, says, "Bullshit."

"Besides, it's only for the summer." My third and final defense.

"Summers become winters," Rebecca concludes.

But first, the Fall.

"I think there's been a misunderstanding," says Elisabet.

I have cleverly disguised myself as a law student, hoping I can avoid her for the next nineteen months, but to no avail. She has tracked me to the mailboxes, homing site for all law students.

"I thought you were waiting for me; when I didn't see you, I went home," she continues.

I shrug nonchalantly. Women flee from me at drunken parties almost every weekend.

A small crowd has begun to gather. Eduardo leads them in a protest song:

Don't give him that bullshit / Don't feed him that line / You saw him standing there / You did and now you're lyin'.

"Do you want to get out of here?" she asks. "Drink a tea or something?"

I leave my unopened mail for the pigeons. Let them fly it home.

We find a quiet corner in the basement of a brick coffeehouse favored by undergraduate film studies majors, the Saudi royal family, and disillusioned existentialists.

Elisabet orders hot chocolate. Tea, she says, reminds her of northern winters when the sun doesn't rise and snow covers houses up to their windows.

She is not British, I tell myself, despite her accent. She is not even French or Italian. A different subcontinent entirely, without common law or Romance language. Her fair skin and hair are familiar, yet the folds above her eyelids and the tilt of her cheekbones cast her face into a remarkable plane. Hers is a curious beauty, comprised of the obvious and the alien. I listen as if to a strange woodwind.

Her parents live in the balmy south, Oslo, where temperatures climb above freezing for a good portion of the year. Her grandmother refuses to move, remaining up north with the dwindling population of cousins and other relations.

"They can't live in a city. They bump into people and get run down by buses."

The coffee is strong enough to power a small village. My eyes are bones in my skull. My tongue lies in a delicatessen case. She continues her family narrative, oblivious to my imminent implosion.

Her father buys minks from the small farms that dot the northern countryside. Nasty little rats with fur like oiled velvet. He spins their skins into gold.

"Poor Mama," she says. "She loves animals."

"A JAP's dilemma," I say.

She rests her hands like a steeple on the table. "I don't understand," she says.

Did the Norwegians save the Jews or was that the Danes? Did they fight with the Germans or was that the Finns? History fails me.

"It's a joke," I say. "My mother is Jewish."

"Ah."

"So is my father."

Her gray eyes blink catlike in rapid calculation. One plus one equals one.

"Grandmother always said that Jewish men were wonderful lovers."

I climb to the edge of my coffee cup, peer down into the murky depths, and jump.

"Of course she never slept with anyone besides my grandfather."

I sputter to the surface, lungs laced with grounds, face scalded.

"And only two or three times, at best."

Her grandfather drank while her grandmother praised Martin Luther, a man whose anti-Semitism was so rabid that even his disciples claimed he suffered from a brain disease. Elisabet gave up religion about the time she gave up tea; she couldn't stand the taste.

"No God, not even a Christian one, would permit the Holocaust," she says.

I take a tentative breath, allowing oxygen to clear my lungs and cool my face. Tiny rivulets of sweat trickle down my neck and dampen my collar.

"I'm sorry," Elisabet says. "I know it's a terrible subject for Jews."

I shake my head. "It is terrible," I agree. "But so is what the Turks did to the Armenians, the Khmer Rouge to the Cambodians, Stalin to his own people."

Elisabet nods. Even Christians have been persecuted, she tells me. She has only one question:

"Why did they go to their deaths so quietly?"

The front door explodes in a detonation of fury. I throw myself beneath the kitchen table, burying my head between my legs. Eduardo and his nationalist compadres have taken their jealousy too far.

"Where is he?" screams Alexandra. "Where is that scumbag?"

I rise to my knees, wiping the plaster from my face.

"The fucking pig! I've been calling him for weeks!"

Nathan's room smells like an old can of tennis balls. Dust bunnies cavort across his floor. Alexandra kicks through his bombed-out closet, raining shirts and suits in a dirty heap.

"Those are his clothes," I say stupidly.

"Fuck his clothes!" She rips the blanket and sheets off his bed. "Fuck him!" She struggles with the mattress until I finally grab her wrist and sit her down. She sputters once, then bursts into tears.

"I'm not crying," she sobs. "I'm angry. I always cry when I'm angry."

I offer her a glass of water. She refuses. Where has he been? she asks. Why hasn't he returned her calls?

I say that he's been busy. He's tried to call her several times, I think, but she hasn't been in.

She knows I'm lying. "Why are you lying for him?" she says. "Why are you lying for that liar?"

I have been hiding in an attic. I've been scribbling inane notes in a diary. There's a war on outside. Haven't I been listening?

"I'm pregnant," she says.

"With a baby?"

"And he's fucking someone else!" she wails.

I look around the kitchen for an instruction manual, a flare. Break glass in case of emergency.

"Do you want it?" I ask.

"Don't be ridiculous."

"Does my brother know?"

She laughs. A dry rasp. "Poor David," she says.

I weigh full disclosure against innuendo and imagination. Ignorance, I decide, is bliss, or at least mildly opiating. I tell her I haven't seen Nathan in days.

She asks if I remember the day we met near the river. Nathan seemed in perpetual motion: his hands, his arms, his mouth. He ate more food than anyone she had ever seen. It burned right through him like jet fuel.

"Everything about him was oversized," she says. "Everything."

I tell her I don't need the details.

"He was like a giant piston."

"Please."

She slumps suddenly into the bed. Her shoulders fold under her chin. Her head collapses into her chest. I crook a tentative arm like a grappling hook over her narrow back. A knob of bone in her neck presses against the inside of my elbow.

"If I murder him," she asks, looking up at me from the V between biceps, "will you take my case?"

"I don't know why she's so crazy," says Nathan. "I said I would pay for the abortion." He brushes dust from his suits and hangs them back in the closet. "It's not like I was the only guy she was sleeping with."

I tell him I'll wait for the videotape.

"She's extremely unfair," says Elisabet, as we walk toward the Square. "It's not his fault she's pregnant."

Whose fault, I ask, could it be? Jews don't believe in an immaculate conception.

"She can take protection."

"Maybe she did."

"Then let her have an abortion."

I am being tested, I know, by a women's advocacy group that, when I fail, will move to have me expelled from law school for crimes against one half of humanity.

A woman, Elisabet continues, is responsible for her reproductive liberties. She cannot shift that responsibility to a man.

"But he got her pregnant," I protest.

My attitude is typically chauvinistic. Men don't "get" women pregnant in consensual relationships. That logic justifies paternalistic laws that prohibit women from participating in traditionally "male" fields with the excuse that women's biological role requires men to protect them from certain harms.

A warm burn buzzes across my back. I am being observed from a doorway, a stairwell, the window across the street.

"Even your rape laws focus on the man's state of mind rather than the woman's," Elisabet says. "If a man 'reasonably believes' a woman consented to intercourse, it doesn't matter what the woman believed; he can't be guilty of rape. Men always define the harm to women by reference to themselves."

"I see," I say blindly.

Deep in a salt mine, scores of technicians evaluate the data. Subject male retains slight potential for rehabilitation, they conclude. Operative instructed to proceed with prejudice.

"My flat is just down the street," she says, stopping at a corner. "Would you like to come up for a tea?"

There is no observer; the windows are clear. I am free to move through enemy lines.

But high above the earth, in an orbiting satellite, an assimilation expert measures our progress with a parabolic microphone and a pair of tweezers.

Tweed, Tartan & Plaid will make me an offer I can't refuse.

"They're the best firm in the city," says Nathan. "They kicked ass in the Oil Refinery Litigation."

An enormous oil refinery exploded off the coast of Mexico, Nathan explains, killing hundreds of workers, spraying the coastline with toxic chemicals, and destroying the ecosystem for generations. Tweed, Tartan, relying on obscure principles of international law, argued successfully that U.S. courts had no jurisdiction over the incident. Then, in front of the Mexican Supreme Court, they argued that the case should be tried in the United States. They won, and the case was dismissed. Without legal recourse, hundreds of impoverished families were left penniless while poisons continued to foul the food chain.

"It was a brilliant defense," claims Nathan.

Robert Stockard, Jr., chairman of the recruiting committee, agrees. "*Oaco* raised troubling questions about a foreign sovereign's right to compel adjudication of an essentially domestic dispute," he tells me over the telephone. "A high-seas version of landgrabbing."

But what about their argument before U.S. courts? I ask, retreating into the bathroom with the phone.

"Different jurisdictional posture," he explains. "Simple breach of contract. No domestic injury."

A dazzling display of legal sophistry, I tell him, as I try to mask the sound of the toilet flushing.

"It's what we do best," he says proudly.

They'll fly me down, he offers, put me up in an expensive hotel, take me out to an extravagant dinner, and beat me with a barbed club of interviews.

"Are you married?" he asks.

"Engaged," I lie.

He proposes to bring my ersatz fiancée along for the ride. "Give her some money and let her loose," he guffaws.

I thank him for his kindness and the size of his wallet. I will be sure to notify him when the bill arrives. Gas, grass, or ass, he tells me, nobody rides for free.

When I emerge from the bathroom, I nearly decapitate Nathan, whose head is resting two inches from the doorjamb.

He scurries into the kitchen like a fleeing cockroach.

The cab bounds along the avenue, a lunar probe navigating the cratered surface. The driver, who can't speak English, hasn't let that impede his conversational proficiency; he reads aloud from a book of his own poetry. Elisabet clutches my hand in the backseat as he swerves into the oncoming lane. He looks up from the book just in time to avert a collision with a truck. Her fingers slacken in my palm.

"We would have to share a bed?" she asked after I outlined my plan.

The balloon of my boldness suffered a pinhole. I corkscrewed about her apartment, making small whistling noises, until I landed, deflated, on the floor.

"There's no ridiculous American law against it?"

At the hotel I hesitate before signing our names. The clerk peers at my signature, then asks if I could print more legibly. The smell of a small animal dying wafts from my armpits.

There are two large beds in the room and two bathrooms with two phones in each, one near the toilet, one near the bath. Elisabet sits on one bed, then rises and sits on the other.

"Firm or soft?" she asks.

I cannot speak. My throat has constricted from some foreign allergy. Let me die right now, I think, before the hotel detective bursts in, two policemen at his side. Let me perish in anticipation of a bath, warm soap across her lovely skin, the dizzying heat, the silence of water. Let me float into the crackling sheets, cool and smelling of fresh laundry.

"I can't stand a soft bed." She draws back the bedspread and plumps the pillows.

I stand dumbly in the middle of the room, too paralyzed to move, too numb to speak coherently.

Elisabet stretches onto the bed, her long body unfolding like a telescope. "What shall we do first?" she muses.

In the control room technicians scratch their heads. Subject does not respond to transparent signals, they report. Check circuits for malfunction.

Eduardo strums his guitar. Nathan rumbas across the carpet. She stands at the top of the stairs, her eyes darting like fish in a bowl.

"Why did you run away?" I blurt.

"Ah, this?" She laughs, shifting on the bed. "Would I be here if I had run away?"

I know there's a fallacy in her logic, some premise left unstated. If I could isolate the flaw in her reasoning, I would save myself from heartache. Instead, I succumb to the syllogism and the color that has risen to her cheekbones.

I move as if through water. She anchors on my neck. We kiss, long, hard, like divers at an oxygen tank. Nitrogen bubbles in my brain.

"There's something I should tell you," she says, breaking away.

I freeze, imagining boyfriends, husbands, venereal diseases.

"America is not my home."

I breathe, my patriotism unoffended.

"Nothing," she warns, "can come of this."

Her hair is gold; her skin is gold; a slender gold chain falls across her breasts. She rises above me like the midnight sun.

I have always wanted to live in the north, I tell her. A Jew among the Norse. I can hide in your basements and barns, flee through fields by moonlight. In the depths of the Scandinavian subcontinent, my blond hair and blue eyes distract the sentries. My dark roots in balkanized Europe concealed by parents who know how to forge a passport.

Her mouth is a vow of silence. Her hands grieve.

There is no moon in summer, I will learn.

lox

watch

He slinks through campus, a cap slanted low across his forehead, his eyes shaded in dark glasses.

"He's positively gnomelike," says Elisabet, squinting over the top of a book from her aerie in the library.

Breath mints clutter our bathroom sink. Condoms spill from the medicine chest. Scribbled telephone numbers zigzag down the wall.

"Tuesday night's great," says Nathan, penciling a Carol next to a Lois. "Wait for me if I'm a little late." Alexandra doesn't call anymore; it's freed up his schedule.

Important judges consult him. Partners at prestigious firms ask his advice. Nathan, they ask, how do you do it? You're a short guy who looks like a gargoyle but there's always a beautiful woman by your side. I'm fat; I'm bald; I'm domineering; I'm a bore; I've been having an affair with the same woman for ten years. What is your secret?

"Women love attention," Nathan tells me. "Even the most beautiful women love to hear how beautiful they are. I know I'm not great-looking, but if I convince a woman that *she's* great-looking, I've got her made."

"His attitude is rather refreshing," decides Elisabet. "At least he's honest."

"If you ever get tired of Elisabet," says Nathan.

I laugh; I believe he is joking.

My parents would love to meet this important person in my life. They have just one question: What have I been waiting for?

After a year of successfully smuggling Elisabet through the heavily patrolled waters of my social life, I've finally surrendered to the immigration authorities. They promise to grant me time off for good behavior after I submit to house arrest.

I tell Elisabet my parents are crumpled, ignorant, hunchbacked figures.

"I'm sure you exaggerate," she says.

"They think Quisling is a Norwegian game show."

Elisabet scowls. Her cat eyes like gray slashes. "We resisted the Germans," she insists.

"What about the Swedes?"

"We resisted them too."

If everyone helped the Jews, I ask, why were they so helpless?

"Yes, yes," says Elisabet. "We all know history. But one reason for the Holocaust was Jews kept themselves separate from the rest of Europe. They made it possible for others to see them as outsiders. If they had integrated better into the cultural life of Europe, people would have seen that Jews were not strangers and Hitler couldn't have fed on their ignorances."

I remember watching a *Hasidic* boy skating at a public rink. On the ice, with his black coat and *payess* flailing, his grin looked like any other kid's. His mother stood alone at the crowded railing, a scarf tied around her head, her skin swathed in black.

"Maybe they wanted to be different," I say.

Elisabet weaves her fingers together; her hands make a basket for her chin.

"Do you?" she asks.

"I'm an American," I say.

"But your grandparents were Jews."

"My grandfather was an anarchist."

"He wasn't Jewish?"

"He was a Jewish anarchist. And an American," I add. "A Jewish American anarchist."

A strand of hair, like a blond filament, in the corner of Elisabet's mouth.

"This is a strange country," she says, shaking the hair free.

Strange and wonderful, I agree. With a liberal immigration policy.

For Scandinavians.

"We're so happy to meet you," coos my mother as she helps Elisabet out of her fur. "Colin has told us so many nice things."

"You're Norwegian," says my father, deft conversationalist.

I haven't seen my parents' house since the summer. As I take Elisabet on the tour, I am struck by the sudden emptiness. Bookshelves stripped of books. Beds stripped of sheets. Walls stripped of posters. As if my parents' children never existed.

"Everything was so cluttered," my mother explains.

"Are you renting the rooms?" I ask.

Her minimalist zeal, however, has not extended to her own office. Books spill over the floor. Papers cover a small couch. My brother's album collection is stacked in a corner.

She is revising her dissertation. There may be an interested publisher.

Elisabet asks about the topic, and my mother launches into a ten-minute abstract, complete with footnotes and bibliography. "You have such a rich history," Elisabet says when my mother has finished.

"We have many storytellers," concurs my mother.

"Norwegians are the same."

My mother smiles politely, indicating her complete lack of agreement.

"Hamsun, you know, won the Nobel Prize," says Elisabet. "As did Sigrid Undset. And of course there's Ibsen."

"Wasn't Hamsun a Nazi?" asks my mother.

"He was never a Nazi," Elisabet protests. "Later in his life he was photographed with Hitler. But he was never a Nazi."

"He wouldn't belong to a club that would have him as a member," I explain.

"No," says Elisabet uncertainly.

"They said he was a sissy."

"What is a sissy?"

I tell my parents the Norwegians smuggled Jews to Canada, rarely refusing anyone with a sack of gold.

"I thought that was the Danes," says my mother.

"Didn't the Norwegians fight with the Germans?" asks my father.

"That was the Finns," says Elisabet.

My father asks if anyone wants a drink. I say I'll have two. He laughs, thinking I am joking, and brings me one instead. I drink quickly and pour myself a second.

We sit in the living room, eating raw vegetables with onion dip, talking politely about European politics and the American electoral college system. My father dozes off discreetly in a wing chair, his eyes at half-mast, nodding every now and then to keep up appearances.

Elisabet radiates loveliness from her perch on the sofa, clipping her sentences like rosebuds. I sit tensely beside her on a cushion of thorns. My mother stiffens her back, straightens her shoulders, folds her hands politely on one knee. She labors mightily in the Queen's English, conscious of the slovenliness of her native tongue.

I wonder why I have subjected us to this slow form of torture. In seven months Elisabet will be gone, a blurry stamp on her passport the only documented proof of her presence. I should have insisted on a driver's license or green card. Instead, the foreign exchange program in which we enrolled has taken our money and closed down shop. What did you expect? the man from the embassy asks; these are the perils of the journey.

A timer sounds, signaling dinner or a bomb. My mother jumps quickly to her feet, grateful for the reprieve. She disappears into the kitchen while we shuffle into the dining room, scraping chairs across the floor as we struggle with the mathematical possibilities.

My mother returns with her famous broiled chicken. One part chicken. One part heat. She claims to be following a recipe. She sets it next to what she declares are peas but are just as likely to be spinach or broccoli.

"Colin told us you're moving back to Norway in June," she asserts as she ladles a scoop of green onto Elisabet's plate.

"I've a job in Oslo," says Elisabet.

"Wonderful," says my mother.

My father awakens from his nap and asks if I have made any decisions about the next year.

I do not tell him about the transatlantic phone calls this past summer while my officemate pretended not to listen, or the tedious hours in the library researching whether the Filed Rate Doctrine proscribes damages for a utility's breach of an oral contract. The Mossad must be looking for operatives in the Scandinavian countries. Lox Watch must need Jews to monitor the curing of salmon caught off the Norwegian coast.

"The company seemed anxious to have you return," he says, as if I worked for the mob instead of The Firm.

I explain that I am cannon fodder. Underneath the masks of collegiality deformed beasts lurk. "They take you to lunch to fatten you up for the kill," I say.

My mother claims I exaggerate. Every job requires its share of monotony and hard work. "It took me twelve years to complete my dissertation," she says.

"Eighteen," I say.

"You remember what happened to my adviser."

"Actually, I thought I might spend next year in Europe," I say nonchalantly.

The bomb explodes in the middle of the vegetables, hurling olive blobs in all directions. Sirens sound. Panic ensues. A mob tramples unsuspecting children underfoot.

"I've been looking into Foreign Service jobs," I lie.

Everyone begins talking at once, their voices a three-part cacophony. What do I mean, Europe? Where in Europe? What kind of job in Europe? Out of the din a harmony emerges.

"You have no visa," says Elisabet.

"You can't speak the language," says my mother.

"You'll need vaccines," contributes my father.

The life of an expatriate is never easy, I tell them. One must maintain a constant vigil against terrorist attacks and bouts of drunken nostalgia. On a dark night one can easily be crushed by wild bulls running in the street.

"I'll travel light," I say.

"Don't come to Norway next year."

"Who said anything about Norway?" I say, my arm suspended in mid-embrace.

My mother has herded us into separate bedrooms, laying razor wire in the trenches. My hands bleed from scaling the barricades; mud cakes my face.

The bed squeaks as Elisabet rolls away from me.

"Norway's not even part of Europe," I add.

"We had the Olympics," she says.

"I want to live with you."

The words slip from my tongue like ball bearings from a broken wheel. They drop one by one through my hands and scatter across the floor. I chase after them, rainbows in the half-light, but spin them farther beyond my reach.

"We could live someplace neutral," I quickly add. "London."

She turns back to me, a speck of toothpaste on her lip. "I hate London."

"Paris, then."

"I can't speak French."

I inventory European capitals like a travel agent on commission. No tipping, fabulous weather, lovely people. But she's not interested in the package tour. Too many concessions to other people's schedules. She wants the one-way fare.

"I'm tired of being the foreigner," she concludes.

"We'd both be foreigners," I say. "We'll learn a new language."

Her hair fans the pillow like a spray of water. "It's not romantic," she says, "forgetting words, living without family, losing your identity."

"We could lose our identities together."

I am slipping in grease. Steel marbles bounce off my head, crack my jaw, lodge between my teeth. If I don't shut up, I will find myself buried beneath an axle.

She twines one willowy leg around my waist. I dangle below the branches.

How can she be so composed? Was the last year simply another elective to add to her class schedule? Am I merely Her First American?

"You knew," she says. "We talked."

Once upon a time we discussed many things, few of which I remember. Year to year I renounce all promises, all oaths, all vows. I create myself anew. This may not be what the rabbis had in mind, I tell her, but it's the wonder of our country, with its foreshortened history and idolatrous conventions. A man can mix and match from any convenient bin.

"This is not my home," she reminds me.

"No one lives here," I say. "We stole the land."

The stairs creak. My mother's voice calls. Does Elisabet have everything she needs?

I leap from the bed, vault the trenches, dodge small arms fire. I crawl across no-man's-land. In my bunker I can hear Elisabet telling my mother that all is well, there is no cause for concern, call off the air strikes.

"They're getting divorced," announces Nathan, laying a sheaf of papers on the kitchen table. "My dad sent me the briefs. He wants me to do some research."

I stare in disbelief at the legal documents in front of me.

"My mom's filed a motion to remove to federal court," he continues, pulling another stack of papers from a leather satchel. "She's claiming federal question jurisdiction since my father's been sleeping with Clothilde, the au pair, who, it turns out, is an illegal alien, which I never knew. Mom's making a claim for jurisdiction under 28 U.S.C.§ 2282(a)(1). I don't think she'll be successful, but it's a good argument."

He plunks himself in front of the briefs, a highlighter in one hand, a pencil in the other.

I remember the open door, the naked figure by the window, broken dishes in the morning. At the time I thought it was a dream.

"I'm sorry, Nathan," I say.

"It happens," he says. "It's a good opportunity for me to get some hands-on litigation experience before I start work."

He flips through a treatise on family law. Irreconcilable differences, cruel and unusual punishment, infidelity.

"Of course," he continues, "there's the potential for conflict. But I'm not actually representing both litigants; I'm acting as an adviser. I've fully disclosed my role and obtained informed consent from both parties."

He places all calls on hold. His other clients will have to wait. This case is big, the one that will make his reputation.

"Can't blame my dad, though. You've seen Clothilde. She's great-looking. And she's got a great body. Turns out he's been knocking her for nearly two years."

He whistles appreciatively.

"Some guys have all the luck," he adds.

At our tiny corner table, in a brick nook, stray notepads and paper are scattered like crumbs. Elisabet highlights passages in her Con Law casebook. I black out the Internal Revenue Code.

Outside, darkly dressed undergraduates scurry past like mice on a sinking ship. Graduation is nearly upon us, and they are frantic with the prospect of unemployment. They glance through the window, watch us comfortably reading and drinking coffee and chocolate, and decide they will go to law school. Years later, as they face the prospect of a lifetime of boredom and oppression, they will wonder how they ever came to such a rash decision.

Elisabet rubs the end of her nose with the highlighter cap. Her scheduled departure through the security gates and over the horizon has been posted on the big board. Why am I the one with the parking ticket, slumping back to the garage to claim my car? I should take to the air, a surprise flight to Hungary or Russia, a return to my own country. You say good-bye. Tell me how you feel. Is it love or the desire to still the spinning firmament? We grasp at the stranger, spurning the familiar, and braid our dreams from imagined threads.

I picture myself saying the words; I hold them in my mouth. They tickle like tiny fireflies in the back of my throat.

"Elisabet," I begin.

Her face, a Venn diagram. Find a common point among over-lapping spheres.

"What are the two of you mooning about?" Nathan's voice booms. He rumbles to a halt in front of our table. "Mind if I sit down?" He sits down.

"This divorce is difficult," he sighs. "Can you predicate federal jurisdiction on one party's employment of an illegal alien if the cause of action accrued prior to employment?"

"What are you talking about?" I say.

"Turns out Clothilde wasn't the only woman my dad was bang-ing."

I watch Elisabet's spheres contract and separate.

"That's awful," she says.

"Yeah," says Nathan. "I think my mom's going to be forced to file in state court."

Elisabet blinks. I explain that Nathan is researching the law governing his parents' divorce.

"You can't be serious?" she says.

Nathan nods. "It's very complicated."

Elisabet reaches across the table and takes Nathan's hand. "This is a tragedy."

"I know," says Nathan. "When I said I would take the case pro bono, I never knew it would be so much work." He snatches the remains of a scone from Elisabet's plate and pops it in his mouth.

"Do you need some help?" asks Elisabet.

There are therapists who specialize in the treatment of law-related personality disorders: *argumentitis, insufferitis, amoralitis.* Patients are shocked into normalcy by constructing an argument even they cannot refute.

"Can you use a computer?" asks Nathan.

"Of course," says Elisabet.

She blows me a kiss as they race toward the library.

The State Department can't imagine what skills I could possibly have to offer. The Israeli secret service has all the operatives it needs in

Scandinavia. Lox Watch is overwhelmed with applications from Jewish men who want to spend time curing salmon.

Elisabet has her ticket. One way. She claims she can buy the other half in Oslo.

I am jobless, penniless, loveless. I am belly up to the bar.

"I've never seen the fjords," I say.

"I won't have time to travel," she says.

"It's a perfect time of year."

My parents, on the advice of their accountant, have cut my umbilical cord. I have a brother and sister in college, in case I've forgotten. Why don't I work for a year, then take my trip? There are so many wonderful cities in Europe.

Instead, I make my deal with the devil. He loves to travel. Vienna, he tells me, now there's a city from hell. A ring for every occasion. I should be sure to include it on my itinerary. Though I'll have plenty of time to visit it later.

"Terrific," says Stockard. "I'll tell the partners."

Should I sign in blood, I ask, or will tears be enough?

"You'll need cash for the summer," he says. "Sow some oats after that exam."

I tell him I might reap into the fall.

"Take as much time as you need." He promises the shackles will be open until I return. "I was young once too," he claims.

And darkness was upon the earth.

I collapse on the sofa, halfway through my final set of academic calisthenics. The tiny muscles in my palm ache from the endless repetition of pencil lifting. My brain is a dried sponge by the side of the sink.

Voices drift into the hallway. A bed creaks.

I walk to the kitchen and pour a glass of water. Gray bubbles filter to the surface. No light penetrates.

Laughter from Nathan's room. The squeaking bed. A woman's voice.

Elisabet.

I jump. The glass cracks on the linoleum, a dull splintering like wood.

In the silence, dripping water.

"Hello?" says Elisabet's voice.

The door peeks open, and Nathan's head emerges.

"Colin," he says. "I thought you had an exam."

"Finished," I say.

Nathan's robe edges through the crack.

Elisabet laughs. "Let him in, Nathan."

The curtain rises on the tableau: Elisabet, fully clothed, sitting on the bed; Nathan standing, robe partially open, a monstrous erection peering through the folds like a sea creature come up for air.

"Your robe, Nathan," says Elisabet, now in hysterics. "Your robe's come undone."

Nathan looks down, not without pride. "So it has," he says.

I stare from beauty to the beast. I should be horrified like Alexandra who ripped his possessions from their moorings. I should burst into tears and fling myself through a window. I should demand justice, equity, constitutional reform.

I have rooted to the floor like an ancient barnacle. Sea vessels scrape over me; my bare and bloody scalp stings with salt. I cannot survive in the merciless ocean. Like a shucked hermit, I crawl from the room and decline.

"Don't be ridiculous," Elisabet says as she stuffs clothes into a suitcase. "We were having an entirely normal conversation until his robe popped open."

Her shabby dormitory room looks even more drab without the dance posters, the sick plants, the picture of me.

"He was depressed about his parents," she continues. "He couldn't even get dressed."

I tell her Nathan rarely dressed before noon; slippers, he believed were a sign of aristocracy.

"If I'd meant to, I would have slept with him months ago. He'd made that clear."

I open my mouth, but the sound that emerges is a thin croaking noise, a frog with a tonsillectomy.

"I've seen his penis before," she adds. "It's quite remarkable."

I grasp for forgotten bits of emergency medicine: head in your lap, head below your heart. Avoid sharp and piercing objects. They are closer than they appear.

When consciousness returns, I am in her bed. The room is in semidarkness, the last traces of daylight on the treetops and windowsill. She lies beside me, her mouth open and pressed to the pillow, her breathing regular and deep.

How long have I been here? I wonder. What have I dreamed and what just badly remembered?

I curl along her spine. She stirs. We make love slowly, silently, as the light leaves the sill and then the earth.

Sometime during the night, the telephone's muffled ring wakes me from my illusions. She fishes it from a box. Her voice, speaking Norwegian, is a jig across a xylophone, a dance from vowel to vowel. I listen through the haze of semiconsciousness, awash in lilting consonants, and suddenly I am graced with a pure, primeval understanding.

Home, she says, *I'm coming home.*

"You don't own her," says Nathan.

We stand, chin to chest, in our boxed-up kitchen.

"It wasn't working out for you guys," he adds.

June heat builds in the unventilated room. Normal objects appear woozy and vertiginous, as if seen through colored glass. I can smell him.

"Anyway, that's history," he concludes.

A passing airplane rattles the windows. Nathan looks up. I punch him hard, once, in the belly. My hand springs back lightly as if from a trampoline.

"You shouldn't have done that," he says, his curled grimace like a feline snarl.

He toes the tile and winds up. I watch the rotation of his fist as it approaches my head. I can see every line in his knuckles, like the seams on a baseball, and the solid muscle that runs up his forearm. I take a step into the batter's box, adjust my helmet, tug at my crotch.

The pitch explodes in my face.

✿   ✿   ✿

"What happened to you?" asks David.

I tell him I bumped into a cabinet.

He shakes his head. "Where's Nathan? Where's Elisabet?"

I explain that everyone's gone. Nathan's moved out and Elisabet's probably in Oslo by now.

David lifts a box as she walks from the taxi. Her father carries the suitcases into the house. Her mother, hands covered with dough, embraces Elisabet with her elbows. *Uff da!* How they've missed her!

Her bedroom is untouched. The cross-country skis in a corner. The collection of famous Norwegian authors on one shelf. She sets my picture on her desk next to the Code of Civil Law, Volume One.

David huffs toward the door. "You sure you bumped into a cabinet?" he asks. "It looks like you've been beaned."

I shake my head, motion him down the stairs. My brother has never seen me cry.

A thin layer of grit covers the apartment. The smell of sour milk lingers behind the cabinets. The lights don't work. The gas has been switched off. I move to unplug the phone.

She sits on the bed and unlaces her boots. Her brother, robust fellow on leave from military exercises in the north, conscript in the mighty Norwegian war machine, bursts into the room. *Har de?* he gushes, a warm, friendly Scandinavian welcome.

Glory to their craggy finger of a country, crooked on Europe's edge, battered by frozen seas and imperialist neighbors, land of Vikings, rats, fjords, and traitors.

The telephone rings.

She has made a terrible mistake. She can't live without me. She is taking the next plane back.

"Hello?" I say.

On the other end, the ocean, a glacier, a long-distant voice.

a jew
among
the norse

We fly east into a false dawn.

Flight attendants bustle down the aisles, feigning good cheer and distributing towelettes. Your face is the window on your soul, they say, wipe, wipe.

Dirk snorts on my shoulder. I roll his head to one side and clean the drool from my shirt. He struggles awake, an encephalitic child on a field trip. "Coffee," he manages.

Oxygen masks mist caffeine into our mucous membranes. Plastic arrives microwaved in aluminum. Slowly our cells recover from the stunted night.

"Isn't it illegal to pack us in here like aliens?" asks Dirk as he unlocks the tray table from his sternum.

I explain that if I didn't pass the bar, my counsel would constitute the unauthorized practice of law and subject me to disciplinary action.

"*Ce n'est pas important,*" says Dirk. "*On y va à Paris.*"

The vast expanse of blue below has given way to crabby lumps of brown that we guess are Great Britain.

"Could be Norway, though," says Dirk. "Depends on our flight plan." He looks at me like a dentist who has just yanked his patient's tooth.

I run my tongue over the gaping hole; the salty taste of my own blood is not unpleasant.

Dirk turns back to the window. "No," he says. "It's Great Britain. If it were Norway, we'd see the smoke signals."

I settle into the cab and let Dirk's pidgin French guide us to our hotel. "Trust me," he says, and I do.

The sunlight is sharp as needles. The air thick with the promise of heat. Dirk keeps up a steady patois with the cabdriver while I watch for familiar signs of Paris. I've never been, but when I see the Eiffel Tower, I know we've arrived in the correct city.

We careen through cobbled streets, narrowly avoiding unruffled pedestrians, who step aside like toreadors. The cab screeches to a halt at a red light, then bursts forward when it changes to green. A young woman, a foreigner, scrambles for safety on the sidewalk. Her blond hair ripples like a cloak about her features. I look back, blood jumping, until her face is unmasked.

At the hotel Dirk pays the driver. We lug our suitcases into the lobby and up to the registration desk. Slick-faced and grimy-eyed, we plead with the concierge for a bed.

"No thing, messieurs," she assures us. "The rooms are not available until the noon."

In the street scraps of food and paper stream down the gutters. Headless chickens and eviscerated pigs hang from hooks in a butcher's window. A woman carries a baguette in one arm, a screaming child in the other. She steps over a man asleep in a doorway.

"Isn't Paris beautiful?" says Dirk.

I am too tired to respond. If Paris has opened its heart, my eyes are closed.

We sip espresso at a sidewalk café. Slowly we sputter and lurch back to life.

"I could live here," says Dirk.

"What about your friends?" I ask.

"They could too."

"Your family?"

"Who needs them?"

Across the street a man and a woman embrace. She kisses him

on both cheeks, then lingers over his mouth. His hands on the back of her shirt pulse like folded wings.

"It's twenty hours by train to Oslo," I say.

Dirk is silent for a long time. Then he says, carefully, "She might not want to see you."

I digest this bit of information as if it were an unknown delicacy rather than the usual cassoulet.

"What if she does?"

A sleepless night. Dirk snoring like Napoleon's army. Shouts from the alley piercing our windows. When night finally falls, it is daybreak in Paris.

"*Les croissants avec confiture,*" announces Dirk. "*Du pain, du fromage, le café au lait.*" He props the tray against my chest, hovering above me like a nurse in intensive care.

He's been awake for hours, taken a stroll along the Seine, read the newspapers, called the Coast. All is quiet on the western front.

While I slather my bread with jam, Dirk regales me with tales of battles with rogue viruses, plagues, and pestilence. A permanent skin graft to a beeper seems a small price to pay for true passion.

"I love San Francisco," he declares. "It feels like home."

I remind him that college was a warm and fuzzy experience.

"The worst four years of my life. It was like living in a box."

"The rooms weren't that bad."

"You, at least, fit in. I was the square peg."

I don't remember my shape. It seemed elastic and shifting. "Forced into the round hole," I offer.

"So to speak."

I feel a fever rise in my neck and spread across my cheeks. That Dirk is gay I've known since the night I found him in bed with another man. But that he might have his own passions and desires separate from my own I never considered for more than an instant. Has he loved, lost, promised, wanted? What cadavers has he buried in the woods? Without sound, loss is forgotten.

The yellow heat of summer yawns across our beds. The gray facade of shuttered windows on the building opposite stares blankly back at us.

"I'm going to call Elisabet," I announce.

"Was it something I said?" asks Dirk.

The foreign pulse of a European telephone like an alarm clock swathed in bandages.

"Hallo? Familie Andenasen."

A woman's voice. Elisabet's mother? Aunt? Neighbor? She's never mentioned a sister. Could I have the right family, wrong number? Wrong family, right number?

I gush through my story, tumbling over the words, not stopping to consider whether we speak the same language, share a vocabulary. If I halt, I may never regain my footing. I'll slide back down the hill and collapse in the ruined fields and mud.

"The train?" she asks in perfect English. "Do you think that is a good idea? Elisabet is not well. Perhaps you should write first."

Stunned by the intrusion of this assembled woman, a mother/aunt/neighbor whom I've never met, whose voice I've never heard, I babble responses in fourteen languages, none of which I speak.

"Good, then," she says. "I will tell her you called and that you will write." She wishes me good health and happiness. She has enjoyed conversing with me.

I sink to the floor of the telephone booth. Gum wrappers, cigarette butts, and bottle caps welcome me. I stare into the eye of a used condom. Someone pounds on the door. I wave him off.

But monsieur, he insists, if I don't get up, then I am gravely ill, or I am a vagrant, or he has to make a phone call. If only I could understand *la langue d'amour*.

I will lie here all day with my copy of *Paris from the Floor of a Phone Booth*. Small animals will sniff me, decide I am not their type, and leave me in peace. I am not unhappy. I have my square yard of corrugated metal and a large debt to a pawnbroker.

Dirk's face appears in the gloom. "Do you need a doctor?" he asks.

I explain that Elisabet's mother is Cerberus at the gate. She has shredded my trousers, chased me off the hill.

Dirk helps me to my feet, wipes off my knees.

"The only solution to Scandinavian pragmatism," he decides, "is Jewish irrationality."

The night train sways like a drunken Swede while the Swedes themselves are surprisingly steady as they navigate drunkenly down the aisles. The two motions cancel each other like sine and cosine.

There is no hope for sleep. The train passes through postcard villages, sweeping up vacationing Swedes in its passage. Come home, Lars, come home, Bjorn, calls the train. Come home to a winter of darkness and alcohol, work at Volvo and Saab, tennis heroes and pornography stars.

Ah, but one last taste, proposes the six-foot blond, one sip before we pass into night. It's still summer, man, drink. Drink!

The duty-free shop is eight deep with Swedes, fishing for their last krona. Even the Danes cannot keep up with their northern cousins. They bid fond farewells as the ferry docks in their island country. What a night we had, coughs one, spitting on his shoes.

My seatmate, short and dark, a mutation in the species, offers me a bottle of vodka. When I take a sip, he says something in German.

"*Ich bin ein American*," I say in my best imitation of John F. Kennedy.

He repeats his question in English.

"Oslo," I tell him.

"*Ach*, the most terrible city," he warns. "Why do you think they are so unhappy?" He points behind him, where a group of four men sit drinking sullenly.

"You could be German," he says. "We are friends now."

He hands me the bottle. I match his massive gulps with birdlike swallows. Soon he is telling me a rambling story of unrequited love in a linguistic babble comprised of Swedish, English, and German. I feign comprehension through the heartache.

"Do not love a Norwegian woman," he concludes. "She is like winter."

I sit up, startled, but his eyes are glazed and focused above my head. White foam has gathered on the corners of his mouth like a beach stained by roiling waters. He drains the bottle, sighs, belches, and begins to sing.

The train whistles mournfully, calling all Nordic dwellers back to their frozen lands, distinguished only in their bleakness. I press my face against the swift, rushing blackness and fall asleep to a soulful and tuneless rendition of the Swedish national anthem.

I awake stiff-necked and thick-tongued on the Norwegian border. The seat next to me is empty except for a small package of lozenges and a scribbled note: "Headache cure."

Two frontier guards, their faces smooth and hairless, guns bulging from girlish hips, search the car for contraband, aliens, undesirable elements. They examine my passport with unflinching sobriety, intent on discovering the drug smuggler beneath my placid exterior.

"How long will you stay in Oslo?" one asks.

I hesitate, unsure of the answer, and my hesitation becomes evasion. I see myself sweating nervously in the guard's mirror glasses. I imagine prison, torture, my cause taken up by Helsinki Watch.

"Seven days?" I squeak.

The guard stares at me impassively, his bug eyes unblinking.

"Business or pleasure?" he asks.

"Pleasure?" I say as sweat gushes from my forehead like a lawn sprinkler.

He hands my passport to his brother-in-arms, then turns back to me and says, "Elisabet can't love you."

I nod dumbly, convinced that in this country of cousins everyone knows my plight.

"Then you must declare it," he says, handing me a form.

DECLARATION OF IMPOSSIBLE LOVE
Declarant _____ (your name) declares that he/she is hopelessly infatuated w/ _____ (name of beloved). Declarant states that his/her affection is unreciprocated. Declarant agrees not to torment him/herself or his/her beloved and to leave the country quietly when asked.

I scribble my name across the bottom.

The guard nods, clicks his heels smartly, and moves on to the next passenger. Poor man, I can hear him screaming as he cracks under interrogation. He loves her; he'll do anything for her; why did she leave him?

A name, an address, but no warning.

I wander the streets of Oslo like a man on a newly frozen lake. One wrong step; she could be anywhere. A group of students emerge from a café. A woman reads on a bench. Blond faces pack a streetcar. I rush through the mathematical possibilities: in a small city, the chance encounter. If I sat in one place, unmoving, for how long?

The stolid stone buildings. The square corners. The unadorned facades. Streetlights blink in regular intervals; pedestrians wait for the green.

Cabs slow, their dark-skinned drivers asking first in German, then English if I need a ride to the hotel. No hotel, radio, I say, as if I made perfect sense. They nod; they know that eighteen percent of all foreign visitors will suffer depression, anxiety, schizophrenia.

Five o'clock. The stores close. She walks briskly from the library to the tram station. She doesn't see the thin American, his face in a crumpled letter, a duffel bag at his feet. She's promised Mama to help with supper tonight. Her brother has summer holiday. Her father can't be bothered. Poor Mama, she's all alone.

I climb aboard the streetcar. The neat blue line leads straight to the suburbs. Her town, the last stop. Boxy apartment complexes, each with flower arrangement and balcony, line the tracks. Small children on bicycles wave at the train. The passengers stare glumly back. A drunk man snarls and mutters at a young woman. She sits stoically, and no one intervenes.

The conductor, a Sikh, sings each station in a Punjabi-accented Norwegian. He hasn't heard from his wife for nearly a year, yet each month, confident that he will have good news soon, he sends deutsche marks wrapped in old newspaper.

The ranks are thinned. Her stop is called. Everyone but the drunk and me scrambles for the exit. I watch him pick his nose, his

fat fingers halfway up his head. He sees me and growls, rising unsteadily from his seat before he flops back down. I skip off the
train.

She could be anywhere. I walk one hundred meters in one direction, then walk back. Commuters bustle past, heads down, eyes
averted, loaves of bread in their arms. Finally I stop a man, mouth
Norwegian sounds. He stares at me impassively. I pull her letter
from my jeans, point to her address. *Ja, ja*, he knows where that is
and gestures in the direction. A neat white house. A gravel path.
Small hemlocks, recently planted, form a barrier from the street.
In Norway, she told me, no one is wealthy, but my parents are
well off.

I zip my jacket. Though the sky betrays no hint of dusk, the
greedy landscape absorbs all warmth. Winter and Not Winter are
the only seasons. Parsimony the national pastime.

A figure floats in a first-floor window. Not as tall, not as blond.
I move to the door, my feet scraping gravel. A knock. The echoing
silence. A pot banging or a gunshot. Footfalls on creaking floor. A
lock clicks.

"Yes?"

I have seen photos. But is it possible she doesn't recognize me?
For a moment I could be anyone, do anything. It's not too late. Run
away. Wrong address. Encyclopedia salesman.

"Colin," I say, pointing to myself like a missionary among the
natives.

She blinks, the same catlike quickness, her features impervious.
Then: "But you said you would write."

"I was in town."

Translation neurons, long withered from disuse, struggle to fire
coherent messages across decayed synapses. Irony and pathos take
a backseat to comprehension.

"But Elisabet is not home."

"Will she be back soon?"

"A fortnight."

I do not speak the Queen's English. If I did, I would understand
that Elisabet will not return for fourteen days and nights. But I am
an American—ignorant, savage, illiterate.

She tried to tell me when I telephoned, she says. Elisabet is north, visiting her grandmother.

I grasp the doorjamb; the house wobbles. Mrs. Andenas, former nurse and psychiatric social worker, clutches my wrist and eases me into the entryway.

"*Sitte du har,*" she commands as she propels me into a chair. She returns a moment later with a cup of tea and a buttered sweet roll. "*Spise,*" she says. "You have had a long passage."

I do not cry. I am oddly content sitting in the paneled entryway of the Andenas house eating a *Berlinerbolle*. It would have been too simple to take a train from one European capital to another. I am convinced my journey requires additional hardship, adversity, mishaps, and drunks. My father's father walked one thousand frozen miles, slept in graveyards, dodged bullets, to reach his promised land.

"You should not be sad," says Elisabet's mother. "This is what I told Elisabet. Let the teenagers have their love. For you there is the university."

She offers me another *Berlinerbolle*. While I eat, she scribbles Elisabet's address on a piece of paper. There is no telephone, she tells me; otherwise I could call. I do not ask what she does in an emergency: a neighbor's phone or the corner store? I have already made my decision.

I thank her for the tea and rolls and decline her offer to stay the night. I have friends in the city, I lie. She doesn't try to persuade me.

"It is better," she says at the door. "You will be happier with your own."

As I walk down the driveway, a man in an expensive German import drives up. He nods tentatively; hasn't he seen me before? I lower my eyes and duck into a neighbor's yard, leaving Elisabet's father to ponder my existence in his rearview mirror.

The town is so small that the ticket agent takes fifteen minutes to find it on his map. There is no train service that far north, he tells me. I will have to ride the night train to Tromsø and then a bus. Bus service is sporadic; he can issue a ticket but cannot guarantee passage.

I am poised between Paris and the unknown. Twenty-four hours from a NATO outpost or a sidewalk café. To return is to abandon all hope; to venture forward, sheer madness. Old men are crammed into freight cars. Cannibals and Pygmies sell children to Gypsies. Unspeakable atrocities are committed at night.

I buy a ticket.

We leave the city and climb into the mountains, sluicing through jagged peaks, swooping above dizzying drops to fjords below. The water, still and clear as a teardrop on a granite slab, hums with sunlight. In a landscape of vertiginous beauty the inhabitants have no choice but to seek balance in a solemn gravity; otherwise, land and people would be as untethered as kites.

My fellow passengers are a joyless lot. With no alcohol and no border crossings they stare glumly out the windows or down the aisles. When night falls, they smoke rancid cigarettes between cars, laughing in staccato bursts and spitting tobacco onto the floor. Their teeth, fingers, and hair are the color of dirty bathwater. Their speech is filled with hiccups and sighs. They have just emerged from forty years in the forest, blinking into town, carting provisions back to mud huts and lean-tos.

I roll my thin coat into a pillow and fall asleep on the vinyl couchette. She flees down the stairs and out the door, her feet skipping manically over pavement and ascending into the starless night.

I tell my parents I'm having a wonderful time in Paris. I give them Dirk's room number and hope they won't call back. The barren terrain. The idling buses. If I died now, who would claim my body?

"Colin?" asks my mother. "Has something happened?"

I reassure her that we have a bad connection. That lachrymal sound she hears is merely a thousand pulses of light competing for space along a microscopic fiber optic cable. That huge bill on their calling card from a town they cannot pronounce is my penultimate resting place. I promise to call again when I am safely entombed.

A light rain falls. Two seasons: mud and ice. To freeze in the depths of summer.

I board a bus. "North Pole," I say to the driver, showing him my ticket. He nods. All roads lead to the Arctic.

We rumble onto a two-lane highway. Scrawny vegetation dots the roadside. The landscape looks newly formed, as if recently heaved from the earth. Everything is rock and water. We pass a sign in English and Norwegian: Farthest Northern Point You Would Ever Want to Attain. Beyond, all is wilderness and frontier. I scratch my name and the date into the seat with a key, a record of my passage. I will not be forgotten.

We board a ferry. We disembark. We board another ferry. I fall asleep. When I awake, the faces around me have changed, but the bus lumbers northward. I am traveling to the edge of the world; the driver will wake me when we fall off.

The highway becomes a dirt path. The bus humps one rutted shoulder. At any moment we will overturn into a ditch and sink in a cloudberry bog. Sheep crowd the road, pulling at weeds in the cracked earth. The bus bumps them politely aside. They shake their cloven hooves and bray. They know who I am.

The driver shakes me from my reverie. The bus is silent and empty.

"Tilså," he declares.

I stagger from my seat, dragging my duffel bag and jacket. The street is mud; the sky gray. A knot of buildings huddle for warmth. Children peer at me from the windows of a shop. I am a notorious gunslinger returning for vengeance.

I walk toward the saloon. The doors swing open, and two women carrying potato sacks emerge. I step aside as they brush past, then slip inside.

"Andenas," I say to the man at the cash register, pointing to the slip of paper with Elisabet's address.

"You are her American," he says in faultless English.

He directs me to the last house at the end of a small peninsula. I thank him. "No problem," he says.

Curtains flutter in the houses I pass. Faces glimpsed in the shadows. It is high noon, but it could be evening; the light through the clouds is pale and thin.

From her window she sees a familiar figure walking down the road: the angular tilt of one shoulder, the high forehead. She would run if there were an exit. She would hide in the attic if they had one.

I unlock the gate. Two dogs bark. The ground is uneven and clumped. I stumble several times. The front door opens.

A smile, not joyful but polite, as if she has received a book she's already read. A smile on which I can read the true foolishness of my journey, the impossibility of any reconciliation. I would run if I could, if I hadn't traveled so far and bus service weren't so erratic. Instead I trudge forward through the mud.

"Mother said you had come," she says. The telephone, apparently, has been invented overnight.

She grants me a perfunctory kiss, a quick brush of the lips, and invites me inside. White surfaces glare. Windows shine like burnished aluminum. Even the wood floors are bleached. I leave my shoes at the door.

An old woman drinks tea in the living room. Elisabet introduces her grandmother. She says something in Norwegian that I assume is a greeting but could just as easily be a curse. I tell her that I am happy to meet her too.

"Are you hungry?" Elisabet asks. "You must have had a long trip. All the way from Paris."

We sit in the kitchen. She feeds me bread and cheese. I ramble nervously about the bar exam, my pending job, Dirk, my family, the taxis in Paris, the weather, the Swede who insisted I was German. Elisabet says little. Her grandmother pours another cup of tea and joins us at the table. Her chair scrapes against the wooden floor.

Elisabet leans toward me. "What are you doing here?" she asks.

I look to her grandmother as if waiting for an answer, hoping to deflect the question mentally.

"She doesn't understand English," Elisabet says.

I realize that the answer she expects and the one I am about to give are a mere approximation of what I can't name. The truth is something concealed, mysterious, ineffable. Three words to represent the unrepresentable.

"I love you," I say anyway.

Elisabet is silent.

"Don't you love me?"

She breathes. "No," she says finally. Her chair creaks. "Like a brother, yes. Not like a lover."

"*Te?*" asks Grandma, holding up her cup.

"*Nei takk, Bestemor,*" says Elisabet.

My shirt is a damp towel. My toes throb in wet socks. In the kitchen an ancient doctor sharpens a wood saw. Water boils on the stove. He can't amputate a frozen heart.

"I didn't come all the way up here to argue you into going out with me," I lie.

"No?" says Elisabet.

"I missed you."

"I missed you too."

"Then why aren't we together?"

Elisabet hesitates. For a moment I allow a drop of hope like ink to squirt into my blood. Black ink.

"I'm Norwegian," she says softly, sadly. "You're American."

"*Ja, ja,*" says Grandma. "*Akkurat.*"

I have traveled five thousand miles, abandoned friends, braved drunken bores, borne miserable weather, suffered inedible food, lied to my family, and swallowed all pride. Nothing can stop me.

I swivel to Elisabet's grandmother, her expression as solemn as a sacrament.

"Shut up," I say.

The day will not end. A grainy light seeps through the windows. I flop about on the hard bed like a herring in a basket. Elisabet sleeps an arm's length away. Her breathing is steady and deep. Her mouth tilts open. She has one hand flung into the space between us as if to ward off unwanted crossings.

"You saw me," I said.

"Yes."

"But you ran away."

"Yes."

"That's how it happens? You just decide?"

"Go to sleep, Colin. You'll wake up *Bestemor.*"

The old woman has my watch and schoolbooks. They do her no

good. She can't read a word. Fortunately her hearing's not great either.

"How can you sleep?"

"Close your eyes."

The midnight sun is a yellow star stitched to my breast. Night will not fall. Dawn breaks and breaks.

I bury my head in the feather pillow. I do not dream.

In the morning, snow.

The mountains capped in white. The fjord an angry gray. Everything between is just a degree.

Elisabet is gone. It may have been days. My watch is missing.

I am snow-blind, afraid to move. I need food, water, my daily dose. I will die of exposure, starvation, malnutrition, the usual deprivations.

Downstairs I hear voices, my name. The demands of nature drive me to the bathroom. The voices halt, hesitate, then resume. I release my bladder.

I pad down the stairs, cough loudly at the bottom, make my entrance.

"*Morgen*," says Grandma, who apparently has turned the other cheek. "*Har de?*"

"Fine, thank you; I think I'm leaving today," I say to Elisabet.

Elisabet translates, ignoring my announcement. "*Bestemor* says you should stay the week," she says. "You only just arrived."

"What do you think?"

"It's up to *Bestemor*."

"Ask *Bestemor* if you'll sleep with me."

"I won't."

"Why not?"

"Because it's none of *Bestemor*'s business."

In southern parts of the Northern Hemisphere, I tell myself, children play beneath open hydrants. Couples stroll in parks. Dirk sits at an outdoor café. The days are hot; the nights breezy and warm.

"It snowed," I say.

"Just a little," says Elisabet.

"I'm leaving."

"I know."

There is no teary good-bye on a runway. Years from now we won't meet in an exotic locale and remember how we always had Tilså. A piano won't play our song because we don't have one.

I stuff my underwear into my duffel bag. Brush my teeth. Elisabet gives me a loaf of bread and a wedge of cheese for the journey.

"There's an afternoon bus," she says.

I search for a heartbreaking response, a howl to rend the soul. The earth will split and crack to the core.

"I should use the bathroom," I say finally.

My face in the mirror looks tired, creased with age. I suck in my cheeks until they are hollow and gaunt. I run my palms over the unfulfilled promise of a beard.

I sit on the edge of the tub. I believe I will cry. Tears well in my eyes. I sneeze.

"Hurry, Colin," Elisabet says through the door. "We don't have much time."

I blow my nose and rinse my face in cold water, hoping it will sound as if I've emerged from the depths of a prolonged weep. I open the door.

Elisabet's lovely face: the intersecting circles and arched vertices, the moon forehead, the gray stillness of her eyes.

She takes my hand and leads me down the stairs. I follow, my feet scuffing wood.

At the front door she fishes through a pile of umbrellas and gives me one. "Take it," she says.

"I'll mail it back."

"Don't be silly. We have plenty."

"I won't keep it."

"But we don't need it."

"You may."

We both hold the umbrella for a moment, staring at the curve of the black plastic handle.

"Fine. Do as you like."

I shrug on my coat, mash my feet into my soggy shoes. Elisabet's grandmother watches me from the vestibule. When I am ready, she hugs me farewell.

"Thanks for letting me stay," I say.

She hugs me again. "Have a good trip," she says.

I am halfway down the road when I realize she speaks English.

And all that day it rained. The windows were sprayed with mud. A brown light came through.

She walked home in the mud. She was neither happy nor sad. Years later, when she remembered him, she would see him through the smudged windows, his hand in a half wave, dirt or memory obscuring his face.

No statues were smashed. No one was banished from his father's house.

Dirk asks me to wait on the ticket line while he finds a newspaper. I gather our bags and corral them toward the counter. All around me the familiar twang of nasal voices.

I toe-push the bags across the dirty floor. A young woman and her mother discuss the wonderful weather, the beautiful city, the charming gardens. They both are tall and fit, the young woman's face unmistakably American: upturned nose, clear blue eyes, straight teeth.

She smiles when she notices that I am looking at her, props her hair behind one ear. "I hate lines," she says.

"*Pardon?*" I say.

She hesitates; something is wrong with my accent. "*Allemand?*" she asks.

I shake my head sadly.

She shrugs and gives up. "I can't speak French," she apologizes.

I kick our bags forward another inch.

Dirk appears, newspaper in hand. "Last copy," he says. "I snagged it right before some New Yorker. He offered me five bucks."

The woman's face slides from surprise to suspicion, narrow eyes slitting to blue scratches.

"Great," I say, turning from her. "What's news at home?"

Dirk, observing our silent exchange, drapes his arm across my shoulders, crooking my neck in his elbow. His lips brush my ear. I can hear his blood.

"It's an epidemic," he says. "They think you can get it from kissing. There's no cure, no recovery."

I don't laugh. He is not funny.

"Tomorrow," he prophesies, "everyone you've loved will be dead."

wandering

tone-deaf
and
color-blind

"You have to do something," insists my mother. "She's *ruining* her life."

A plastic dinosaur trots across the shifting desert of white on my desk. The paperless office: the false promise of the computer age.

"It's just a year," I say, walking the dinosaur. "What's the big deal?"

How can I not understand the magnitude of this transgression? she demands. One year leads to another leads to vagrancy and illegitimate children.

I check my watch. A therapist would be cheaper, I suggest.

It was bad enough when I switched majors, she continues; at least I stayed in school. But all that tuition for a musician? They could have bought tickets to the symphony for life.

"She can't even sing," my mother adds.

I agree that though she's not completely tone-deaf, she's musically impaired.

"She sounds miserable."

Paying clients are calling, I tell her. I promise to phone back when my hourly rates are lower.

"We just want her to be happy. Would you let her know that? She can do whatever she wants if it makes her happy."

She has never been a good liar, my mother.

"She's ruining my life," says Rebecca.

We are an odd couple, Rebecca in black and me in a blue suit, sitting in a dirty downtown café like urban bruises.

"It's none of her business if I drop out of school. She should be happy I'm doing what I want to do."

I tell her our mother is ecstatic. "She's so delirious she's deranged," I add.

Rebecca disavows responsibility for our mother's mental state. "She's not going to force me to go to law school like she forced you," she says.

I thought my legal career represented a lack of imagination, I tell her, not volition. In my search for first principles I found the law.

"You could have been anything," Rebecca continues. "Remember those pamphlets you and Joshua used to write?"

"They were ridiculous," I say with false modesty.

"Sure," agrees Rebecca. "But at least you were addressing the Big Subjects. Now what do you do in your blue suit and yellow tie?"

"Do you mind?" I say. "I came to discuss your angst, not mine."

"I'm blessed," says Rebecca. She jams a fork into a packet of sugar.

"You have a terrible voice," I say.

"You've never heard me sing."

"And you can't play an instrument."

"I played cello."

"In sixth grade."

"I'm learning guitar."

"That's encouraging."

"You sound exactly like Mom."

I inhale a hot gulp of coffee directly into my lungs. I gasp and spray brown liquid over the white tablecloth.

"Don't be gross," says Rebecca.

Caffeine blazes through my nostrils. Automatic sprinkler systems discharge in my sinuses. My lungs flood with coffee grounds and saliva.

The waitress arrives with a rag and a fresh pot. "Shouldn't bite off more than you can chew," she says, winking at Rebecca as she wipes off the table. "Another cup?"

Rebecca shakes her head. "We're working on hot liquids."

"Thanks for your help," I say to Rebecca as I dry my forehead.

"You seem to be able to handle spitting up on your own."

I blot a brown stain from my white shirt. It looks like an ink spot shaped like a brown stain. "Everyone thinks you're crazy," I say.

"I'd be worried if they thought I was normal."

"You can't sing."

"Angel's playing Saturday at Hell. I'll put you on the guest list."

I don't need an invitation to eternal misery, I tell her. Twelve hours a day are enough for me.

"RebelAngel, my band," she explains. "We're opening at Hell on Saturday."

Despite my suit, my surrender to convention, my embrace of bourgeois culture, I refuse to acknowledge that my sister may be hipper than I.

"You can meet David," she says.

"David's going to be there?"

"Not David. David."

"David, as in David?"

"But not that David."

"Of course."

"You'll see."

She kisses me on both cheeks. "Friends?" she asks.

I agree to pencil her into my buddy book.

"Tell Mom to quit tormenting me." She pats her pockets. "Do you have any money?"

I give her a ten for cabfare.

"You should thank me. There's one fuckup in every family. Now it won't be you."

"Thanks," I say.

"By the way," she says as she turns to leave, "everyone calls me Reb now. No last name. Just Reb."

Volume 624 of the Federal Supplement whizzes past my left ear, thudding into the bookcase with a sad splintering of its binding.

"*Aronson* v. *National United Federation, Inc.!*" thunders Robert Stockard, Jr.

How could I have missed the most important decision on the applicability of the *Keogh* doctrine to state law claims that do not challenge the reasonableness of rates? I am profoundly ignorant and sorrowful.

"Your memorandum!" he bellows. A crumpled wad of paper ricochets off the same bookcase and bounces to my feet.

I compliment him on his ingenious filing system.

"When this ship goes down, Stone," he says, "we're strapping you to the deck."

"Aye, aye, sir," I say, expanding on the nautical theme.

He regards me sternly. "Are you being insolent?"

I shake my head quickly. Last time, I think, he wasn't aiming.

"Where did you prep, Stone?" he asks.

I admit that I am a victim of our public education system.

His rat eyes squint. "The State University as well?"

I shake my head, grateful for the small shield of ivy covering my heart. He interviewed me at the tower, I remind him. The brocaded curtains, the ivory walls. We chatted wittily about declining standards and the single-parent family.

"Yes, well," he says, "I've recruited so many young men. The best and the brightest." The proud strains of marching music fill the room from speakers hidden somewhere behind his bookshelves.

"The competition is fierce," he continues. "But it doesn't end when you walk through these doors. Only the best and the brightest of the best and the brightest survive all the way to the top. Hard work. Intelligence. Drive." His glazed eyes stare past me toward the river and the cityscape beyond, imagining future glories, attractive secretaries, three-martini lunches.

He snaps back to attention. The music dies.

"No soldier ever marched on his ass," he barks. "Now get cracking on that memo."

His fingers drum time on his desk as I scurry from the room.

Rebecca can't sing.

She howls. She wails. She caterwauls. Her lyrics are indecipherable, punctuated by curses and growls. A drummer, bass player, and guitarist screech a nightmare accompaniment. The dimly lit basement pulsates with dark bodies and dank odors. The walls ooze slime and beer.

My little sister snarls and spits about the stage. Jet black hair, paper white face, tattered clothing, nails and pins.

"We're RebelAngel!" shouts Rebecca as the band thrashes into a convulsive cacophony. "Fuck you!"

The audience seethes like angry gelatin. Bodies ride the wave, then collapse into the tide. Bare arms and slick torsos coat me with human grease as I wade through the crowd.

"That chick is excellent," grunts a bald man with a tattoo on his skull.

"Reb rules!" agrees his hirsute neighbor.

I push past a bouncer who regards my scrawled backstage pass with boredom. I scale a small mountain of wires, amplifiers, and crates. Strange, druglike odors waft down the corridor. Young men glide past, their arms loaded with musical implements and heavy machinery.

Rebecca's laugh. A white stab through an open door.

"Hey, hey, brother," she says as I blink in the bright light. She sits, black bra and black jeans, balanced on a man's thighs, her feet planted firmly on the floor. "David, Colin. Colin, David."

I slowly grasp, like a stroke victim recognizing his own name, that she is introducing me to the man on whose lap she sits, a man I now recognize as the guitarist.

A black man.

We shake, our hands a public service advertisement for racial harmony.

"That was loud," I say, to say something, anything, hoping that my voice doesn't squeak, that I don't suffer a sudden Tourette's attack, years of good liberal training washed away in a torrent of neurological confession.

"You liked it?" says Rebecca.

"I didn't know you were so angry."

She laughs, her voice hoarse and throaty. "I'm supposed to be angry. There's a lot to be angry about."

The sonic boom of another band taking the stage pummels the walls. I locate the nearest doorframe.

Rebecca rises from David's lap and introduces me to the rest of the band: the waiflike, neurasthenic drummer; the bass player, five pounds heavier. They tilt in my direction. The drummer asks if I'm the lawyer or the doctor.

"I sue people," I say.

"My old man's a lawyer," says David. He plinks away on his unplugged electric guitar, his fingers racing between the frets. I watch his face for signs that he is joking.

"He wanted me to go to law school." David continues. " 'That's all we need,' he said, 'another guitar-strumming Negro.' "

"You could still go," I suggest earnestly, the nerd brother.

"Yeah," he muses, his eyes on his strings. "I'd be a good lawyer."

"You'd have to wear a suit," says the drummer.

"You don't have to sleep in it," says David.

Rebecca turns from the mirror, her face masked in cold cream, whiter than white. "Play that line again," she says to David.

"What line?" he says.

Red spider webs spin beneath the cold cream on Rebecca's cheeks.

"You know I can't sing it."

David stops plinking. "Hum a few bars."

A cat would be more musically gifted, I decide.

I tell my mother I've got bad news and bad news.

"Give me the bad news first," she says.

I tell her that Rebecca can't sing.

"And what's the bad news?"

"She sings."

She blames my father. If he had not sung Broadway show tunes in the kitchen during our formative years, Rebecca would be earning her bachelor's degree today.

"She'll outgrow it," he promises, his voice a distant echo on another line. "They all do."

My secretary makes the universal phone signal—a tilted fist, thumb and pinkie extended, positioned two inches from ear and lips—and mouths Stockard's name. I make the universal talking-to-him-would-be-certain-death signal—an index finger swipe across the neck.

"Your sister needs to settle down, find a nice young man," claims my mother. "Don't you have any lawyer friends you can introduce her to?"

I protest that Rebecca's only twenty, she's not interested in my friends, she has a boyfriend.

The static over the telephone lines is the calm before an electrical storm. Into the eye my secretary makes the universal he's-going-to-kill-you gesture. Then all squeals break loose.

Who is he, where did he go to school, what do his parents do, where's he from, what's his name, his family name? My mother's questions swirl like tornadoes.

"His name is David," I say. "And that's all I know."

"David," says my father.

"I wouldn't put too much faith in names," I say. "Mine is Colin."

My second phone line blinks an insistent red, the same color as my secretary's face. I tell my parents that as delightful as I find their conversation, the executioner calls.

"You know," says my mother before she hangs up, "your real name is *Cha'yim*."

"Colin Stone," I say into the squawking receiver.

"You told Mom," moans Rebecca. She blows dust from a wineglass.

"His name," I protest.

David laughs. "She's not the FBI."

"You don't know," says Rebecca.

He is taller than I remembered, and heavier. The tiny apartment feels cramped in his presence. His fingers strum tabletops, walls, his thigh. He selects some music from Rebecca's malnourished collection, listens a moment, then chooses another. He fiddles with the volume and tone controls until the limpid notes of a piano ring through Rebecca's tinny speakers.

He apologizes. "It's the only classical recording Reb's got."

"David gave it to me," she says from the kitchenette.

"Your brother, she means," says David.

His fingers, I notice, have stilled.

Rebecca serves spaghetti. David fills my glass with wine. The music ends, then begins again, an endless ivory loop.

I tell them about my work: the hours hunched over documents, closeted in the library, squinting at a computer screen. David says his father spends weeks preparing a case for a jury. He practically lives in the office before a trial.

I explain that I will never appear before a jury. No cases have gone to trial in my firm in the last three years. If one did, a partner would handle it.

"I stack papers on my desk and push plastic dinosaurs across them," I confess.

"There's good work you could be doing," says Rebecca.

"He needs experience," says David.

"And money," Rebecca says derisively.

"Sure, why not? What's wrong with money?"

I listen to them debate my future. I want to discover if I will be happy, find true love, connect my genetic string to the cosmos. The present is the future; the past, an amnesiac's memory. We tread inexorably from job, to car, to house, to death.

"Nothing good comes from prosperity," says Rebecca. "Our parents were corrupted by affluence."

"They had dreams."

"Racist ones."

"Mine had anti-Semitic ones."

"We should get them together for dinner," I suggest.

David shrugs. "Jews say they're shocked by black anti-Semitism, but blacks aren't surprised that Jews are racist. Everybody hates somebody, and they'd all kill each other if they could."

"That's a pleasant thought," says Rebecca.

"People are poor, nasty, brutish, or short," I contribute, my first lesson from law school.

"At least I'm six-four," says David, draining the last of his wine.

Later, as Rebecca and I wash dishes and David plinks his guitar on the couch, I give him the brotherly stamp of approval. I suggest that she break the news slowly to our parents.

"Start with the worst and work your way back," I advise. "Tell them he's a Nazi."

Rebecca thinks I may be overreacting.

"You heard how they treated Elisabet," I say.

She nods, her hands bobbing in the soapy water.

"It was like Nuremberg."

Her hands submerge, disappearing into the depths. "You miss her," she asserts.

I don't see the blade, its black handle protruding from my abdomen. How quick her hands, peacefully scrubbing a pot! Air squeaks through my swollen throat; noises emerge from my mouth.

"Even if she was a Nazi," Rebecca adds.

"I've got nothing against minorities," says Stockard. "They've had a tough time in this country. But who invited them?"

I explain our liberal immigration policy, the civil rights movement, pervasive discrimination, and mob violence.

"Sure, this country's not perfect. But it's the best one around. Let them go back home if they think it's so great. Pestilence. Famine. Civil war."

The United States, I suggest, is equally brutal.

"Plenty of minorities have made it. Irish. Jews. Orientals. Look at the Orientals."

I promise to take a good hard look at the Orientals.

"This is our country," says Stockard. "They should be grateful for the opportunity. Other immigrants are banging on our doors, knocking them down to get in. Why should we have a law requiring minimum quotas? We don't have one requiring maximum quotas. That's discrimination." He pushes the file to the side of his desk.

I dutifully scratch notes on a yellow legal pad.

"We've got private attorney generals crawling all over this, ready to roast our weenies," he continues. "No statutory mandate. No federal jurisdiction. But our client can't afford the bad publicity."

He tells me we're going to fight the legislation in court until we crush the spines and pulverize the kneecaps of a Communist-dominated Congress. "We'll make them sorry they didn't let Reagan serve a third term."

I strap the holster around my waist, spin the barrel of my gun. One hundred eighty dollars per hour or mile of paper generated, whichever comes first.

Clients are lined up outside his door as I gallop past: asbestos manufacturers, tobacco companies, pharmaceutical and chemical interests, Nazi war criminals.

Cash or certified check, I tell them. Justice may be blind, but it isn't cheap.

A rare free weekend. David, Rebecca, and I walk through Central Park. The usual assortment of jocks, lovers, and freaks. David's fingers thrum time on Rebecca's neck.

"Doe ray me fa so la tee doe," he sings.

"Doe ray me fa so . . ." scratches Rebecca.

"La tee doe," continues David, carrying the notes into a higher register.

Rebecca pouts. She'll never increase her range. She's doomed to snarl in the basement.

"Think castrati," David suggests. "You know how much you like those little boys."

She punches him in the chest, shrieks as if she's the one been hit, and races off. David peels after her, his sneakers squeaking on the damp grass.

They caper gleefully like porpoises in an aquarium, performing for their audience and a fishy treat. I clap on cue, express my delight in their gaiety. The lovelorn older brother, broken and bitter, reads Kafka in the park.

I slump on a bench. Rebecca calls for help as David carries her off like a sacked city. Farewell, sister, I wave, may a thousand ships be launched.

Two men gaze at me. I avert my eyes and open my book.

A dog races past, yapping sideways while rushing forward.

An older couple approach, hand in hand, the man tall and gray, the woman thin and well dressed. They smile familiarly, as if wealth and privilege and a sky so blue it might crack make us family. They look like my parents.

They are my parents.

I freeze, force myself not to look in Rebecca's direction. I scan for surveillance cameras, parabolic microphones, satellites. How have they tracked us?

What a surprise, claims my mother; they just came from the museum, garaged the car, took a walk. What a lovely day.

My neck, stiffened with resolve, manages to move my head.

But what am I doing in the park with Kafka? my mother wants to know. She imagines despair, gloom, melancholy, cockroaches. How could I, a neonate suckling at the tit of the bar, be unhappy?

Before I can open my mouth to lie, David dumps Rebecca at my feet.

"Ta-da," he announces. "One Jewish princess at your disposal."

"Oh, shit," says Rebecca.

My jaw unlocks. I thank David for retrieving my sister, introduce him to my parents, tell him I'll see him in the office Monday.

"Stanley?" he says densely. "My name's David."

"David," sighs Rebecca as she rises to her feet.

"David?" my parents say in unison.

"Did I say Stanley?" I say.

My mother says they are thrilled to meet him, they've heard so much about him. Rebecca glares at me.

"I play guitar," David says.

"Wonderful," says my mother.

"In the band," he adds.

"Terrific."

Captivated by David's witty repartees, my mother invites us to lunch. David accepts. We flock to a flowery restaurant where recorded birdsongs burble like gas through cracks in the ocean bottom. My mother chatters giddily about the weather, the city, bohemian life. My father nods, though he could easily be napping. Rebecca sulks, slinking low in her chair. I kick her beneath the table and she looks at me with disdain, the diseased carrier of bourgeois culture.

Coffee is served. David's hand lies on the white tablecloth, his long fingers tapping a secret rhythm on the fabric. Rebecca's hand settles on top, her palm spooning his knuckles. My mother's eyes skip lightly over their misdemeanor.

"We never knew Rebecca could sing," my mother says, her eyes straining nonchalantly to revisit the crime scene.

"We met in the choir," says David.

An explosion rocks the restaurant, followed by an earthquake and a tidal wave. My mother clasps the side of her chair. My father grabs his napkin. They both talk at once, barking relief orders and emergency procedures.

"You were in a choir?" my father finally manages.

"University choir," says Rebecca. "I wanted to learn to sing."

"You were at Yale?" my mother says to David.

They stroll across campus, arm in arm, debating whether to go to a fraternity party or a barbecue. David is tired of the Deltas. Rebecca thinks they're cute. Big football game this weekend. Go, Elis!

Why shouldn't my sister be a college dropout, her boyfriend an Ivy League grad? We live in a beautiful world of educational opportunity where the privileged are free to default on their entitlements.

"I graduated," says David, "when Reb quit to sing in the band."

Rebecca lifts her hand from David's. "Not everyone sells out," she says.

My mother, sniffing blood, asks if Rebecca has reconsidered her decision.

Rebecca kicks back her chair and stands up. "If this is pick-on-Rebecca time," she says, "I'm leaving."

David tells her to calm down. Motion will only agitate the sharks.

Rebecca sits. "They've got nothing to teach me," she says.

The greatest thinkers surely have something to contribute to her education, my mother suggests. Why else have their words endured?

"Books are just bound paper," Rebecca says. "They don't protect you against ignorance and hatred."

"It depends how big they are," I volunteer.

"True knowledge"—she ignores me—"comes from the barrel of a gun."

My mother shakes her head at such naïveté. Rebecca obviously never finished her class in political theory, or she would know that history has completely discredited her ideology. "Violence doesn't solve anything," my mother reminds her.

"Neither does nonviolence," says David. "I think the civil rights movement proved that."

"Wait a minute," says my mother, her right hand chopping air. "I marched on Washington. We all did. And I beg to differ, but a great deal changed."

"Now blacks can *vote* for politicians who let the cities burn," says David.

"Lodz burned. Warsaw burned. Krakow burned."

"That proves my point," says Rebecca. "Nothing changes until there's war."

"African Americans are dying every day," says David. "No one's building them a memorial."

"They forgot to ask politely," I say.

My father leans across the table and reaches for the check. He holds it to the light, examining both sides as if reading a tea leaf or fortune cookie.

"Why build a memorial?" he asks, his wrists like unbent wire. "You can't read—when you're dead."

I switch on every electrical apparatus when I return to my apartment. They hum and buzz with a reassuring presence, filling the empty room with the crackle of energy. My windows glow with tiny charges, beacons to a darkened city. Other windows blink back, warning of rocks and narrow inlets.

Papers scattered across the kitchen table. Two coffee mugs, half filled with a brownish-green liquid, anchored like bookmarks. Pages stick and tear when I remove the cups. I gather the ragged remains and cram them in my briefcase.

White shirts billow in my closet. Red ties hang like entrails. Blue and gray suits, Civil War soldiers, salute across plastic hangers.

I pad from bedroom to bath, reluctant to turn off my electrical friends. They drone happily, unaware of their pending demise. One by one I cut their lifeblood, silencing their siphoning glee. Soon the apartment is in semidarkness, lit only by flickering crystals from dying appliances.

A siren warbles. The roof creaks. A man's gruff voice barks once. The toilet flushes. Water courses through pipes as on a capsizing ship.

My sister traveled tone-deaf and color-blind. No dark rivers to ford or frozen mountain passes to climb. She found true love in the last row of the bleachers singing Handel's *Messiah.* Her journey ended when they hit the same note, round and harmonious, a circle of two.

I lie in bed, the covers up to my neck. I can feel every woven cotton fiber, every shifting air pocket.

I open my mouth. I begin to sing softly, off-key, my voice squeaking with the effort. I sing one of my father's show tunes, substituting words where I've forgotten them. It's a sad tune about lost love and broken hearts, and I sing it with my father's remembered phrasing. After several verses I gain confidence, and by the final chorus I am crooning out the heartache.

I don't sing badly, I decide.

secret
jew of
the month

"Abracadabra," says Joshua. "Zombies."

He swivels across my office in a leather chair. Sparks fly from the carpet as he conjures the undead from the dark recesses of boxes and cartons of documents. They walk the silent hallways in dark suits and ties.

My tax dollars fund his research into the arcane practices of Jewish medievalists. Fellowship after fellowship, he's draining the treasury. Without me, I tell him, he'd have to get a job.

"In the Middle Ages," he says, "the entire community worked to support the scholar." He sighs and stares through the windows into an airless atrium.

The first two chapters of his dissertation compete for space on my desk with the first eleven chapters of the bankruptcy code. I glance at his title page, a quote from Martin Buber: *God can be beheld in each thing and reached through each pure deed.*

He looks unhealthy, his face blotched with fever, his hands pale and agitated. A strange virus acquired in the bowels of the Bodleian Library. Three years in England have done nothing for his complexion.

He claims he feels fine. His illness is the logical outgrowth of a certain philosophical inquiry. "These guys are the true pre-

Socratics," he says, lifting his dissertation and riffling the pages at me. "The triumph of passion and spirit over reason and rationality."

"Since when did you become such a Jew?" I ask.

"I've always been a Jew," he says. "So have you."

I never received an invitation to Joshua's conversion. Was it lost in the mail with the packages for the thirteenth tribe?

"Hitler was your hero," I remind him.

"I don't think so," he says slowly.

"Without him, you said, there'd be no Jews."

"I never said that." He laughs. "You're making it up."

His giant brain, I learn, is capable of prodigious feats of forgetfulness.

The subway spews me onto a graffiti-encrusted platform. I shoulder through a mass of humanity, labor up the grimy stairs. Emerging from the dank hole, I nearly collide with a baby carriage. I kick its tires and elbow the driver out of the way.

"Colin?" she says.

A dark-haired woman who resembles Marjorie's mother stands behind the carriage. Her belly pillows against the handle.

"It's Marjorie," she claims.

Six months pregnant, with a ten-month-old baby and a nineteen-month-old marriage.

"Things happened a little quicker than we planned," she explains.

Wisps of gray trail through her hair like smoke signals from her scalp. Olive eyes like ripe avocados. A thin sheen of perspiration on her brow.

She asks how I am, what I've made of my life. I confess that I'm a lawyer.

"Look at me," she commiserates: "Who'd've thought I'd have two babies?"

Except for me and everyone else who knew her, I think, probably no one.

Instead of becoming an actress, she explains, she married an investment banker/screenwriter. "Wally's going to be famous," she says about her fecund husband. "Right now, though, we're just wealthy."

When she asks if I'm married, I flip her an unadorned finger.

"Same old Colin," she says. "Funny, funny. You'll see, you'll be married in a year to one of your paralegals and you'll love it."

I tremble at the accuracy of her predictions.

"Weren't you going out with some Danish woman?"

I nod. I don't have the energy to correct her.

"I dated a Swedish guy once," she says. "Blond. Tall. Accent. The whole thing."

Her baby whimpers, the beginning of a whine.

"It was great," she says, ignoring the baby. "But everything changes when you think about marriage, about having kids," she says. "You don't want them singing about the baby Jesus."

I remind her that her parents celebrated Christmas.

"That was different. We were Jewish. Christmas wasn't religious; it was festive, a festive holiday," she says, proud of having found the right word.

"Joshua's practically Orthodox."

"He is not," she says.

I describe his dissertation: *Hasidism and the Kabbalah: Authenticity Through Mystical Unity.*

"He's never gotten over Nell's death," Marjorie explains.

"I think it's God's death that bothers him."

"It was random, meaningless," she continues. "No one could do anything about it."

I'm not certain whose death she is talking about, but I agree anyway.

A fresh brood of underground dwellers emerges from the bowels of the city and shoulders us aside. Marjorie swears at an older man who has bumped her against the carriage. "This city is killing me," she says as she walks east.

I follow her to the park. I am silent while she chatters about Wally, his job, his agent, his screenplay. She invites me to her apartment to meet this genius husband.

"He'll talk your ear off," she vows, as if to entice me.

I promise to visit another day.

We exchange the obligatory greetings to family, the air kisses, the expressions of mutual fondness and undeserved absence.

"Call me," she urges.

"I will," I lie.

"Bankruptcy," begins Marty Rose, senior associate, Stockard's hatchet man, "was the litigator's crazy aunt, locked in the attic."

His Adam's apple bobs in his throat like a lobster trap. Wiry hair springs from his head as if from an electrical outlet. Frayed shirt collar and cuffs. Who dressed him? Who let him out of the house?

"No one wanted to admit to the practice, but every firm had its specialist," he continues. "Then the laws were liberalized, the federal judiciary established specialized courts, and attorneys discovered that bankruptcy could be an effective weapon in litigation or in fending off a hostile takeover."

The walls are covered with certificates of merits: testimonials from famous judges and politicians; attestations of pedigree from institutions of higher learning.

"Corporate reorganization is the preferred term. Bankruptcy has its negative connotations of destitution, insolvency, and ruin."

Today's conundrum, Marty explains, is how to assist a struggling health care organization from paying the long-overdue medical bills of its crippled and ailing patients.

I write on my yellow pad: *screw the dying and disabled.*

Marty directs me to a wall of boxes where he tells me I will find the necessary documents. He asks his secretary to call a trucking company to transfer the wall to my office. She looks at me poignantly, foreseeing misery and an early death.

"Bob has only terrific things to say about you," says Marty, lowering his scratchy head and scrutinizing me from under his brows. "He thinks you're the Great White Hope."

I mumble something about not being worthy.

"He says you'll be around here for a long time."

"Thank you," I say.

As I click down the hushed hallway, I wonder whether I've just been given a promise or a warning.

✼   ✼   ✼

Marjorie claims I'm depressed and cynical because I'm lonely. "And you think too much," she adds, her voice jumping at me like a telephone ambush. "You always have."

I barely think at all, I protest. I live by wits alone.

"You've got to meet more people, different people," she insists.

In a city of murderers and madmen, I tell her, I'm happy living on an island.

Wally and she are having a dinner party, "literary types," she declares, and I'm invited.

Apparently she has forgiven me for driving into her porch, screaming at her neighbors, besmirching her good name. We are adults, she claims, and her parents always liked me.

"Besides," she adds, "there's someone I want you to meet; you can't pine for me your entire life."

Later, sorting through suits in my closet, I decide Marjorie was joking. Yet as I toss gray fabric after blue, I resolve to limit my lamenting to alternate Tuesdays and Thursdays. Elisabet has probably married by now, the strapping mother of two, my name a page in a photo album.

I choose a pair of battered black pants and a black turtleneck, the remnants of a bohemian aspiration. I drink a scotch or two. Antiperspirant rolls along my biceps. A small rototiller churns through my stomach.

I'm not nervous, I tell myself. I enjoy nausea and restlessness.

Marjorie lives in an enclave of serenity protected by killer guards and armed dogs. The doorman frisks me before walking me through a metal detector. He looks slightly disappointed when I tell him I haven't brought my dental records. He lets me go only after typing my tissues and coding my DNA.

I ride the silent elevator fourteen floors. The doors open on a vestibule that opens onto two other doors. I hesitate—the lady or the tiger—until one door opens and Marjorie appears.

Dark hair coiled above her head. Her eyes a burnished olive. A black dress caresses her belly like a hand. She smiles, offers me her arm, and we glide into the apartment.

Though I'm only twenty minutes late, everyone else is grazing and chomping when we enter the room. They regard me sternly while Marjorie makes introductions. Some of the men wear blazers and ties, and all the women are in long dresses. I search furtively among them for my secret date, but if she's there, she is well camouflaged.

Marjorie's husband, round and bald, shakes my hand. "So you're the one who deflowered my wife," he says, grinning.

"Wally," scolds Marjorie.

"No hard feelings," he adds.

He tells me Marjorie always felt bad about breaking my heart and my nose but that it looks as if I've recovered well.

"My heart has a slight bump," I say.

He crooks his head and barks. "That's good," he says, pulling a pad of paper and a pen from inside his blazer. "I'll have to use that."

The apartment is large and clean with matching leather sofas, stainless steel blinds, and plush carpeting. Marjorie apologizes for the decorations, but explains that they bought the apartment and everything in it from Wally's agent, who recently declared bankruptcy following his divorce. Even the picture frames still have his family photographs.

"We killed him on the price," says Wally.

A foreign-accented woman interrupts our conversation to tell Marjorie that dinner is ready. I stare after her, and my heart jumps with recognition.

"Clothilde," I say.

"She's wonderful," agrees Marjorie.

"You know her?" says Wally.

If Clothilde has recognized me, she gives no indication. She bustles around the table with another woman serving soup and pouring wine. She has gained weight but otherwise looks unchanged.

I wonder if Clothilde is the person Marjorie wanted me to meet. I survey my bland dinner companions and conclude it couldn't be any of them. They discuss the fat and cholesterol content of foods; they recommend jogging routes around the park; they compare calf muscles. If there were a lawyer among them, she would blind the table with personality.

"Marjorie said you have a friend who's going native," burbles Wally through a mouthful of soup.

"He's searching for his roots," I say.

"Isn't that the plague of this generation?" Wally clucks. "We think we have roots, and they're worth finding."

"Wally's writing a screenplay," says a pale man with an ill-shaved neck.

"It's about the Here and Now," says Wally. "None of this roots crap."

Clothilde withdraws into the kitchen, double doors swinging behind her. I excuse myself for the bathroom and sneak in through the side entry. She is bent over the stove, her face flushed, hands covered with oven mitts.

I say her name. She looks up. She is not surprised.

"I am working," she says.

She shovels tiny chickens onto a platter while I grill her for information. She has not seen *"la famille* Weiss" since Mrs. Weiss fired and reported her to Immigration. Mr. Weiss and Nathan abandoned her before the deportation proceedings. Without a lawyer, fearing banishment from the kingdom, she fled the courthouse during a lunch recess and never returned.

"I am a secret," she says.

The air shimmers woozily. Tiny beads of water line her upper lip. Her hand is damp and small, the bones like birds'.

I will contact the embassy, file for asylum, apply for a green card, I gush. She will not be abandoned. I will never forget.

Clothilde disengages my hand. My zealotry impresses her, but she has to serve dinner. She promises to call my office when she gets a telephone. I am a very sweet boy.

She flutters from the kitchen behind a tray of chickens.

Marjorie regards me warily when I return to the table. "Dating the help is a breach of the social contract," she warns.

I remind her that the date was her idea.

Her laugh arrests dinner conversation. She lowers her voice. "Why would I want you to meet the cleaning lady?" she asks.

I shrug and slice a wing from my chicken. Who can explain the ticking of the heart's machinations?

The doorbell rings. Wally stands, waving Marjorie seated with his wineglass. He ambles toward the door, wobbling slightly like an egg with shoes.

A woman with dark red hair bursts into the room. "Sorry, sorry, sorry," she says breathlessly. "Sorry I'm late."

"Everyone," announces Wally, "this is Kathleen."

"They wrote about assimilation," says Joshua. "I'm writing about excavation. Why did our parents bury their souls, and how can we exhume and breathe life into them?"

I stare at my face looking at his face in the bathroom mirror. Doesn't he have a home, someone else to torment?

"Have you ever thought what it means to be a Jew?" he continues. "Why we've been persecuted and slaughtered yet still managed to survive and pass on a tradition through the generations? Does it bother you that your tradition is now being murdered by Jews who celebrate Christmas and date *shiksas*?"

I tell him it's a date, not a wedding.

"Soon there'll be no Jews left. What Hitler couldn't do, Jews will."

I slam down my razor, spraying tiny hairs and foam across the sink. Joshua steps back, his arm raised as if I might hit him.

"You're such a hypocrite," I say finally. "One day God is dead, Hitler's your hero; the next day you're a rabbi."

We look at each other in surprise.

"These are my beliefs," Joshua says quietly.

"Bullshit," I say, anger building on anger, years of listening to Joshua's theories and exploding brain. "You don't believe anything. Tomorrow you'll finish your dissertation and you'll believe something else."

"How can you ignore our history?"

"What history? We grew up in the suburbs. The only anti-Semitism we've ever seen is on TV."

"But you're a Jew."

"And I'm white. And I'm American. And I'm a lot of other things. You are too."

Joshua looks stricken with a sudden intestinal disorder. "You're trivializing five thousand years of tradition," he says.

"Compared to a million years of humanity."

"But you're not just an animal who's evolved. You're a thinking, reasoning being. To deny your Jewishness is to deny your humanity and to live inauthentically."

"You read that in a book."

"Why do you hate Jews?"

"Me?"

"You."

"I don't hate Jews," I say. *I don't hate them. I don't.*

She's late.

I twirl a wineglass between my forefinger and thumb. I listen to the couple behind me argue whose in-laws are more intrusive. I watch the waiters practicing their lines.

She's changed her mind, forgotten the restaurant, lost my phone number. When I called, I had to remind her who I was. She claimed she knew two Colins.

Marjorie warned she was unreliable. In college Kathleen regularly locked herself out of her studio and would climb the fire escape and crawl along the narrow window ledge to open the door.

Marjorie exaggerates, Kathleen said. They barely knew each other at school. Marjorie camped with Brits and Swedes, a veritable foreign exchange program.

The waiter sneers when I tell him I'm expecting someone. He's seen me before: lonely, forsaken, awaiting an imaginary date. I'll have two beers and then stumble home alone, muttering to myself.

I stare through the glass. Outside a man digs for change to toss in a beggar's cup. His companion, the purple welt of disease on his face, clings tightly. They glance at me, haunted and pursued, their hidden lives exposed like wounds.

"Sorry, sorry, sorry."

Kathleen's voice jars me from the window.

"I'm a terrible mess. I lost the address. Couldn't find your phone number. I'm sorry, sorry, sorry."

I shake myself to life, wave off her apologies. I tell her I enjoy ruminating on loss.

Her hands on the white tablecloth. Nails bitten to the finger. Knuckles flecked with paint.

She scans the menu, and I use the opportunity to breathe. I have forgotten how to make conversation. I search my memory for clever phrases or charming anecdotes. Instead I recommend the tuna.

Her head bows coolly, hair red as medieval tapestry.

"The lamb is also excellent," I venture, buoyed by my initial success with speech.

She winces. "I don't eat anything with eyes."

"They take the eyes out."

Her nose wrinkles into three shades: red, white, pink. She imagines a gaping hole in a lamb chop where an eye used to be. The eye rolling around the plate. "Food by Dalí," she offers.

She orders a glass of wine, quizzing the waiter in great detail about the selection. She settles reluctantly for a California Chardonnay, disappointed that her first choice isn't available by the glass. I suggest she order the entire bottle.

"If you want to order three," she says.

"The Merlot?" I ask, pointing to the third wine on the list.

She explains that she has to drink in intervals of three. Three glasses or three bottles.

"What about three sips?" I suggest helpfully.

"I've done that, in an emergency. Six, actually, after I cut my hand on a broken glass."

It occurs to me she may be serious.

"But I paid for it later," she adds.

There are twenty-seven steps to her apartment, which she takes in nine jumps of three going down, and forty-eight steps to her studio, which she takes one at a time because they're steeper. In her old studio she would walk twelve steps beyond her door and then back again to make sixty-nine. She always hails the third cab she sees and sits in the third subway car from the front. If she eats an appetizer, she has a salad before her main course or a dessert afterward; if her main course doesn't include a vegetable and a potato, she divides it into threes.

She settles back into her chair. "That's probably more than you want to know about me. I thought I'd get the worst out first."

"I don't believe in numerology," I say. "Or astrology," I add. "Now you know the worst about me."

"You're a rationalist," she says. "That's why you're a lawyer."

"Law before order," I say.

"And you're almost blond," she adds.

"Thank you."

"I don't usually date blond men."

I ask her to make an exception for the nearly blond.

"The truth is, I'm not very interested in the blond, blue-eyed, all-American type."

"I never played football," I offer.

"Most of my boyfriends have been Jewish."

I crack an ice cube between my teeth. Or maybe it's my teeth.

"I am a Jew," I say tentatively, my tongue swishing for broken molars.

She smiles. "The lost Anglo-Saxon tribe."

"Really," I say. "*Shema Y'Israel adonai elohainu, adonai echad.*"

She considers my prayer, my call for unity, the rejection of false gods and dualistic philosophies.

"My brother is a doctor," I add. "And my mother wants to meet you."

She scrutinizes me for a minute, her nose wrinkling into threes again. "You're not a good Jew, are you?"

I agree. "I used to think *Kristallnacht* was a brand of bottled water."

"That's not funny," she says. "Six million Jews were murdered."

"Including my great-grandparents."

She presses for details, and I'm embarrassed to admit I don't know. "My father doesn't talk about his family," I say.

"Have you asked?"

"No."

She tells me her father is writing a family history. Since he retired, he spends his days searching records in libraries and court-houses. She grew up in every college town in Illinois and Indiana, wandering with his peripatetic appointments.

"After my mom died," she says, "he couldn't bear settling down without her."

She taps her wineglass three times.

"If he doesn't write, he says he'll forget everything. He wants me to remember."

She pushes her half-eaten fish around her plate. The waiter measures her progress, debating whether to pounce with coffee and dessert.

"I've always envied Jews," she says, shooing the waiter, "their sense of family and tradition. Christians, especially Catholics, talk about family, but really their relationship is with God and Christ. Jews focus on the home while Christians focus on their church."

"All the temples were burned," I say.

She spears her last asparagus. "The day my mother died was my last day in church."

The waiter swoops in to remove her plate. Silver jangles against china, glass against glass. The remains of our meal swept from the white tablecloth.

The dinner crowd dissipates. Our voices swell and ebb in the encroaching solitude. The coffee grows cold, is refilled, and grows cold again. Kathleen laughs, her knuckles pressed to her teeth. White indentations on blue.

"Thanks for dinner," she says as the check arrives. "I had more fun than I thought."

I'm grateful for low expectations.

"Lawyers invite you out all the time," she explains. "You don't look forward to it."

I sign the credit card, tipping generously in case she is watching. She slings a black backpack over one bare shoulder; the strap bites against her neck. I follow her to the door, past a chorus line of busboys and waiters. The maître d' winks at me.

Outside, shiny bits of glass sparkle in the street. A tree blows a breath of fresh air in our direction. A mounted policeman trots past on a horse.

Two vacant taxis slow, but Kathleen ignores them. When I step off the curb, she clutches my elbow. I lower my arm and let them pass. Kathleen hails a third.

"Coming?" she asks as she holds open the door.

We ride in silence up the glimmering avenue. The cab dips and rises like a small boat in choppy water. We sit in the middle of the seat, a thin membrane of air between us, barely enough oxygen to breathe.

"I live here," she says when the cab pulls up to her building.

I reach for her hand, but the door is already open and she is skipping out it. I scramble across the seat. She pops her head back inside, an afterthought, and kisses me quickly on the mouth. "I'll call you," she says, and she is gone, her hair the color of brick as she vanishes behind the wall.

I can do immigration pro bono, Marty tells me, if it doesn't detract from my other work.

"You're still expected to bill your hours on paying clients," he says.

I assure him I will toil into the night, my visored forehead wrinkled with concentration, my fingers stained black with blood and ink.

"Who is this woman?" he asks. "Not a girlfriend, I hope."

I narrate Clothilde's ill-fated history.

Recognition roils his brow like a cannonball shot into a swimming pool. "Steven Weiss's girlfriend?" he says. "The catwoman? She ruined his life."

I protest that Mr. Weiss left Clothilde without money, a job, or a place to live.

"I know Steve Weiss. Everybody knows Steve Weiss. Steve only wanted what was best for his wife and his family."

I keep my mouth shut.

"Steve may have made some mistakes," Marty continues. "Who hasn't? But our families go way back. His father was my Hebrew-school teacher."

I can't help myself. "You're Jewish?" I say.

A bird flutters inside his cheek. "My mother is," he says vaguely.

"But you went to Hebrew school."

"Years ago."

"When you were a kid."

"When I was Marty *Rosen*."

Already I understand as he rushes into an explanation: a secular society; unfounded prejudice; easier to spell.

"Don't say anything to Bob," he concludes. "Do me a favor. It would make him uncomfortable."

"I'm a Jew," I say, my daily declaration like vitamins.

The bird flutters again. "You're kidding."

"*Cha'yim*. My parents called me Colin."

He stares at me, as if he could read it in my cells. His lips locked between faith and incredulity. I smile, and then he laughs, the suppressed tension erupting in a staccato burst. He wipes his face with the back of his palm and explodes again, laughing hysterically as tears roll from his eyes.

"That's good," he says. "Oh, that's good."

He knows I can keep a secret.

We lean into the concrete wall, her thigh between my legs, my hands raked across her back. She finds my mouth, my nose, my eyes. I sink onto her hip, riding her kisses like a swelling wave.

"I should go," she says.

"Stay," I say.

"We're on the street."

Someone whistles from the shadows. A man and a woman slow, mark our presence, continue past. A bus grinds down the avenue.

"Come inside," I say.

"It's my apartment."

"Invite me then."

She breaks away, leaving me knuckling the wall. "There's work," she says. "And sleep."

I can file my appeal elsewhere, she advises. No additional evidence will win my suit.

"Really," she says, pulling me from her sweater like a bur. "I have to go."

I consider sobbing, pleading for mercy. Life is short and we all die young and there's no one to write the obituary. Without a past, some human thread, the finely sifted sands of our lives are dust motes on a wing chair. Blow them off so someone else can sit down.

She kisses me once more. The faint tracing of her lips like an outline on my mouth. My teeth feel too large for my gums; they press stupidly forward while the rest of my face aches to catch up.

I am alone on an empty sidewalk.

I trudge down the street, beating my penis into a plowshare. She loves me; she loves me not. Each step a promise fulfilled or broken.

At the corner a one-legged man asks for some spare change. He tells me the government is trying to kill him. I fish through my pockets and hand him all my coins. He stares unseeing into his palms and curses me.

I trip up the avenue. He calls after me, screaming my name. The tortured and insane know who I am.

"Colin! Colin! Colin!"

I leap at the hand on my wrist.

"I've never made anyone run so fast," says Kathleen.

I stammer an explanation involving one-legged men and political conspiracies. She nods, preoccupied by her own predicament.

She's lost her keys, probably somewhere in her studio. There's no doorman, and the owner is a corporation in New Jersey.

"It's not the most romantic invitation," she says. "But it's late."

Stunningly, like the advent of spring, weeks of dull rain followed by a sudden burst of color, I realize that she's inviting herself to stay at my apartment.

"It's just for the night," she continues, with what I now recognize as nervousness, "until I find someone to unlock my studio."

"Sure, sure," I reassure her, just as nervously. "I'll sleep on the couch."

Her wrists snap. She looks up. My heart stops.

"You don't need to do that," she says.

Kathleen does everything in threes.

golem

We walk south past forgotten piers, abandoned cars, leaking tunnels.
Across the river the failed promise of suburbia sinks into the marsh:
Apartment buildings crumble; luxury homes burst into flames. Overhead, birds drop from exhaustion into pools of oil. A giant billboard
billows into the air like a discarded tissue.

Kathleen's paint-flecked knuckles guide my elbow past the detritus of urban existence. "I moved to the city at the worst time in
my life," she says.

I step gingerly over a human form slumped across the sidewalk.

"Everything frightened me: noises from the street, clanks in the
pipes in my studio, the subway."

"The subway still frightens me."

"I couldn't drive a car for three years. I was afraid of going
downhill."

"You took a lot of cabs."

"I was afraid to sit in a cab. I felt out of control. I'd stare out
the window and pretend the street was moving, not me."

"No wonder you felt out of control."

"I didn't date. I didn't work. I avoided everyone I knew."

We step around a pool of dark liquid. It could be anything.

"My father worried about me. But I worried about him. Once,

when I came home for Christmas, I found him sitting by himself at the window, staring into space. It was Christmas Day, we were supposed to go to my aunt's, and he was staring out the window. And the shades were drawn."

I measure the clicks as our heels strike pavement. She is silent for two long blocks. When she speaks, her voice drifts to the surface.

"When I left, I swore I wouldn't come back. I didn't want to be reminded all the time." She breathes. "It was bad enough being here with all the decay."

I follow her arm across the dirty street where a crumpled man hunches over the embers of a trash can fire.

"But the next time I saw my father, he seemed fine. He had even started dating. It was as if he had gotten all the mourning out of his system and was ready for life again."

We stop in front of a squat gray building. Kathleen jingles her keys.

"So I began to think about the dead. And then I started painting."

"Now is the time for all good men to come to the aid of their beleaguered clients," says Stockard.

He directs a barge filled with documents into my office. Dump it anywhere, he tells the skipper. A flood of paper rises to my desk like an angry tide. I work until the early morning, sandbags stacked around my head. But at dawn all is lost; my possessions float out to sea.

"This is the big one," says Stockard, "the one that will make or break you. I'm counting on you, Stone."

"Thank you, sir," I say, clicking my heels and responding in my best military fashion as I always do when Stockard gives me one of his "rousing" speeches.

I hunker down behind the sandbags. From best I can determine, the case involves a suit by beneficiaries of a pension plan against their bankrupt former employer. They claim the employer owes them their pensions; the employer claims that it is bankrupt.

Not too bankrupt to pay our legal fees, however.

Thousands of retired clerks, typists, and sales assistants eat watered-down soup and scrapple while Stockard and I frequent elegant midtown restaurants at our client's expense to discuss its plight.

"The whole system's unconstitutional," belches Stockard after he drains his third martini. "You can't impose future indeterminate liabilities on a reorganizing entity."

I suggest that perhaps the bankruptcy laws are being used to avoid obligations already assumed in the collective bargaining process. In that sense the liabilities are past, not future.

"You sound like my son with that socialist hogwash," says Stockard.

I imagine Stockard's hippie son, parading about his family's Park Avenue apartment. Karl Marx in one hand, the *Social Register* in the other. Get a job, his father screams. Get me a summer house, yells the son.

Stockard rises unsteadily from his seat. "You're my senior associate on this one," he says, scrawling his name across the check.

I tell him I'm not worthy. I'm incapable of commanding legions of minty-faced younger lawyers and mewly paralegals. I tremble before file clerks.

"Rose is off; you're on," he continues, ignoring me.

I scramble to keep up with him as he lurches across the restaurant. Waiters dive for safety. The maître d' lashes himself to the mast.

Slow down, I plead. Has the client decided that well-fed inexpensive lawyers are cheaper than hungry expensive ones?

Stockard shakes his head. "He's been passed over."

We skirt an air-conditioning vent. A cold breeze vents up my leg. The air smells like plastic.

"He was good. And a hard worker. But he wasn't partnership material." Stockard combs his scouring-pad hair with his fingers.

I imagine Marty with a sack on his back, his lawbooks making awkward rectangular bulges, his thumb out on Wall Street. Nobody rides for free, honks a passing suit.

"I'll get you a couple of first-years," says Stockard. "Your own sharecroppers."

I nod, still in shock.

"Just be careful you don't make any promises when you fuck them up the ass."

"He screwed me," says Marty. "I worked my ass off for him, and he screwed me. He'll screw you too."

Marty rifles through his files. Papers fly into boxes, the trash, onto the floor.

"Eight years I worked for that bastard. That psychopath. That anti-Semite."

I tell Marty that over seventy partners voted.

Marty looks at me: Poor, poor, dumb, naïve Colin. "I was his boy," he says bitterly.

He can't throw everything away, I insist. I may need his files.

"I never should've been a lawyer." He crumples a piece of paper, shoots for the wastebasket, and misses. "In college I had my own business," he says, his voice thick with memory. "I rented this little storefront in town and made bread. Pumpernickel, rye, sour dough, whole wheat, raisin. Fresh bread. You couldn't get it up there."

A worthy pursuit, I tell him. Wholesome food for the masses.

"The kids loved it. They loved bread." He misses another basket. "And I was making something." He looks at his hands. Soft. White. Doughy. "Do you think Stockard knew?"

"How could he?"

"You didn't tell him?"

"Of course not. You told me not to."

He shakes his head. "I can't think of another reason. I billed thirty-two hundred hours last year."

I claim that Stockard is an equal opportunity bigot.

Marty misses for the third time. "It comes back to haunt you, doesn't it?" he says.

We both look at the growing pile of paper.

"Today isn't my lucky day," he says. He sinks to the floor, crumpling first to his knees, then to his elbows, then collapsing facedown on the carpet.

"Marty?" I venture.

A howl, like a dog in a deep well, emanates from his prostrate body. I stand awkwardly above him, uncertain whether to approach or keep my distance. I've never touched him. What does his skin feel like? His secretary peers over her cubicle; several paralegals pause in the hallway. I shut the door.

"Marty?" I try again, tapping him lightly on the shoulder.

"Awwwwlllll." He shudders.

"It's nothing," I say. "It's just a job."

"Hooooooooollll," he says.

I look around his office for something to slap him or shock him from his catatonia. Gold-lettered bound volumes line his bookshelf. *Big Corporation v. Giant Corporation. In re Huge Corporate Bankruptcy.* One of those would knock him senseless. I push them aside and nearly topple a small silver frame. Picking it up, I notice a mousy woman with indeterminate colored hair holding a tiny baby. The baby's luminous face glows with an unearthly shimmer, as if it has sucked all of its mother's vitality. But the mother, whose complexion recalls Nosferatu, looks like a grateful victim.

"*Your son loves you,*" I whisper to Marty, guessing at the baby's sex.

Marty's howls taper to whimpers. His legs stop twitching. He raises his head slightly like a sleeping dog sniffing dinner.

"Daughter," he says.

"She's beautiful," I say.

He's alive now, sitting up and gesticulating with one hand while the other fishes through his wallet for more photos of his androgynous progeny. He's got the entire set, a collector's trove, buy 'em, sell 'em, swap 'em. I smile vaguely, fearful of what I've loosed, while he steamrolls through a litany of miracles, promises, and hopes.

"She's not going to be a lawyer, I'll tell you that." He concludes.

In the promised land, I remind him, there won't be a need for lawyers. The lion will lie with the lamb, and disputes will be resolved through the use of laser-guided weaponry.

"I hope you're right," he says. "But until then she's going into medicine."

We agree that children are the future.

He takes my hand, and for one moment I am afraid that he will start crying or kiss me. *Or will he explode?*

"Colin . . ." he begins. His eyes are misty and round with self-pity. I stare out at the skyline: City of hope, city of dreams; bring me your tired, your poor, your wretched refuse.

"Thank you," he concludes.

I look back tentatively, a bomb squad detective unbelieving of his good fortune. "You'll be okay?" I ask.

"I'll be fine," he says.

I close the door behind me and run for cover.

Lucifer leers, his elongated face a Modigliani nightmare. Smoldering fires billow black soot. Sulfur and iron rain on a charred landscape. The dead rise from watery graves.

"What do you think?" asks Kathleen.

Her studio smells like a truck stop: hydrocarbons and coffee. Paint chips from the walls and ceiling. The floor bulges where a pipe has burst. The windows are cracked and brittle. But sunlight washes the dusty corners and brackish sills with a yellow glow. And the warm promise of day illumines the dark beads of oil in her brushstrokes.

"It's based on medieval representations of the golem," she explains, "the Kabbalists' zombie."

"I know all about golem," I say, slightly annoyed at her lecturing tone.

"The golem is the material rendering of a spiritual reality," she continues, pausing only slightly to scrutinize my mood. "I thought it ironic that in all the representations I saw, he was always male and always looked like a zombie."

I finger a corner of the canvas.

"In a way he seemed to me an allegory for spiritual torpor rather than infinite wonder. More of a metaphor for modernity than anything else. Lack of faith, decay, poverty, AIDS. He's a walking embodiment of the ills of our age."

The fabric bristles against my fingertips.

"He arises, like Christ, bearing the sins of our age."

"What does he do with them?" I ask.

"I don't know. I'm not a theologian."

"Does he carry them to heaven in a sack?"

"I doubt it."

"Maybe he packs them in a truck and leaves it double-parked near St. Peter's."

"Maybe."

"Or maybe he dumps them in an illegal landfill."

"Colin," Kathleen says. She raises one battered knuckle to brush at her eyes.

"I'm just expounding a theory," I say.

"Don't get angry."

"I'm not angry," I say angrily.

"We don't have to talk about it."

"About what? What are we talking about?"

Kathleen edges toward her easel. She pushes her sweatshirt up her forearms. "Did I say something?" she says.

I'm surrounded by conspiracy theories, creation theories, consciousness theories, extinction theories. No one ventures outside without a mythology strapped to his forehead like a prosthesis.

"Marty didn't make partner," I say.

"That's what you're upset about?" says Kathleen.

"He thinks Stockard's an anti-Semite."

Kathleen's nose wrinkles. She taps her knuckles three times against her teeth. "I believe it," she says.

"That's ridiculous. Stockard didn't even know Marty was Jewish. And even if he did, that wouldn't affect the decision. There're dozens of Jews in the firm."

"Don't count on it."

"What does that mean?"

"It means 'don't count on it.' "

We stare belligerently at each other: infidel and apostle. One false move and the scimitars rattle.

"People don't discriminate against Jews," I say. "Blacks, yes. Women, okay. Gays. But no one cares if you're a Jew anymore."

"Six million died so you don't have to care," she says softly.

I sputter helplessly in the face of her blatant violation of the International Rules for Domestic Debate.

"I'm the Jew," I finally manage.

"You wouldn't think so," Kathleen continues, lashing my prostrate body. "You've forgotten everything."

"My great-grandparents were killed by Nazis."

"Your badge of authenticity."

"At least I didn't grow up in Podunk, Illinois."

She shades pink, then red, an angry bloom that powers her electric hair.

"You're a snot, you know that? You're not very nice and you're a snot and you're filled with self-hatred and mockery." She slaps her hands against her jeans. "Now get out. You bore me."

I stand in the headlights, frozen, my body tense with flight. I have violated some unwritten code sworn to by those who occupy the vast land between the coasts. A fealty to earth and its bounty and the solemnity of soy.

"Get OUT!" she commands.

I edge backward toward the door, tripping over a canvas that rips with a sickening moan. When I lift my foot, a painting is attached to my leg like a rectangular manacle. I hobble a few steps, trying to shuck the canvas with my good leg, and fall on my face with a loud crack.

"Oh, my God," says Kathleen enthusiastically. "Did you break your nose?"

I feel my face, my teeth, my jaw. Everything seems in its proper place. I shake a leg. I shake my other leg. The painting wobbles.

"I cracked the frame," I say fearfully, anticipating another barrage.

She looks at me aghast. "You tore the canvas."

"I'm sorry. I'm really, really sorry."

"It's not my painting," she says, her fury suddenly dissipated. "It's Sara's. We share the space."

I realize that the jumble of boxes and old auto parts I thought Kathleen had inherited with the studio are, in fact, *art*. My foot pokes through the exact center of a painted tire.

"Will she kill me?" I ask.

"We'll tell her you're the great-grandson of Holocaust victims. She'll understand."

Kathleen helps slip the tire off my leg. Her nails are chewed flat and rimmed with paint. Her hands are red and recently scrubbed. I can smell turpentine in the creases of her palm.

"I didn't mean what I said about Illinois," I say.

"Sure you did," she says, her eyes grayer than green. "But you were wrong. I was born in Boring. And grew up in Normal." She twists a thread of hair in one finger, pulls it tight. "At least I haven't forgotten where I'm from."

✿   ✿   ✿

My sister warns she may get married. "I'm telling you," she says, "just in case."

She's practically swimming in David's leather jacket, a hermit crab in a conch shell.

"I'm not telling Mom," she says. Instead, she claims, she'll hop a bus for Vegas and find an Elvis impersonator.

Our mother would never forgive her, I tell her.

"I know. She'd hate the Elvis impersonator."

She drains her coffee cup, looks around for the waitress, signals for a refill, and stirs in two packets of sugar.

Slowly, like a man rising from sleep and stitching together the pieces of his dream, I tell her about Kathleen. She nods, the edge of a smile bending her lips.

"I knew you'd get over Elisabet," she says.

I agree before I know what I am doing, then vigorously shake my head in denial. The combined convulsions lead to sudden whiplash and paralysis. If I could move the left side of my mouth, I'd tell her she doesn't know what she's talking about; I haven't thought about Elisabet for decades; I never think about Elisabet; I don't miss Elisabet; Elisabet who?

Instead I say out of the right side, "Until I met Kathleen, I wasn't sure."

"We worried about you."

A symposium on my emotional well-being worries me. What were they all worrying about? Who was worrying?

"First Nell, then Elisabet," Rebecca says, ignoring my questions. "You've had a lot of bad luck with women."

"Nell wasn't my girlfriend," I protest, desperately trying to avoid the badge: Bad Luck with Women.

"I said you might be gay."

I straighten my spine, suck in my cheeks, join the YMCA. But the men eye me strangely in the pool: They worry about me; they know I have Bad Luck with Women.

"Of course I wouldn't care." Rebecca reassures me. "You're my brother."

"What about Marjorie?" I manage.

"Didn't she dump you for some Brit?" Rebecca asks.

"It was mutual," I say.

"You dumped each other for a Brit? The same Brit?"

"We broke up."

"All we were saying is that you were attracted to women who were elusive."

I explain that by pursuing these women, I was attempting to gain control over my mother. Or conversely, I was fleeing my mother and was attracted to the most distant women I could find: foreign women, women with boyfriends, dead women.

"But now you're in love."

In love. I roll the words in my mouth like an oddly shaped candy.

"I love Kathleen," I say, experimenting with the words.

Rebecca claps. "You should see your face," she says. "You look like you've had a revelation."

A luminous spirit rises in the material world. The infinite is composed of single spheres, it says. There is magic in the numbers. Look both ways before you cross the street. Wash behind your ears.

Rebecca and I blink, clear our noses and throats, wipe our eyes. We are so happy we can barely breathe. Gas canisters rain tears. The National Guard must be called in to suppress our riotousness. Lawlessness prevails.

"Have you told Mom?" coughs Rebecca, emerging from the smoke.

"I have to tell Kathleen first," I say.

"That's a close call. How did you decide?"

She's funny, my sister. She claims it runs in the family like an incapacity for sugar, a nerve disorder. Bad diet, inbreeding, poor grooming habits. We are born free, she says, but everywhere our genes are bound by dumb wit.

"I asked Mom."

I have often walked down the street she lives, but I have never been able to sing as well as my father. He serenades my mother from beneath her fire escape as the neighbors giggle, poke each other in the ribs, then give him a rousing ovation. If only, like Cyrano, he could put the notes in my mouth.

My feet scuff the sidewalk outside her apartment. I scrape the words from my throat. Trill through the scales. My larynx has never been cleaner, but my mouth feels like the inside of a sandbox.

Sing! The rousing melodies from the homeland. Songs of joy and jubilation. Every man must lighten his heart with his own true tonelessness. No matter that he sounds like a screeching bat. Love admits no hearing impediments.

The intercom squawks its musical accompaniment. I push through the clanking door, skating over a floor of menus and discount flyers. The hallway smells like a potpourri of Asian cuisines: ginger, lemon grass, curry, and garlic.

I clomp up the stairs, counting threes aloud. At twenty-seven I stop, an odd satisfaction with the unity of numbers. Nine times three. Three times three times three. Three to the power of three. And three itself, indivisible by any other number.

I ring the doorbell. A single chord comprised of three tones: root plus major third and perfect fifth.

Her gleaming eye through the peephole. A ruby strand of hair. Nose. Mouth. Lips. Nervous fingers on my neck. We kiss in the hallway, her hands on my fluttering collarbone, my hands on my fluttering heart. A door slams. She jumps. I pull her off my toes.

"Guess what," she sighs. "We're locked out."

"Do you have your toothbrush?"

She shakes her head. "Can I use yours?"

Forever and ever and ever.

"Nothing lasts," says Stockard. "One day you're king of the hill, the next you're bottom of the heap."

I admire his profound and learned observations.

"You make them pay while you can," he continues, encouraged by my fawning obsequiousness. "Put a little aside. A war chest. Later you can cash it in. That's good business advice. It's good personal advice."

I reassure him that I have a personal bomb shelter in which I've dried and reconstituted every kindness.

"Consolidated didn't plan for the future; now they've got unfunded pension liabilities. Rose didn't plan either; now he's doing PI work."

Has Marty gone over to the other side? Has he really taken up with the ambulance chasers, his toll-free number hanging in the subway next to 1-800-MD-TUSCH?

"He found himself a personal injury firm," explains Stockard. "It's in his blood."

My ears buzz while my head lolls autistically. I cannot process certain information in my brain; my hemispheres are split, and no connection will render them whole. Stockard continues to talk, but the words are just noise. If I close my eyes, the babel will go away.

"Don't worry," concludes Stockard, misinterpreting my panicked expression. "He'll survive. He's the chosen people."

I could punch him in the head; I could twist his nose between my fingers until the cartilage snaps; I could kick him hard in the groin.

"Freed from bondage and left to wander the desert," I say.

Stockard is thick and slow, his reactions dulled from his days as a football star at a minor men's college. Too many sacks, his head colliding with the frozen earth. Too many beers after the game, his future wife dragging herself and then him out of the back of her father's automobile. His military bearing is a sham; he dodged service with a feigned eye injury. His father-in-law bought him a spot at the law school, then situated him at the same firm where the father-in-law had been a partner since the War Between the States. Two wives later, Stockard himself made partner.

Now he looks at me, amusement slowly lighting his dull eyes.

"That's funny," he says. "Very clever."

Forty years, I think, it took to reach the Promised Land.

"I love you," she says.

Her skin makes my leg jump. "What?" I manage.

"Please," she says. "Don't make me say it again."

Her hair fans the pillow like a velvet curtain. A light spray of freckles across her shoulders and chest. She draws a hand like a veil beneath her eyes.

I curl into her. "Why?" I ask coyly.

"Because it's embarrassing."

Shame is no basis for a lasting relationship, I tell her. Don't lock me in the closet with the Phantom and other Broadway freaks. Who will hear my song?

"Not you," she says, taking pity on my cracked and tuneless melody. "I'm embarassed by what I said."

"Why, then?" I brighten.

She blinks three times, tiger lashes beating her eyes into focus.

"Because you're a Jew," she says.

My ears buzz like a harp. I have never been an object of religious devotion. Will I have to hang from a car mirror, my eyes shifting with the view?

"It's shorthand, I know." She rushes into explanation. "I don't mean all Jews are like you or even that you're like all Jews. It's just those qualities I associate with Jewishness: humor, learning, family, a sense of the absurd. Probably all wrongly, but there you have it." She bites nervously at a fingernail. "Call me an anti-Semite."

"You said I was a bad Jew."

"I did. And you are. I love the good parts of you."

"The Jewish parts."

"Those especially," she says, finding me beneath the blanket.

"Ah," I say.

Her lovely back. Her champagne skin. She rises in the east.

I am beneath her. I am beside her. I am inside her.

She groans, a rib-creaking moan from an unearthly body.

"Do you love me?" she asks as she carries me from the bed and into a violet night.

The sky opens, and the stars fall like rain. We climb across the city, into the heavens, a Chagall bridegroom and bride. We sail beyond unsettled regions, strange lands of unfamiliar sights. Animals sniff uncertainly as we pass overhead. Birds avoid us. Land and sky and water, a blurred purple veil. Sound is forgotten. Light is all that remains. And then even the light is gone.

"Yes," I say. "Oh, God, yes."

the
law of
return

Come back to the Church this Christmas, bids the advertisement on the side of a bus.

Kathleen and I wait for the air to clear of diesel fumes, then cross the street into the park.

"We practically live together anyway," I say.

"It's not the same," she protests. "We each have our space. If we fight, I can leave."

"You have your studio," I say.

"I can't sleep there."

"It's a waste of money." I try another tack.

"My grant pays for it."

Does anyone work anymore? I wonder. She can't live off the largess of the state forever. Eventually they'll cut the budget, eviscerate the arts, put their money where the money is.

She kicks a loose piece of gravel. "I need time," she says.

"Time. Space. It's like dating Albert Einstein."

"Ask him to move in with you."

A breeze sifts through the trees like the rustling of skirts. Two women jog by us. A man and his dog bark at each other. A riderless horse thunders past.

"I'm a man," I say. "I have space. I want to share it with you."

Kathleen frowns. "And why does it have to be your apartment?"

"Yours is a closet."

"It's cozy."

"You barely have room for a bed."

"I have two chairs."

We climb a short path to the reservoir. I stare out over the water, gray and flat as a steel door. We need more than two chairs, I want to tell her; we need a dining room set. Life is not potluck; bring a dish and sit on the floor. There's salad bowls and soup tureens and gilded china patterns. People expect more than nuts.

"I can't live cluttered by your possessions," she says.

"I'll sell everything I own."

She wraps her fingers around a wire loop in the chain-linked fence. She leans back, and the fence puckers toward her. She lets go, and the fence rebounds, sending her stumbling backward.

"Kathleen!" I warn as a three-hundred-pound jogger swerves to miss her.

She straightens. Her face flushed a shade of her hair. The jogger looks back, shakes his head at the eccentricities of the human species.

"I'm not moving," she says.

A pigeon flaps about drunkenly. Two men pass behind me. One declares that everything is relative.

In an expanding universe there are few constants. Gravity. Mass. Density. The attraction of foreign bodies. Who can argue with the law?

I take Kathleen's hand. "Don't move," I agree. "It's too dangerous."

We continue our slow trajectory through the park. The immovable object and her orbiting companion.

Stockard slaps a time sheet on my desk.

"One hundred seventy-eight hours," he says.

"It's pro bono," I say, reviewing the records.

"I know what it is," he says. "I want to know *why* it is."

His breath smells of alcohol. His hands rest calmly on the edge of my desk, but his head sways slightly.

I give him the lite version of Clothilde's immigration woes. Tiny beads of sweat pearl across his forehead.

"I never approved this," he growls.

"Marty did."

His neck bulges from his collar. A vein swells in his temple. I rest my finger on the paramedic alert button. Imminent injury, to himself or me, looms.

"That little shit had zero authority," he says, quivering like a taut string.

I tell him that all the right people signed the proper forms.

"I don't care who signed what. You're not wasting our time on some French maid."

"She's not French."

"Whatever she is."

"I billed twenty-five hundred hours for the firm," I say.

"And you owe us one hundred seventy-eight."

"We have a commitment to pro bono."

"Save that crap for the law students. We've got a motion for summary judgment to oppose."

After advancing Clothilde's case to the Board of Immigration Appeals, I know I can't abandon it. But to complain to the partners about Stockard would be like complaining to the barracudas about the piranha. I decide to take the only action available.

"I'll drop it," I lie. "Consolidated needs me."

"Good boy."

He pauses by my door, his military frame blocking all egress. "One thing about the French," he says, "they know how to lie on their backs." Then he turns and stumbles from my office.

A day in the country. My parents at the kitchen table. The suburbs have never seemed cleaner, more rustic, positively quaint. A herd of deer gambol in the backyard. Songbirds mate out front. All is well under a smog-free sun.

Kathleen chats amiably with my mother. No unsheathed swords or broken bottles. My father asks about work. I describe the summary judgment opposition I've just written, the impending document production, the big client who keeps me on a leash, the partner whose poop I scoop.

"He's the terror of the firm," Kathleen interrupts.

"I'm not," I say modestly.

"Not you," says Kathleen. "Stockard. The anti-Semite."

"Kathleen," I plead. The conversation veers dangerously toward the abyss. Another moment, and we will teeter into the pit of international conspiracy and papal collusion.

"You said so yourself."

"I said he terrorized his associates."

"Why don't they fire him?" says my mother.

I explain that you can't fire a partner; he owns the firm. Stockard is no worse than most, just slightly more monomaniacal.

"But he's an anti-Semite," my mother says.

"He's not," I say, glaring at Kathleen. "Anyway, what he does in his private time is his own business. He could collect Nazi memorabilia for all I care."

"Does he?" asks my mother.

"Yes," I say. "Jews' teeth too."

"Your great-grandparents were killed by Nazis," Kathleen reminds me.

Everywhere I turn I'm confronted by the Third Reich. Their shiny uniforms folded in a shoebox beneath my bed.

"Actually your great-grandfather survived the concentration camps," says my father.

Like Lord Chamberlain, my father will concoct anything to keep the peace.

"But after the war," he embellishes, "they tied him to a horse and dragged him through the streets."

"Dad?" I say.

"The Nazis?" asks Kathleen.

"His neighbors." My father warms to his task. He claims his grandfather lived in a small village in the Ukraine. His wife, my great-grandmother, died there in 1938. My great-grandfather outlasted most of the Nazi occupation by bribing other farmers. But when he ran out of money and farm animals, they turned him in.

He survived Treblinka only to be killed when he returned to the village after the war.

"You never told me," Kathleen says.

"I didn't know." I beseech my father. If I don't stop him, he'll have cousins fighting in the Resistance and uncles working the Underground.

"After the war my father got a letter from his sister," he says. "It's the only time I ever saw him cry."

I'm afraid my father will start crying himself. Instead, Kathleen bursts into tears.

For an instant all movement is frozen in Kathleen's hands. Then, as one, we extend our arms. We spill over the tabletop. We gather cloth in our outstretched hands. We fold into each other's palms.

"I'm sorry, sorry, sorry," she sniffs, waving us back into our seats.

"You dear girl," says my mother.

"I imagine the lives," says Kathleen.

My mother drapes her arm over Kathleen's shoulder. From somewhere a tissue is produced. Kathleen wipes her eyes, then excuses herself for the bathroom. My mother leads the way.

I clear the plates from the table. My father sinks back into his chair.

"She's an artist," I explain.

"She'll be fine," he says. "They're always fine."

He hums softly from his favorite musical. I don't remind him that he's not getting married in the morning. Not in a church. Not on time.

"Why didn't you tell me?" I ask.

He looks across the kitchen, into the snow and wind. "My father walked with his cousin through Russia to Finland. In the winter. That's about all I knew."

I can feel a tiny click near the bone in my elbow as I set the plates in the sink. The slightest mechanical twinge, reminding me that we are, after all, nothing but hinges and screws, banging loosely in bad weather. We rust; we stick; we crack. Only our families hold us together. Glue, oil, and paint. This is called love.

"He didn't talk about it." My father continues. "Neither did my mother. They forgot, or made themselves forget."

"Grandma said she couldn't speak Polish," I remember.

"They spoke Yiddish, or English. They were Americans."

"Did anyone die?" I ask. "In the Holocaust?"

"Everyone died," my father says.

I sit down next to him, so close I can hear his eyes blink. "Tell me," I say.

Another marathon walk, circumnavigating the island. Kathleen impervious to the miles. I struggle to keep up, my shoes tattered and soleless. My breath ragged and short.

"Absurdity is the human condition," she says. "We push rocks up the hill and they tumble back down." She steps into the street, narrowly averting a collision with a bicycle messenger. "There's no explanation for the irrational."

I scratch at the scratchy hat on my head, pull it over my eyes.

"You spend all day crafting words," she continues, "building a fort around the reasonable. When was the last time you did something really foolish at work?"

"I lied to Stockard."

"Good. Lies are good."

I never thought I would love a woman who encouraged lying, numerology, and neurological disorders. I was always such an obedient boy.

"Love is an absurd leap," she says. "I think Kierkegaard said that. Or maybe Sartre. It doesn't matter." She grasps my left arm and drags me through traffic. "Moses brought the word to the people of Israel while Aaron made a golden calf. Everyone remembers Moses. Why? What's so great about limiting the world to ten rules? Moses was the lawgiver. But Aaron was an artist. An artist, a good artist, isn't reductive. Aaron knew that. The Jews were wandering in the desert without a plan, wondering whether they'd made a serious mistake. Aaron gave them something to gaze upon, something beautiful, an image that expressed all their hopes and fears. In the end it was too much responsibility; they would rather have rules than rely on their own imagination. They were afraid of irrationality, of making an absurd leap.

"But think about them, for just a minute, dancing in the desert with fires burning all around, the golden calf gleaming—everyone singing, everyone drinking, the pure joy of living."

She stops on the sidewalk. Her face is flushed. Her hair is the reddest I've ever seen, a fiery sun gathered in a bundle atop her head. Several strands fall loose around her face. Her lips are dark as the inside of a bottle of claret. Her eyes shimmer with the reflection of a thousand flashbulbs. I have never loved her more than I do at that moment.

"I found it," she says.

"Found what?" I ask, imagining religious cults, Eastern sects, strange liturgical rites. She has crossed into the light.

"The perfect apartment."

I fly into the dwarf city of the north on a mission of utmost banality: Deliver the documents or die. As the plane taxis to the gate, I can see my brother's angular face pressed to a terminal window. It's not me he's looking at, I know, but the complicated maneuverings of jets and their airport companions. I fold my newspaper and slip it back into my briefcase.

Alexandra waits with him as I step into the noisy hush of the waiting room. He mentioned her casually, as if she were just a friend, but their clasped hands tells me they have dissolved their friendship and reincorporated as a different entity. Rebecca threatens marriage every day, but her siblings may beat her to it.

"Brother," David greets me. His skinny arms and bobbing head shock me like an old photo of my father come to life. Alexandra smiles at us, and I realize we must look to the world like two photos of our father, shaded differently but from the same album. After years of thinking of myself as the blond one out, I know I am simply a lighter piece of toast.

His dark eyes pinched with fatigue. He closes them as Alexandra drives and I detail my important mission. He nods periodically, but he could be dreaming. Alexandra glances at me once in the rearview mirror. Our eyes agree on a silent pact; years ago we both were much younger.

"Have you seen Joshua?" I ask David.

He awakens. "The rabbi?" He says he saw Joshua at a movie

theater last week. "I didn't know they were allowed to watch movies," he adds.

"He's not a rabbi," I say defensively. "He's getting a Ph.D. in philosophy."

David shrugs. "He looked like a rabbi."

When did Joshua metamorphosize into a bearded and black-hatted figure, an austere version of Jacob, our Hebrew-school teacher? We ate the same food, drank the same beer, kissed the same girl. But when the party ended, Joshua stayed behind to scold the parents.

"I have to see him," I say, with a sudden, piercing longing, like a thirst for salt, the oasis of my adolescence.

David is fully awake now. His eyes, as we sit in traffic, are hazel, the same color as our father's. "He may not want to see you, you know. You're the unwashed."

I've trembled under the *mohel*'s grip. I've blessed the wine and bread. I've said the prayers over the sacred parchment. Who is Joshua to decide what's holy?

"This is America," I say. "I can do whatever I want."

Once, when we were kids, David ran me down with a sled. He didn't mean to do it, he lost control on the snow, but as he careened toward me, his face expressed the same sequence of emotions: confusion, concern, acceptance, delight.

"He was always a pain-in-the-ass know-it-all," David says. "Tell him to fuck off." Then he closes his eyes again.

Forget Stockard's documents, I decide. I've more important business to attend to.

His house is like every other house on the block: three-story, wood-shingled, a small balcony at each floor. No banners proclaim the Messiah's imminent arrival; no Repent! signs flutter from his windows. A small *mezuzah* hangs crookedly along the front doorframe. The house, the street, the entire neighborhood look like a photograph from my father's childhood. If I squint, I can make out my grandfather clomping up the steps.

I ring the doorbell. The stairs creak. Joshua coughs.

He opens the door and takes two steps onto the porch before he stops. "Colin Stone, I presume."

He is not unlike his former self, only darker and hairier. His apple cheeks speckled brown. A *yarmulke* perched atop an unruly shag mop.

"Come in," he says.

I have not yet spoken.

"I'll make some tea," he offers.

"You know I can't stand tea," I say finally.

"I thought you might have changed."

Did we argue? I can't remember. I claimed the world was round; he said it was spherical. We were held by gravity; spinning and spinning and spinning. When we let go, we tumbled to our feet.

"What transgression darkens our city's fair gates?" he asks once we're inside.

I display the stack of documents, the standing invitation to deliver, my marching orders. "Bankruptcy," I say.

"Moral or financial?"

An ancient resentment flares like an arthritic joint. If I move too much, I'm liable to crack. Instead I bind my bones with a baleful glare and tell him.

"I saw the young Hippocrates last week," Joshua continues blithely.

"I'm staying with him. He sends his love."

"Sweet kid."

"He's a doctor. He has a girlfriend."

"I saw her. She's a beauty."

"She reminds me of Nell."

A breath passes between us, fainter than memory, fading into a teapot's whistle.

Joshua rises.

"Do you think about her?" I ask.

"Sometimes."

How could I know that years later her death would mark the beginning of history, not the end, the coda to an era when anything was possible? Or that I would be sitting with my friend of five thousand years marking it?

"It's her parents I think about," I say.

Joshua pours hot water into two glass teacups. "To lose a child," he agrees.

"She said your parents wouldn't talk to her."

"She said that?" He drops two cubes into the water.

"Is it true?"

Joshua's laugh is a forced burbling that I've never heard before. The teacups rattle, punctuating the burbles with a high-pitched tinkling.

"My parents loved her. They still talk about her. I think my father had a crush on her." He sets a cup in front of me. "It was *her* parents who wouldn't talk to *me*. They hated me because of who we were."

"Her father was Jewish."

"It wasn't about religion. It was economic. Class. Her father never forgave anyone for his poverty. He drank."

"They had money," I protest.

"He didn't think so. In that town nothing seemed enough."

I imagine Nell's father, embittered, cursing his middle-class luck, blaming the bankers and the doctors and the lawyers whose children raced their shiny cars through circular drives. Would he have brightened if someone told him his only child would be dead within the decade? Would he have snapped from his lethargy, awakened to the possibility of living without everything? Life, only life, precious life.

"What's this about?" I say to the teacup.

"Chicken broth."

It's my turn to laugh, the old laugh, until my face aches and the tiny bones in my wrists thrum. I laugh the way an explorer might when he discovers the natives don't mean to eat him but are just preparing dinner.

"Not the broth," I say. "This house. This place. You."

"I am what I am." His arms spread wide.

"A Jew."

"Yes," Joshua says, letting the sibilant drag, a world of meaning in the letters.

"What happened to Nietzsche and Marx?"

"I was wrong about Marx," Joshua says. "He was a deeply religious person. They both were." He looks at me as if waiting for me to disagree. I don't. "Marx believed we were alienated because of the false dichotomy between our public and private selves," he continues. "We're not Americans, but we're not really Jews either. We have no community, no identity, no connection with other people. I *am* a Jew," he concludes. "It's an active state, not a passive one."

"You think I'm passive." A statement, not a question.

He shakes his mop. I wonder how his *yarmulke* stays in place. Bobby pins? Glue? Hair weave?

"I think I talk too much," he says.

"You always have."

I raise the cup to my lips. Her breath, salty and warm, fogs the view. Freeze-dried and reconstituted, memory in a bouillon, the hot liquid rushes deep into my belly.

"Any cheesecake?" I ask.

He smiles. He remembers. My grandmother labored nights to whip the eggs into a froth for him.

"Where are they now?" he asks. "The new dead and the old?"

His teacup has left a perfect circle of water on the table. It trembles slightly from the vibrations of a passing car. Light shimmies along the water's edge, a luminescent dance of spheres.

"They're here," I say.

I will never work in this town again, Stockard tells me.

"I spoke to the committee," I say. "They approved it."

His face twists through the five stages of anger: temper, passion, fury, wrath, revenge.

"Fuck the committee," he says. "I am the committee."

I shake my head. "No. Sir. There's a pro bono committee, and they approved it."

He sways like a drunken boxer. For a minute I'm afraid he will hit me. Then he says, "You're billing firm time on a Jew's whore."

The moon revolves around the earth. The earth spins around the sun. The sun rotates about the center of the galaxy. The galaxy speeds toward the edge of the universe. The universe expands into the void. These are the laws according to physics. I am the son of a scientist. I believe in gravity and mass and density. I cannot explain why I am floating above the earth.

"I'm a Jew," I say quietly.

Stockard seems surprised. Perhaps he's never seen a person rise unencumbered into the heavenly spheres. He stares at me for a long time, trying to make sense of this new phenomenon.

"So you are," he concludes. Then he turns and leaves my office.

The sun floods a small living room and foyer, bathes the bedroom in light, washes through a newly tiled kitchen. White walls. High ceilings. Wood floors. A person could live here.

"What if I hated it?" I ask.

"I would have moved in by myself," says Kathleen.

"What if we fight?"

"My name's on the lease," she answers.

"What if I lose my job?"

"I'll kick you out."

She will paint her demon portraits while I wander the streets with my suits balled in a satchel. Associate for sale, I wave at the busloads of tourists outside the Stock Exchange. Take one home before the Crash.

She hands me a set of keys. "Don't lose them," she says.

"Are you sure?" I ask.

"There's no spare."

For a minute I consider the practical implications: breaking my lease, moving my possessions, informing my mother. Maybe I could just forward all calls. Who would know? The strange woman on my telephone? Crossed lines, poor service, sunspot activity.

Live together. I practice the variations like a fugue. The woman I live with. My live-in woman. The woman who lives in. And I'm her live-in man.

What do I have to fear? I have wandered, sought warmth like all creatures, fled false prophets and broken idols. Crossing the sea was nothing, a mere breath, the speck of effort. My feet barely stuck in the reedy mud. Mosquitoes and dragonflies buzzed above my head, their incessant drone like hunger. We built a bonfire. Torched our prayer books. Sang the bitter songs. In the morning, still drunk, our mouths clamped shut with clay, eyes pillowed in blinding sand, we trudged from daybreak, smashed our heads into the mountain, broke our spines, our septums, lost sleep, lost lives, lost hope.

"It's perfect," I say.

"Live with me?" she asks, her formal invitation.

Should I get down on one knee? Should she? How could I refuse such an elegant offer? Could anyone?

"Anywhere," I say. "Everything."

She kisses me. Her mouth tastes like rain. The waters course through my aching legs, carrying me farther and farther from the dunes.

Where, I ask, leaving one final question on her lips, where did she find this refuge?

She holds a battered hand to my face. Taps her middle finger three times against my cheek. "Eighty-one," she says in a conspiratorial whisper. "The eighty-one steps."

The hall is jammed with attorneys trying to stick their tongues in their secretaries' ears while paralegals take notes for sex discrimination cases. A band mangles its way through "White Christmas." Waiters circulate with empty hors d'oeuvres trays and bottles of champagne. In one corner, someone from word processing is vomiting.

Kathleen and I weave past a knot of junior partners. I wave, but they are too busy thumping one another on their backs to notice.

"There'll be another case," Kathleen consoles me. "You can't win every one."

I explain that Consolidated is a major client; its liability is potentially limitless; it depends on us.

Kathleen stops. She grasps me by both shoulders. "Colin," she says, her eyes steady, "I love you."

"Stockard is on the rampage."

"Fuck him. He's an anti-Semite, and you never liked him anyway."

"He screwed Marty's chance of making partner."

"You don't want to make partner."

She's right. Like the Israelites at the gates of the holy city, I suddenly understand that I have nothing to flee. Stockard cannot touch me. The walls are built of mud burned hard in the sun. Twenty-eight years of bondage, freedom, worship, and wandering must lead to more than a life of hand-holding, kowtowing, backslapping, and ass kissing. There are worthier clients than a bankrupt pension dodger, worthier causes than profiteering from the meek, disabled, and disempowered.

Résumé in one hand, Kathleen in the other, I slalom past the empty punch bowls, carved ice eagles, and diet soda mountains. The absurd music skitters couples across the slippery dance floor. Kathleen spins me like a clumsy top, my head unraveling across the parquet. When she laughs, the lights dim and all the circuits flow backward. Amplifiers explode; the tuba player is sucked into his horn.

Arm in arm, we dance until the musicians disappear.

At first I don't see him. There are four other couples at our table, and one by one they stand to introduce their spouses. Stockard remains seated. He is drunk, I can tell from his flushed face and exaggerated gestures of normalcy as his wife tugs at his sleeve.

"Bob," she pleads as he stares into oblivion, "look who's here."

He glances at me. For a moment our eyes lock; then he turns away, betrayal curling his lip.

"The Jew," he says.

The conversation at the table dies, then rushes back to life with a manic intensity. Everyone talks at once, a babbling tower of polite trivialities.

"Excuse me?" I say.

Stockard stands, not without effort. He pulls himself up with both hands clenched on the adjoining chairs.

In a suspended second I absorb the entire tableau: Stockard's height and bulk; Kathleen's confused and worried face; his wife's tired eyes resting heavily on me.

I cock my arm and punch him in the head.

It's a right hook. The flawless beauty of its form as it arcs through space, the weight of my entire body behind it, transfixes me. It leaps of its own unbounded energy, singing in the dulled air, knuckles like an unfulfilled promise.

Stockard manages to avert his face, and the blow hits him in the temple. His head snaps up, a quick salute. Then he spins, kicks over a chair, and crashes to the floor.

Liquid from a shattered drink drips in the silence. Someone mutters, "Jesus." Stockard's wife starts to cry, a slow, tuneless sob. Kathleen's hands are clenched to her sides, red wrists and white fingertips. In a moment I will go to her, ask her for forgiveness, but as I straddle Stockard, he stirs beneath my legs.

I kick him, hard, in the ribs.

the
promised
land

the
promised
land

In the morning the silver sedan idles by the curb outside our apartment. Its windows rolled and darkened. A streak of mud behind the tire wells.

I step from the sidewalk and open the passenger door.

"Come in," Eli greets me. He's wearing a new suit, something less tailored, boxy, a Japanese designer. He has shed the greasy look; his hair falls naturally to one side of his face. Gold-rimmed glasses, a silk tie, nails manicured and trim.

The cushioned leather seat grips my bottom like a friendly aunt. The doors lock. Seat belts belt. The engine grinds as Eli turns the key in the ignition.

"It's already running," I tell him.

"Damn Germans," he says as he eases into the busy street.

We head toward the river, then north up the parkway, driving in silence against traffic.

A slight snow has fallen during the night, coating the trees and earth with a fresh coat of paint. A flatbed truck with a cargo of evergreens bombs down the road in the opposite direction.

"Feels like Christmas," says Eli.

I've learned not to question his observations or even to listen too closely. One man's sense is another man's loose change.

"Is this going to take awhile?" I ask. "I've got to get to work."

A frown curls the corners of his mouth. "I thought you knew. You're not going to work today."

"Was I fired?"

"Fired?"

"Laid off. Downsized. De-employed," I offer.

He slices air with his hand like a baker separating loaves. "Nothing like that," he says.

I wait for him to elaborate, but after a while I'm content to watch the road blur.

He exits somewhere beyond the city; the sign is clouded with snow. I ask if he knows where he's going.

"I have a map," he says, fumbling in his lap.

I reach over to help, and he straightens suddenly. "Don't touch," he bristles. I notice, for the first time, a bulging shoulder holster beneath his blue blazer.

After several minutes of consultation he seems to have pinpointed our destination. He throws the car into gear and continues down a steep incline. The road twists and turns like most roads we've traveled. Hemlocks and pines hang low, brushing the windshield with snow. A squirrel scampers across the hood.

The snow is deeper here, a wild white powder. The tires skid and slide across the road. The road itself vanishes into a sea of chalk. No markers, only the spaces between trees. Eli keeps the car moving.

We dodge through the forest, the low hum of the engine the only sound. The steering wheel spins in Eli's hands; the car leaps in its own direction.

Soon the evergreens dwarf and recede, and a vast white valley opens before us. Small houses dot the vista, smoke curling from their chimneys, thatched roofs buried by snow, stone walls lopsided and discolored.

"What suburb is this?" I ask warily.

Eli consults his map. "It's on here somewhere," he says, waving at a section near the corner. When I crane to look, he yanks the map back between his legs.

"I remember the exit," I lie.

"It won't do you any good," he says.

We circle through drifts and banks until we reach a small cottage with a single tree in the front yard. The car stops. Eli turns to me.

"You're here," he says.

"Where?" I say.

He sweeps his arm across his chest to the windshield. "Here," he repeats.

The house is no bigger than a large truck. The crooked chimney will blow down in the next wind. Two silvered and weather-beaten windows stare blankly into the yard.

I open the car door. "Wait for me," I say hopefully.

The door closes.

I walk through the virgin snow, my footprints the only sign of life. As I get closer, I notice two flower boxes beneath the windows, the dried and dead stalks of last year's flowers in the frozen dirt.

I knock. No answer. I enter.

A blast of warm air like an industrial-strength dryer shrivels my skin. I blink in the dim light. A figure sits reading at a wooden table, his large feet extended onto another chair.

"Dirk?" I say.

He slowly sets down the book, reading until the last possible minute, looks up reluctantly, then jumps to his feet. He's so happy to see me. How was my trip? How's the job? The apartment? Life in the big city?

"Dirk, Dirk," I say as if he were an excitable puppy. "What are you doing here?"

"Everyone's here," he gushes. "Don't miss them! It's fantastic!" His double jaw moves quadruple time.

"In this little cottage?" I ask incredulously.

"Everywhere, everywhere," he says.

I grab him by his broad shoulders, stare up into his manic eyes. "Where?" I ask slowly, deliberately, menacingly.

Dirk laughs, a crazed cackle. "Don't take my word for it." He snaps his fingers. "You'll see!"

I follow him up a narrow staircase. It's crooked and old, and dust rises at every step. Did the house have two floors? I can't remember. The stairs open on a long hallway with doors on each side. Dirk pushes through the closest one.

We enter a brightly lit room. In one corner, a small Ferris wheel spins slowly, blinking lights splashing color on the walls. Children race across the floor in miniature autos, honking and revving their engines; one nearly runs me down. "Get outta the way!" he yells. I step backward and bump into a small animal that looks suspiciously like Marjorie's old dog. It bares its teeth and yowls at me. Dirk kicks it away.

Happy songs fill the air. A warm breeze blows. Drafts of cucumber and honeysuckle.

"Dirk!" a woman calls out, and waves to us. As she approaches, I can feel my stomach flip. Her alabaster skin; her black, black eyes.

Nell.

Dirk wraps her in his giant arms. She peers at me from beneath his biceps. "Hey, you," she says, as if we'd just seen each other, as if she hadn't been dead for nearly a decade.

She kisses me twice on the cheeks and once on the lips. "I missed you," she murmurs into my ear.

"You never came back," I say.

"Obviously," she says derisively.

Nothing is obvious, it seems to me. There should be laws to explain the inexplicable. Physical laws, at least, or metaphysical ones. I look to Dirk for confirmation, but he's already wandering off toward the Ferris wheel, a flock of children in his wake, the Pied Piper of this nuthouse.

"What are you doing here?" I finally ask.

"I finished my degree," she says, "and I'm doing some teaching."

"No, no, no," I say. This is all wrong. Everything is wrong. Nell shouldn't be here. Dirk shouldn't be here. What am I doing here? What is here?

"Poor confused Colin," says Nell, kissing me on the mouth. "Come upstairs?"

I know there can't be another upstairs. I also know there can't be a downstairs. Four walls, eight windows, no floors.

"I'm living with someone," I say.

"It's nothing like that," she says.

"You were never attracted to me."

"That's right."

"Just checking."

Satisfied that I'm satisfied, she takes my hand and leads me to another staircase.

This one is narrower and creakier than the last; it sways and totters as we climb. At the top we push through a trapdoor, cobwebs on our fingers, and emerge into an enormous ancient ballroom.

Dozens of circular tables are strung like wooden pearls along an endless timbered floor. Old men hunker over the tables, fistfuls of playing cards clutched in their hands, shirtsleeves rolled to the elbow, bald heads gleaming in the dull yellow light. Empty plates and beer tankards pile up near their elbows. Stacks of chips totter like mountains of crackers.

Closer to the walls old women bustle, scraping half-eaten meals from platters, uncapping jars and bottles, unwrapping bread, fruit, pies, chattering briskly. Their voices a perpetual chant to the goddess of food.

Chandeliers cast the ceiling into gold. Candles burn on sideboard tables.

A young man bumps me, his face buried in a small mound of cheesecake. Looking closer, I realize he's not even a man, but a boy, his face aflame with pimples, his upturned nose an oil-slickened ski jump.

"Excuse me," he says to the cheesecake.

He was never polite. Has he changed? Did he have a postdeath experience?

"Tommy," I say, experimenting, "you bumped me."

"I know," he says, mouth full of cheese. "I said I'm sorry."

"Okay," I say, pushing my luck, "just make sure you never do it again."

He agrees quickly, eagerly shoveling more cake into his mouth. I consider telling him that his dietary habits have not been approved by the American Society of Dermatologists. But then I wonder why he should care.

"He's a sweetheart," says Nell. "And he's got a very cute boy-friend. Don't you, Tommy?"

Tommy blushes, the red pimples fading into a pink background. He holds up his empty plate. "Think she'd give me more?" he sputters.

Nell links elbows with Tommy and dances him toward the old women. I tread several steps behind.

At an oblong and drooping table Grandma Esther slices enormous slabs from a wheel of cake. Beside her Grandma Miriam forklifts the pieces onto plates of random patterns and designs.

"He's an eater," says Grandma Esther warmly as she cuts another piece for Tommy.

"She's all right, this lady," says Tommy.

Grandma Miriam holds out a plate for me. I grasp it like a life preserver. "Grandma," I begin, "am I—?"

"*Cha'yim!*" she wails.

I drop the plate. It crashes to the floor with a tinkle and a muffled thud. How did this happen? I was so young; life stretched before me like a promise. I try to recall if I told Kathleen I loved her when I left this morning. Did she hear me as she squirmed beneath the blanket? When was the last time I told my father, my mother, David, Becca? The endless wasted moments in which love slips by unnoticed rush at me like a wave of sound, crushing my ribs and heart, bursting my eardrums, my eyes, leaving me deaf, dumb, blind, alone. You are born; you die; in a breath life is over. Why count the days? But if I had one more minute, I would gather them all in my hands, wrap them in my arms, carry them to a place of safety, lay their gentle heads in my lap, and sing.

"Stop that racket," says Grandma Esther, clamping her hand on Grandma Miriam's roll-like forearm. "Colin," she says, pointing with the knife at a circle of old men, "tell your grandfather to finish his game."

Five steps away Grandpa Isaac presses his cards against his ample belly. He squints at them one by one as he slides them up to his chest. "Pigs," he says when they are all assembled. His bald crown glimmers with sweat, his white shirt stained dark between the shoulder blades.

I tap him lightly on a clean space of fabric. "Grandpa?" I venture.

"Do you see these pigs?" he asks, holding his cards two inches from my nose.

I see two kings and two aces. If it's poker, my grandfather is bluffing. The enormous pile of chips winks.

"Fold," says a skinny man to the left of Grandpa Isaac, tossing his cards to the table.

There's something familiar about his sleepy eyes, the sparrow chest, his twiglike wrists. A picture of my father aged twenty-five years. Myself in fifty.

His chair groans as he skids away from the table and bends toward me. "Colin," he says, extending a bony hand. "I always liked that name."

"Grandpa *Cha'yim?*" I ask, grasping his dry and calcified fingers.

"Herman," he says. "This is America now." He releases his skeletal grip.

A great roar goes up from the table as Grandpa Isaac rakes the enormous pile toward his belly.

"Crook," says Herman. "He hides the aces."

"Is this what you do?" I ask. "Eat cheesecake and cheat at cards?"

"Instead we should contemplate our existence?"

He has a point. I suppose there isn't too much volunteer work. Charity begins at home, while you're still alive.

"You could learn to knit," I offer.

He plucks at his sweater. "You want one? I have a dozen, different colors."

I admire his skill. But surely there's more going on than an all-night card game.

"I read a book," he says. "They got everything wrong. I couldn't finish it."

I edge closer. Wisdom from the seer.

"You can't learn anything in a book," he continues. "Your father, what does he know? A lot of formulas and chemicals."

"He has a Ph.D.," I say defensively.

"A doctor of philosophy," he snorts. "Not a real doctor."

He tells Grandpa Isaac to deal him out. He scoots next to me, his slippers rasping on the floor. His pencil shins bare between his sagging white socks and the cuffs of his gray slacks. I bow into him.

"When I was a boy," he begins, "we lived in a village in the Ukraine, near the Polish border. Every morning my father went down to the fields. Every day he worked until his fingers were swollen and black.

"One night the Cossacks came. They broke our windows and burned our barns, made off with the cattle and chickens. A Cossack officer tried to enter our house. He kicked the door in with his boot.

"We were in the living room, hiding from the broken glass. My mother and sisters cowered behind the sofa. My father rose up to stop the man, but he knocked my father to the floor with his pistol butt.

"I was fourteen years old, you understand. The only son. My hands were smooth from reading and prayer. But I leaped at that officer like a dog. I was on him before he could even move. When I hit him, I split my knuckles on his face. As he fell, he struck his head against the side of a chair. He lay unconscious on the stone while his men galloped away in the distance.

"I had no choice. He would have raped my sisters. He might have killed me. But now he lay on the floor, not dead but not moving.

"I did the only thing I could. I ran. My mother packed everything. My cousin Misha volunteered to escort me. We left that night. Traveled by night. Headed north through Russia.

"Near Lithuania Misha died. I found him one morning frozen, his lips white with frost. I couldn't bury him, the ground was too hard. I left him in the woods beneath a tree. I continued alone to Riga, then Helsinki, where I took a freighter for Canada."

He brushes his eyebrow with one finger.

"Later, everyone died," he continues. "But I ran. I lived because I ran." His voice cracks. *"Who could have known?"*

"Grandpa," I say, the tears like bitter herbs on the back of my throat.

"Ach," he says. "What's the use? We play cards."

He balances against my shoulders and hoists himself to his feet.

One arm, then the other, until he stands on his own. He wobbles slightly as he moves away from the game. I walk with him toward the front of the ballroom.

Each human life narrates an apocryphal tale. We wake; we rise; we recreate. Our grandfathers deal us their hand. When we shuffle the deck, the same cards peer back at us.

I follow him past the circles of old men, the endless lines of tables. One step, then another, we amble forward. The room expands as we walk, the walls fading into distance. My grandfather leads the way. When I look back, all I can see are swirling eddies of snow.

He opens a door. "Here," he says, "this is what I want to show you."

I am standing out on the front lawn. The sun shines. A steady drip, drip of water from the roof plinks near my feet. Green shoots poke from the holes. Life, everywhere, life.

On the trunk of the silver sedan Eli reclines, his glasses pushed up his forehead, his face directed at the sky. I turn to my grandfather, but he is gone. His footprints already melted. No trail to follow.

I lift my suit trousers and slosh to the car.

"Back already?" asks Eli as he starts the engine.

Smoke curls from the chimney of the small cottage. A shadowed figure darkens the opaque window.

"Eli," I ask, "am I dead?"

"Not yet."

"Is God?"

Eli sighs. "How should I know?" he says.

We sit quietly in the humming car. A bird alights on the hood and regards us quizzically. After a minute, it flies off.

"Where to?" Eli asks.

I look out over the thawed landscape, the melting snow, the bodies buried in the woods.

"Just drive," I say. "We'll figure it out."